15 12

MW00439839

Vial Murders

Other Walker and Company Titles by Marsha Landreth

The Holiday Murders
A Clinic for Murder

Vial Murders

A Doctor Samantha Turner Mystery

Marsha Landreth

**Walker and Company
New York**

Copyright © 1994 by Marsha Landreth

All rights reserved. No part of this book may be reproduced or
transmitted in any form or by any means, electronic or mechanical,
including photocopying, recording, or by any information storage and
retrieval system, without permission in writing from the Publisher.

All the characters and events portrayed in this work are fictitious.

First published in the United States of America in 1994
by Walker Publishing Company, Inc.

Published simultaneously in Canada by Thomas Allen & Son
Canada, Limited, Markham, Ontario

Library of Congress Cataloging-in-Publication Data
Landreth, Marsha.
Vial murders: / Marsha Landreth.
p.   cm. (A Doctor Samantha Turner mystery)
ISBN 0-8027-3199-6
1. Women physicians—Wyoming—Fiction.
2. Coroners—Wyoming—Fiction. I. Title.
II. Series: Landreth, Marsha. Dr. Sam Turner mystery
PS3562.A4774V5   1995
813'.54—dc20   94-16398
CIP

Printed in the United States of America
2 4 6 8 10 9 7 5 3 1

For Pauline Burns, my mother

Acknowledgments

MY SINCERE THANKS to Korey Jorgensen, M.D., and John Phelan, M.D., for reading the manuscript; Patricia Stranahan, M.D., Ph.D., for providing scientific data; Ann Gorzalka for lending her name; Sharan Newman for locating the perfect au pair.

Vial Murders

$\triangledown$

1

Wednesday, April 14

DR. SAMANTHA TURNER, county coroner for Sheridan, Wyoming, depressed the play and record buttons on her microcassette recorder. "Case number 94-00175, David Crider. The body is that of a well-developed, well-nourished seventeen-year old Caucasian male with brown hair and brown eyes. The body is seventy-two inches long and weighs one hundred and sixty five pounds."

Sam closed the boy's medical record which she'd borrowed from the school district. She set the microcassette recorder on the mortician's worktable and prayed that the recorder would have better luck picking up her words than it had for the last autopsy. "Rigor mortis is present in the extremities," she said loudly for the recorder. Working in the preparation room at the funeral home was a far cry from the days of postmortem examinations in state-of-the-art facilities at the San Francisco hospitals where she'd trained. "The skin is covered with yellow pustules and . . ."

The opening door stirred the foul air. Sam turned off the microcassette recorder as old Doc Wallace walked in. He didn't look happy to see her, and she knew it wasn't because the mortician, at her insistence, had suited him up in hospital greens. Their relationship had been strained since she blew the whistle that landed his son in prison for life.

"Thanks for coming, Bob."

"My office is dark Wednesdays. Besides, your message said it was important," he said as he took a place across the stainless steel table from her, struggled into his gloves, and gave the body a cursory glance. "I don't recognize him. He's one of mine?"

"No, the family doesn't have an attending physician. The father's pastor of some religious sect that's into prayer healing."

"So what do you want?" A year ago he would have favored her with a snappy repartee about not praying hard enough, she would have scolded him, and then they would have gotten to the heart of the matter.

"Did you ever see a case of smallpox?"

"Smallpox!" Bob Wallace pushed his glasses up and settled them on his bald pate. He looked closely at one of the pustular lesions.

"Why, Bob, that's exactly what the guy at the state health department said. Except he was *certain* he was talking to a crazy person."

He gave her that sympathetic look of old. What she wouldn't give to have his friendship back . . . "Are they coming to see for themselves?"

"No, they want me to send specimens. They're certain it's a case of chicken pox. Idiots!" Sam reached for a number 11 scalpel. "I don't know what medical school they went to, but mine always taught us to look for the zebra in the herd of horses."

"This is the zebra, all right." He picked up the magnifying glass and held it over another eruption. "Saw a Kaffir pox that looked a little like this when I was an intern, but that was a hundred years ago." He moved on to a skin lesion in the crusting phase. "Impossible."

"I know. Smallpox was eradicated worldwide when I was a schoolgirl." The fluid was too viscous to be collected in capillary tubes. She would make smears on glass slides instead. The health department would want four smears. She would prepare eight slides. No, twelve. "Rational thinking aside, I'd bet my last dollar on variola major." She'd have to ask Kate, the pathology department secretary, to find an

Etiologic Agents label to affix to the outer shipping container. Sam couldn't remember the last time she'd sent anything down questioning cause. The skunk with bubonic plague, two years ago. One of the vets brought it in.

"Well, whatever this is, it was bad enough to kill the kid." Bob settled his glasses on his nose, carefully avoiding an angry-looking sore behind his right ear. "Looks like we've got ourselves a can of worms."

"Tell me about it." She separated the individual slides with toothpicks and slipped a rubber band around the first four. "Death occurred in the late pustular stage. Look how many of the lesions are broken down." Their eyes locked, each knowing the other's thought. The virus had been liberated, the patient highly infective. "When was the last time you gave a smallpox vaccination, Bob?" She didn't bring enough to make twelve slides. Eight would suffice.

"Not for a good long time. Stopped sometime in the seventies."

Way before she started practicing medicine. "Every teen-ager in Sheridan is at risk," she said, collecting crusts. Bob held out the screw-capped vials for her, one at a time. Sam smiled her thanks; he pretended not to notice. "See any scabs measuring five millimeters on that side?"

"Here's a good one," Bob said, pointing. Sam rounded the table and duly scraped. "You always were an optimist, Sam. The vaccination protects three, four years. Only those who have had smallpox are immune for life."

"Oh, an equal opportunity epidemic." She gestured with the screw-capped vial she had just finished sealing with waterproof tape. "Now we play the waiting game."

They fell into silence. Bob scrutinized the corpse, counting eruptions like a child counting freckles. Sam waited until he was down around the pelvis before she made the Y incision across the chest, shoulder to shoulder.

"Just in time for the rodeo."

Sam stopped the midline incision just below the xyphoid to have a look at Bob. "What rodeo?"

"Don't you ever read the newspaper? Listen to the radio?"

"Jeep's radio is on the fritz." She turned back to her work, continuing the midline incision down the entire length of the abdomen to the pubis. "And newspaper is a strange name for that rag. It's still predicting Reagan will be reelected by a landslide."

"They're right. Got to give them that."

"Plug this in for me. please." Sam unraveled the cord to the saw. Bob crawled under the table to find the outlet. "Thanks." Sam sawed through the ribs and cartilage to expose the heart and lungs. "I like my news a little more timely."

"You might not have been able to get today's gold quote, but you would have known that Sheridan College is hosting the regional rodeo the first weekend in May."

"A college rodeo." First weekend in May. That gave Sam two weeks.

He coughed, and then waited until she finished opening the pericardial sac. "Sam, I've been meaning to call you."

"Yeah?" Sam drew a sample of blood from the heart.

"It's your dad. It's time to move him to the north wing."

The north wing of the nursing home was for those patients who couldn't do anything for themselves. A place to go to die. Sam removed the heart, lungs, esophagus, and trachea en bloc. The addition to the house was progressing slowly, thanks to poor spring weather. Sam had hoped to keep her dad at the nursing home until it was completed. "How long, Bob? I want him home at the end."

Bob ran a gentle hand across her shoulders. "Hard telling about Alzheimer's. Once it gets down into the brain stem, it goes pretty fast."

"Maybe we should admit him to the hospital, have Ken do another CAT scan."

"Why put him through it? Let him go, Sam."

David Crider had gotten his height and generous aquiline nose from his father; his mother's contribution was fine, dark hair. The Criders lived in an older neighborhood of single-family homes and well-tended yards. The parish house was catty-corner from the Church of Divine Light.

Sam sat in a straight chair that she'd pulled from the dining room table and dragged over the blue shag carpet. Naomi and Jacob Crider sat stoically on the couch in front of her. She had never liked this part of her job, but now that she was a mother herself and had come so close to losing her own son, she couldn't bear to see such agony. No parent should have to bury a child. To add insult to injury, Sam couldn't allow it; she needed the corpse and would keep it in the mortuary's cavernous vault at 40 degrees until everyone was in agreement as to the cause of death.

"What killed my son?" Mrs. Crider asked.

Internal bleeding was the mechanism of death, the pathological condition within the body that resulted in death, but that wasn't the answer she needed to hear. "A severe exanthematous virus."

"What does that mean?"

A pang of pity hit Sam square in her midriff. "Skin eruptions," Sam said softly.

"We saw them, but what were they?"

Bad enough to have to accept the death of a child, but this mother's tragedy was magnified by the uncertainty surrounding it. If Sam were in her place, she'd be asking herself if she could have done something to prevent her child's death. On the other hand, Sam knew the answer to that. Had they sought treatment for the boy in a timely manner, David might have made it. Sam would not torment the parents with her insight. Nor would she share her smallpox supposition.

"I'm not certain, Mrs. Crider. I've notified the state health department. They'll—"

"Save our son?"

Sam could understand her hostility and didn't mind the woman's lashing out. She searched her mind for words to soften the mother's suffering. None came. "No, Mrs. Crider. But maybe they'll save someone else's son." Sam waited to see if the woman would say something else. Mrs. Crider wiped her cheek with the back of her hand instead. "Reverend Crider, Mrs. Crider, I'm afraid I need to ask you a few questions."

"Pastor," Mrs. Crider corrected indignantly, "not Reverend."

Pastor Crider found his wife's hand and held it reassuringly.

"Mrs. Crider, Pastor Crider, has your son been out of the country in the last month?"

"No." Mrs. Crider buried her face into her husband's chest and sobbed uncontrollably.

The doors of the cuckoo clock opened and a bird popped out and called twice. So much for lunch in the hospital cafeteria, though all of this had caused her to lose her appetite. Sam waited until Pastor Crider glanced at her. "Was David around anyone visiting from any other country within the last month?"

Crider shook his head as he patted his wife's back.

"Did he have a job around imported goods?"

The pastor gave a quick shake.

"Produce?"

"He helps . . . helped out around the church." The pastor's voice broke. "He had no other job."

"Was he friends with a foreign exchange student?"

He shrugged.

She would check at the high school. "Pastor Crider, I'm afraid I won't be able to release the body in time for the scheduled funeral day after tomorrow."

Mrs. Crider stopped crying. "You can't do that. We have relatives coming in from all over the country."

Sam got to her feet. "I'm sorry, Mrs. Crider, Pastor. I have no choice."

"But Thaddeus Smith said Friday would be fine."

"Mrs. Crider, I'm truly sorry. I've already spoken with the mortician, Thaddeus will see that your son's remains are well cared for in the interim. Please be assured that I will do all in my power to discover what caused David's death and do so as quickly as possible."

$\triangledown$

2

"Kate," Derek Turner called to the pathology department's secretary as he walked in. Four-month-old Woody
wailed and wiggled within the confines of the royal blue
corduroy Snugli baby carrier strapped to Derek's chest.

Clacking typewriter keys and jangling bracelets quieted,
unlike the baby, as Kate looked up. "Seems one of the
Turners isn't happy." She pouted until her magenta lips
became a tight circle. The lipstick clashed terribly with her
red hair and ruddy complexion but accented the blond streak
acceptably.

"The other Turner isn't all that happy, either." Derek
rubbed the Snugli, feeling the spine in the little fellow's back.
He wondered if Woody would ever catch up from being two
months premature. Derek nodded to Samantha's desk
across from Kate's. "I'm looking for that beautiful and
charming wife of mine."

"She's in Dr. Gordon's office. Looking for a book, I think
she said." Kate pointed to the closed door that once was
Samantha's office but now housed her new partner, the
not-necessarily-renowned Dr. Eugene Gordon. Flash—a
term of nonendearment used because he was slow in every
way possible—had the office through having taken ad-
vantage of Samantha's good nature. For the sake of har-
monious bliss at the Turner ranch, Derek kept quiet on the
subject. "Can't you hear her?"

Derek certainly could, now that she was yelling her head off.
The patients waiting to have blood drawn in the lab next door

were being treated to her ranting and raving as well. "Guess all the Turners are unhappy. Well, now we know my son came by his vocal cords honestly." He paced the floor, trying to calm Woody. "What's it about this time?"

"Who knows?" She rolled a new report form into her typewriter.

The door banged open, just barely missing Derek. Samantha stomped to her desk with the carriage of an indignant queen, Flash dogging her trail like an impatient court jester. Spending time hunched over a microscope hadn't done much for his posture. "Sam, be reasonable." Her chair shrieked for mercy as she plopped down and jettisoned a heavy medical tome to the cluttered desk in front of her.

She brushed a wisp of golden hair from her face, and then struggled with the longer strands that had escaped the knot at the nape of her neck. She was entirely too thin these days, and it showed in the hollows under her high cheekbones. She looked every minute of her thirty-six years. Even so, she was gorgeous.

Flash sat on the corner of her desk, running nervous fingers through his thinning blond hair. "Not even two weeks."

"Goddammit, Eugene, you're sitting on my glasses."

He pushed up with his arms long enough for her to snake her hand around under his squat trunk. She found her glasses, put them on.

"Are they all right?"

"Yeah, no thanks to . . . Derek!" She threw her glasses onto a pile of reports as she got up and started toward him. "I didn't see you."

Derek was suddenly basking in the warmth of her smile. "We've just been standing here in the corner crying."

"Poor baby," she cooed to Woody as she removed him from the Snugli. "Did that mean pediatrician hurt you with an old needle?" She smothered Woody with kisses before lifting her face to Derek. The kiss she offered him was unexpectedly hungry. "How'd it go?"

"Fine. Martin seemed happy with Woody's progress. Weighed in at four pounds six ounces. Said for a little fellow he's a keeper. He drew Woody his very own growth chart— below the regular one."

She crooked her little finger and stuck it between Woody's lips. The caterwauling halted as the baby sucked greedily. "He seems a little feverish."

"Now don't be a Nervous Nellie," Derek said. "He's just had a DPT and oral poliomyelitis vaccines and I have the baby Tylenol instructions from *his* doctor."

Samantha looked at their son. "You'd think your father never heard of getting a second opinion."

Flash cleared his throat. "Sam?"

"Go away, Eugene." She carried the baby over to Kate. "Look how much bigger I am this week."

Kate picked up one of his twig arms. "You still look pretty scrawny to me. Still cutting your newborn diapers in half, betcha."

"Not for long," Samantha said, rising to her son's defense. "Soon I'll be wearing big-boy diapers."

Flash jumped in front of her. "Sam—"

"No!" She skirted him and carried Woody into the lab, where she was quickly surrounded by people all wanting to see the baby.

Flash turned to Derek. "Two weeks is all I'm asking. Tell her to give me the time off."

"*Tell* her?" Derek looked over at Kate. She quickly turned to the typewriter and started banging on the keys like a war correspondent in the thick of battle.

"It's a great opportunity." Flash clawed at his collar. "It's official business."

Derek had no idea what he was talking about and had no intention of getting involved. How had the young doctor managed to work with Samantha a year and not realize that saying *official* to her was like waving a red flag in front of a bull. "Official isn't going to cut it with her."

Flash hurried into the lab. Samantha brushed past him

and took Woody across the hall and disappeared into the radiology department. Flash was still on her heels a few minutes later when she returned.

"This is a once-in-a-lifetime opportunity, Sam."

An ambulance siren wailed outside. Samantha started to give Derek the baby, but then pulled back. "Pavlovian conditioning." She laughed. "We covered the ER so long, I'll always jump when I hear a siren."

Derek didn't understand. "Sorry?"

"She meant Pavlov, the Russian physiologist. He would ring a bell—"

"Eugene," Samantha snapped, "give it a rest." The frown lines disappeared when she turned to Derek. "We finally have a couple of ER docs. On a trial basis, anyway."

"Larry hired ER doctors?" Derek noticed Samantha cringe at the hospital administrator's name. The two had butted heads for as long as Derek had been in the picture. Longer, actually.

"They showed up out of the blue a couple weeks ago. I haven't even had a chance to welcome them to the staff."

"Sam, I need to let them know." Flash looked as if he'd start holding his breath. Or stamping his feet.

"No, something's come up. I need you here." Sam whirled around to the secretary. "Kate, will you call down to the farmer's co-op and ask them where I can get hold of some fertile hen's eggs?"

Kate turned off her typewriter and started turning pages in Sheridan's thin telephone directory.

"Sam, just think of the mileage the hospital can get out of this publicity."

"Yeah, Larry would milk it for all it's worth. But you still can't go." Samantha settled into her chair with the baby and took out her address book.

A nurse in surgical greens came to the door, giving Flash the opportunity to make himself useful. He relieved the nurse of her steel bowl. "Ah, Patrick's hysterectomy." Flash lifted the corner of the gauze cloth covering the bowl to have a look, then he held up what looked like a bag of marbles attached to a giant ball of tissue. "Looks like he only had to take one of the ovaries."

"Ovaries?" Samantha asked, snapping to attention.

"Stein-Leventhal syndrome," Flash answered, looking at Derek as if he had asked the question. "The other must not have been polycystic."

"Guess not," Derek said. He sounded as if he knew what was going on.

Flash started into the lab with the steel bowl. Samantha called him back. "All right, Eugene, you can have the time off. Leave that here on my desk and go call them."

He abandoned the bowl and flashed into his office, closing the door.

"Where's he going?" Derek asked.

Samantha stroked the spot on Woody's head where the fine hair had been shaved for the IV. "Switzerland. His name was pulled at random as a delegate to the World Health Organization conclave."

"Why did you suddenly change your mind?"

Samantha put a finger to her lip and nodded to the baby. He had fallen asleep, his arms outstretched.

"Sam," Kate called as she put her hand over the phone's receiver, "how many do you need?"

"Two dozen." Woody's arms jerked out in his sleep as Samantha spoke. "No . . .three." Samantha looked up. "Derek, will you go ask Terry for a Dixie cup?" She nodded to the lab technician working at the counter just inside the adjacent lab.

As he stood by the door waiting for Terry to come back with a Dixie cup, Derek watched Kate hang up the phone and cross out the first number on her list. "Fertile hen's eggs must be harder to find than one might imagine," he said to her.

"The only good rooster is a stewed rooster." She dialed the next number.

"Hubby still in Cheyenne for the state bowling tournament?"

"How'd you know that?"

Derek shrugged. "Took a wild guess."

"This is Dr. Turner, county coroner, is the mayor in?" Derek heard Sam just as Terry said, "Here you are," and handed him the specimen cup. He dutifully carried it to Samantha's desk.

"Have him return my call as soon as possible. It's about the rodeo," Sam said into the phone. "Thanks," she added as she hung up.

Derek held the cup out. "What do you want in it?"

She glanced at Kate, and then beckoned him closer. "Seminal fluid," she whispered.

He must not have heard her correctly. He went around the desk and hunkered down beside her chair. "Say that again."

"Fill it with seminal fluid," she whispered in his ear.

"That's what I thought you said." He cleared his throat. "How?"

"God down to the men's room, think erotically of me, and give it your best shot."

Derek rolled the cup in his hands. "Why?"

"For a lab experiment. I'll explain when I get home tonight. Please?"

"I don't think I can do it."

"Derek, you're almost forty. You've probably done it a thousand times in the last twenty-five years."

"Not in a public rest room."

"There're doors on the stalls, aren't there?" She lifted one of her beautifully arched brows, her green eyes dancing. "Do I have to go with you and give you a helping hand?"

Derek straightened to his full height. "That winning double entendre has inspired me." He took off the Snugli. "I'll be right back with your prize." Cup in hand, he gave his wife and baby one last look, and then headed down the hall like a condemned man to his execution.

▽

3

A WALL OF lumber came into the headlights. Sam turned off the engine. It was as good a place to park as any. The inconvenience of having construction materials all around the house was a necessary evil. Two bedrooms had been plenty when she was alone; now she had a husband and child. Her father needed a room. And they would have to have live-in help. Derek had had bitter words over paternity leave rights with the Company, and Sam wouldn't be a bit surprised to come home one of these days and find a note on the mantle telling her that he was off to Timbuktu. Not that he would actually tell her where he was being sent. CIA operatives know how to keep a secret.

"Shh, you'll wake up the devil himself," Sam said to the two yellow Labs as she got out of the Jeep and started up the red shale path. The motion-activating lights Derek had installed after the last snowstorm came on. She looked at her watch—3:17. She'd be hearing about this.

The cat rubbed up against The Little One's front paws, then hissed and growled when she saw Fido. All this before Sam had shut out the cold. The Little One had come to the ranch as a tiny pup, but his litter mate Fido had been six months old before Sam adopted him. The cat bared her claws and swiped at Fido. Before Sam could step over The Little One to grab the cat, the hundred-pound Fido tucked his tail between his hind legs and hurried off to the family room, where he could bolster his pride under the table.

Sam took off her jacket and opened the squeaking door to the hall closet. She tiptoed over the Mexican tile in the hall and was at the foot of the stairs before she noticed the light was on in the library.

She managed to get around The Little One, and found Derek in the rocking chair giving Woody his bottle. Sheets of heavy plastic hung at the far end of the room where the new addition was in the works. The wood in the fireplace had turned to white coals.

"Your dinner's cold." The lines on either side of the bridge of Derek's nose deepened as he scowled. She used to think the vertical wrinkles added character to his rugged good looks, but that was when he was scowling at someone else.

The dog beat her to the rocker. She planted a kiss on the top of Derek's head while the dog sniffed the baby. She brushed a brown lock off her husband's forehead and then ran her fingers through his disheveled wavy hair, trying to repair the damage sleep had caused. "I'm sorry. Had a lot of work to do. The time got away from me."

"Here, finish feeding the baby. I'll warm up your dinner."

Sam put a restraining hand on the sleeve of his robe. "I'm not hungry. I ate in Billings."

"Awful long way to go for dinner. Hope it was worth a hundred and forty miles each way."

"Taco Bell was about the only place open."

"There's a closer one on Coffeen. And if you had driven a mere ten miles farther, you could have had a home-cooked meal at Turner ranch."

"Sorry, I should have called. I needed to use an electron microscope. Billings has the nearest." She plopped down on the floor in front of his slippered feet and sat Indian style. She pulled her skirt over her knees.

The dog rolled over on its back to have his stomach scratched. "Woody feeling better?"

"He was a bit cranky when I was reading Plato to him," he said as he kissed the baby. Kissing her couldn't have made her feel more loved. "You're making precursors, aren't you?"

"Was it that obvious?"

"Right after the ovaries showed up you changed your mind about letting Eugene take his trip. You want him out of the lab so you can grow the cultures without drawing attention. You needed the seminal fluid to fertilize the eggs."

"Supersleuth strikes again!" The ovum divides as precursor cells for the first seventy-two hours after fertilization, until they get their act together and find out what they're supposed to be. He wouldn't have known a damned thing about their use in gene therapy if it hadn't been for all their trouble in that clinic in the Caribbean. If she'd never gotten involved in that mess, Woody would be half his age and twice his weight. Never again would she stick her nose where it didn't belong.

"For your dad?"

She nodded. "I froze half of the eggs in case I botch the first batch." She sighed. "Are you sure they didn't find Dr. Blanca's research papers when they searched his clinic?" If she hadn't been in St. Thomas's hospital postnatal, she could have gone through his files herself. She laughed.

"What's so funny?"

"Nothing." Speaking of whistling in the dark! Nothing this side of hell could have gotten her to go back to that clinic. Not even surrounded by the CIA and guarded by a battalion of marines. But she would have appreciated their bringing her the Institute's research. They'd made an amazing breakthrough in gene therapy treatment. While other researchers in the field theorized what might be, the Blanca Institute was putting it to practice. "Assuming I can persuade the precursors to mimic neurons and get them into the right location how do I ensure that the spliced genetic material I've introduced will be passed on to the daughter cells? The answer has to be in the checking proteins that scan the DNA and direct repairs. Don't you think?"

"Not that I understand any of that, but if I were you, I'd be concerned about the Wyoming Medical Board. They're likely to lift your medical license for unethical practices."

"I'm checking Dad out of the nursing home. I'll treat him at home."

"And he's suddenly cured of Alzheimer's?" Derek held out the bottle for her so he could burp the baby.

"Unexplained miracles happen."

The Little One licked the nipple and got a thump on his nose from Derek. The dog high tailed it. "I put them out for a reason."

"They wanted in. It's cold outside."

"That's why they have fur coats."

"I'll get another nipple." Sam found The Little One in the kitchen lapping water. "Thanks for getting me in trouble." The dog lifted his sad brown eyes to her for a moment and then stuck his muzzle back in the dish to slap some more water on his red nose.

"What's come up?" Derek asked when she returned with the almost empty bottle and new nipple. "Why were you hesitant to let Eugene go to Switzerland?"

Sam took the baby and changed places with Derek. The seat was nice and warm. Derek threw the cloth diaper over her shoulder. She could smell regurgitated formula on it. There was some on the front of Woody's aqua sleeper also. And now that she was getting a good whiff, she surmised that a diaper changing would be in Woody's immediate future.

"Think we're about to be hit by an epidemic of smallpox."

"Smallpox? Third World countries don't have smallpox. How could Sheridan have an epidemic?"

"I saw my first case this morning. A seventeen-year-old boy. That's why I drove to Billings. I found pox viruses when I examined the stained smears under my light microscope. Then I took some lesion fluid grids and some ground scab grids up to the Billings hospital and used their electron microscope. Lo and behold, C's found in the scabs, M's in vesicular fluid. Just like the pictures in the old textbook I found in the hospital library."

"Did you call the CDC?" he asked, as if she didn't realize

she was duty bound to call the federally run monitoring organization.

"They'll be here in the morning." Maybe they'd have more luck persuading the mayor to cancel the rodeo; all she'd gotten him to agree to was a presentation of her case at the Tuesday City Council meeting.

"Then go up to bed." Derek took the baby out of her arms. "Get some sleep."

"Derek," she called as he started out with the baby. He turned at the door. "I know I said I didn't want Dad here until we're finished with the construction, but . . ."

"I'll bring him home tomorrow. And see about finding a discreet nurse."

∇

4

Thursday, April 15

Sᴀᴍ's ᴛɪᴍɪɴɢ ʟᴇꜰᴛ a lot to be desired. She arrived at the high school the same time as the students, ended up parking in a handicap spot, and now as she charged up the hall of the social studies wing surrounded by clamoring teenagers, her beeper went off.

She took it out of her pocket as she unbuttoned her coat. The lab's number flashed. They were to beep her when the general surgeon started the mastectomy. She figured she had thirty minutes before they would be needing her for the frozen section. She turned off the beeper, ignoring caustic comments about dealing drugs. Instead, she looked for room numbers.

Ms. Norton was writing the date on the green board when Sam walked in. She was a young thing, petite, long black hair permed in loose curls. She wore a bulky knit sweater over a flowered skirt that came to her calves. Her boots were laced to above the ankle.

A mob of students sucked Sam farther into the room. The door opened behind her, and one boy got in just as the buzzer sounded. Three more students dashed in behind him and were in their seats before the deafening noise ceased.

"Ms. Norton, someone's here to see you," said the girl in the front seat of the middle row. Sam wasn't sure how the girl had managed to see her through her shaggy bangs.

The teacher looked over her shoulder. "Oh, I'm sorry," she said to Sam as she put down the chalk, and then vigorously crossed to her. Sam didn't know how anyone could be so peppy so early in the morning. Sam was tired from just watching her bubble with energy.

"Ms. Norton, I'm Dr. Turner. The office sent me down. Would you mind if I spoke to you in the hall for just a minute?"

The teacher pirouetted to the class. "Sheila, take roll for me, please." Sheila was the girl with the bangs. "The rest of you, keep it to a roar or you'll be reciting how a bill goes through Congress . . . backwards."

"Ms. Norton," Sam said when they were in the deserted corridor, save for one boy sprinting to the room at the far end of the hall. "I need to ask you a couple of questions about David Crider."

The teacher shook her head sorrowfully, enthusiasm drained. "Oh, yes. We all felt so terrible when we heard. He was one of those invisible kids. And now that it's too late for him to appreciate it, he's the center of attention. Everyone suddenly was his best friend."

"A loner, you mean? David was a loner?"

"More a hanger-on. He wanted to be part of everything, and the other kids tolerated him because he was there."

"I was told by the counselor that you took a group of students to Washington, D.C., last month and that David was one of them."

A crash made the teacher spin around and open the door. "If I were you, I'd take out my notebooks and bone up on how a bill goes through Congress. Right to left." She closed the door and turned back to Sam. "Sorry. The trip. Yes, David was one of the delegates. He almost couldn't go. We didn't get back until Palm Sunday and he had to miss the services or something."

That would have made it three and a half weeks ago. The incubation period was from seven to seventeen days. A couple of weeks for the lesions to crust. Timing was fine. Sam wondered why David's parents hadn't mentioned the trip. "One of the delegates?"

"Student Congress. High schools from all over the nation sent delegates." Ms. Norton closed her eyes and clenched her teeth when a shriek penetrated the walls. She craned to look but resisted the urge to open the door. "Kids!"

"Was he around anyone who might have been out of the country? A foreign exchange student?"

She shrugged. "Maybe. Schools send their brightest kids. It is within the realm of possibility that one of the delegates had been a foreign exchange student first semester."

"No, it needs to be more recent. What about the students? Is there anyone who might know if David met someone who might have been ill?"

"Jess was his roommate. If anyone knows, it's Jess. Jess Gorzalka."

"You wouldn't know where I could find Jess, by any chance?"

She shook her head. "Check with the attendance office, around the corner from the main office. They'll look up his schedule."

Sam held out her hand. "Thank you."

Ms. Norton gave it an enthusiastic shake. "I hope I was some help."

More than the parents had been.

The attendance office was filled with students. Sam cut in front of the line. "Excuse me," she said to the badgered-looking woman at the computer. "Could you please give me Jess Gorzalka's class schedule?"

The woman looked up at her as if she'd asked her to reveal the secret formula for making an atomic bomb. Sam had seen cadavers looking happier.

"I'm Dr. Turner, the county medical examiner. It's official business." Most people didn't know the difference between a coroner and a medical examiner, and the latter didn't sound as deadly. A coroner was anyone who could get elected, and a medical examiner was a physician appointee of the court. Technically she was both.

The clerk frowned and gave the student she was helping

the wait-a-minute sign and worked the computer. The dot-matrix printer started clicking. When it stopped, she tore off the paper and started ripping off the tractor feed edges. "Would you like me to send a runner to his class?" she asked, as if it would be a bother.

"No, I don't have time right now. I'll have to come back. Thank you." Sam took the schedule and pushed against the tide of tardy students.

The main hall was quiet, making her escape easy. She'd been more uncomfortable in a school than she'd care to admit. As if she'd regressed to childhood where she had no control and was at the mercy of the system. She shook off the feeling, only to feel a numbing chill replace it. Would spring ever arrive or would they go directly into hot summer?

Sam looked at the parking lot but didn't see her car. Maybe she was turned around. She walked back to the door. No, this was the set of doors she'd come in. Double doors next to the ramp. The main office was on her right then, and now.

Sticking her hands deep into her pockets, she walked across the roadway and looked up and down. She'd parked right up front. In the handicap space. This was the only row with handicap parking. She'd left her car right here. A sick feeling sank to the pit of her stomach as she realized that her car had been stolen. She flailed around inside her pockets. The key was still there.

As she started back toward the school to call the police, a patrol car, blowing a steady stream of poisonous gas out of the exhaust pipe, cruised up the roadway. No-chin Skip was behind the wheel. Of all the nincompoops on the force, he was Sam's least favorite. He pulled to a stop next to her and lowered the window.

"Trouble, Dr. Turner?" His breath looked much like the vapors coming out of the back of the cruiser, and the smell was as choking.

"Someone stole my Jeep!"

"A brown Jeep, with a red interior?"

He knew perfectly well what it looked like; he stopped her often enough. "You've seen it?"

"Yeah, not more than five minutes ago. Tow truck took it away. It was in the handicap space without a permit." He said it so innocently with his southern twang. He hadn't lived in Wyoming all his life, and Sam, for one, hoped he'd return to the Appalachian rock he'd crawled out from under sooner than later.

"According to this eye-pleasing sign on your door, you're here to serve and protect. Why don't you just call on that little radio of yours and tell him to get it back here? I'm on official business."

"Official business? Did you see where a police*woman* had been added to the roster." Hiring a woman would be a bitter pill for the chief of police to swallow. A pillar of the community himself, the chief granted power and trust only to those who passed the thug-mentality test. Woman like Bonnie Parker came along only once in a lifetime.

"For your enlightenment, Skip, I'm the county coroner. While on official business, I can park any fucking place I want."

He handed her a citation. "Be sure to tell that to the judge."

"You going to call them or not?" She glanced at her wristwatch. She had to get back. "Never mind, just give me a ride to the hospital."

"Did I hear the magic word?"

"The magic word is *up yours*, you asshole."

He sped away, leaving her in a choking cloud of exhaust.

She balled her fists around her citation, crumpled it into a tight ball, and screamed. The hospital was less than a mile down the road. She could see the third floor over the tops of trees in the commercially undeveloped grassland that separated the hospital to the east, the school to the west, and the housing developments to the north and south. She'd take a shortcut along the irrigation ditch, if she could get around the scummy pond, the real reason the field was undeveloped.

5

Sam WAS STILL steamed when she got to the hospital. She turned on her light, to tell the telephone operator that she was in-house, and then headed down the back hall. The administrator's secretary was on the phone but gave a little wave as Sam passed. Larry's door was open, but he wasn't at his desk. Not that she'd stop and chat if he had been. Maybe one of these days, when she had more time, she would stop to tell him how well the ER docs were working out. Whether they were or not was immaterial; the fact that she no longer had to run down to the ER every time an emergency came through the door was what mattered.

"Well, well, well. Look what the cat dragged in." Ken Miller, the radiologist, was haunting the doorway at the end of the corridor. His large frame obscured most of the word *Private* written on the back door to the radiology department.

"And you're the back-hall troll, or something?"

"Hey, don't snap at me. I'm your friend," he said, flashing his easy smile.

Sam took the Styrofoam cup out of his hand and gulped his coffee. "Is that real sugar?"

"And now you're looking a gift horse in the mouth? A hard-core caffeine addict like you shouldn't care how you get it." He gave her the once-over. "You look awful."

"This is what two hours of beauty sleep gets you."

"Try three next time. Isn't parenthood fun before they get their days and nights straightened out?"

"Listen to you! Derek, like your Mary, is the parent who

paces the floor in the middle of the night at our house. For your information, I was working."

"Well, I work just as hard as you."

"Don't look to me for sympathy. I'm tired and cranky, and we both know the other doctors think radiologists and pathologists are gold brickers."

"Is it my fault our learned colleagues weren't smart enough to find specialties where they could work eight to five? Didn't take long into my internship to realize that babies like to be born during the night, mothers panic with sick kids after midnight, and most car accidents occur after the bars close." He went down on one knee. "Give me your foot, Sleeping Beauty."

"I think the foot fetish comes from 'Cinderella.' "

He pulled off a mud-caked pump. "You been chasing buffalo again? Now the other one."

She shook it off for him and followed him into his office. "No, the fucking police towed my car away while I was at the high school. I cut across the field."

He took a letter opener from his desk. "Bring me back a water lily?"

"You're never satisfied. I bring you algae," Sam replied as she pointed to the mud, "and you want a water lily?" She followed him to the wastebasket.

He scraped mud from the first shoe. Sam took a final gulp of the coffee, getting the sugar and sediments that had settled at the bottom, and then threw it into the wastebasket.

"Maybe next year you should send a nice Christmas present over to the police station."

"When pigs fly!" Sam wiggled out of her burr-clinging pantyhose and counted five runs. "These were brand new." They followed the cup. A heavy chunk of mud sank the stockings. "Got to go look at a frozen section for Willis."

"Yeah? Mrs. Murphy's mastectomy?"

"A mastectomy, anyway. I don't know the patient's name."

"Mrs. Murphy." He shook his head. "You should see the

calcifications on her mammogram. Bless her heart. Thought he canceled her surgery. Arrhythmia."

Irregularity of the heartbeat was sound reason to postpone surgery. What was the page for then? "Got to go."

She walked on the balls of her feet around the corner and then down the side hall. Kate wasn't at her desk. But she recognized the back of Larry's bald dome. He was standing in the doorway between the office and the lab. *Wonderful*.

Sam took off her jacket and hung it on the metal tree and then put on her lab coat. She stood behind her desk to hide her bare feet. "Larry," she called as pleasantly as she could manage.

He turned around, a big smile on his face. That was a first; usually he reserved it for those he wanted to suck up to. "There you are." He came to her as if on parade. He took her arm and led her toward the lab. "They keep asking questions," he whispered.

They turned out to be three men. The youngest, a smiling kid in his twenties, had his shirtsleeves rolled up and was sifting his fingers through little pieces of David Crider's innards, which the young, single, and impressionable lab tech Terry, who was happily sitting next to him at the counter, had apparently provided. The bespectacled man, whose intense eyes bored through Sam, wore a morose look. He was small and wiry.

The last man, scrutinizing the lab's log book, seemed nervous, an acolyte assisting his first Mass. He pushed his wire-rimmed glasses up his impressive beak. Terry had chosen wisely.

"Gentlemen," Larry said, "may I introduce our pathologist, Dr. Samantha Turner."

Mr. Morose took a step forward and offered his hand. "Pleased to meet you. Roger Ryder, regional director for the Centers for Disease Control. These are my assistant, Kyle Wells"—he pointed to the acolyte—"and Tom Polvich." Tom stopped playing with the samples long enough to wave.

"Thank you for coming. I'm sorry I wasn't here when

you arrived. Thought you'd be on the midmorning plane."

"We chartered a flight."

The acolyte stepped forward and showed her an entry in the daily log. "Your assistant was unable to find a number of grids."

"I took them with me when I left last night. They're in my . . . car." Great!

"You took them with you?" Roger asked in a tone of disapproval.

"Yes, to Billings, Montana. The nearest electron microscope."

"Could you get them for us, please?" Roger commanded more than asked.

"My car's, ah. Well . . . " She swallowed her pride. "It was . . . it's at the garage. I had some trouble with it at the high school this morning."

"Here you go." Ken dropped her shoes in front of her. "As good as . . . oh . . . am I interrupting?"

Larry made the introductions as Sam stepped into her shoes. "May I introduce Dr. Kenneth Miller, our radiologist. Ken, Drs. Roger Ryder, Kyle Wells, and Tom Polvich, from the Centers for Disease Control."

Ken stopped shaking Rogers hand. "Oh?" He turned to Sam. "CDC?" as if to say, I'm your closest friend and you didn't bother to tell me we have something cooking?

Kyle waved the log. "Can you—"

Roger put a hand on the log, silencing Kyle. He turned to Sam. "Shall we go down to the morgue and have a look?"

Kate came in. "Dr. Ryder, I'm sorry, there don't seem to be any hospital records on David Crider."

"No, there aren't any," Sam explained. "He belonged to a religious sect that doesn't believe in conventional medicine. They called the mortician when he expired." She eyed Larry. "The hospital has no morgue to speak of." A tiny room in the basement where the mortician comes to claim his trophy *was* nothing to speak of. "But we can go to the funeral home." If they could solve the transportation problem.

"Sam," Kate said, "Mrs. Bellows called."

"Who?"

"Mrs. Bellows from the high school. She said to tell you Jess Gorzalka isn't in school today. Wasn't there yesterday, either."

"Is he ill?"

"Didn't say."

Sam looked from one man to the next, finally settling on Larry. "Maybe you could take our guests to the funeral home while I try to find this Jess. He might be infected."

6

SAM SCRUTINIZED THE corner of the high window in Eugene's office. The spiderwebbed crack she'd hollered about for seven years was gone, replaced with new glass. If this were still her office, not Eugene's, Sam suspected she'd be looking at the crack even now. It infuriated her beyond words. The nerve-soothing music as she waited for Judge Moots to come on the phone line wasn't helping, either.

"Hello." Moots's bellowing baritone made her miss the music.

Sam took her feet off the desk and placed them flat on the floor. "Stanley, it's Samantha Turner."

"Samantha, nice to hear from you."

She knew that wasn't so, but it was tactful of him, if not judicial. "Stanley, the police took away my Jeep while I was at the high school on official business earlier this morning. Will you call them and tell them to give it back?"

"They took away your Jeep?"

"I had to park in one of the handicap spaces, and Skip took that as leave to tow it to God-only-knows-where. And surprise of all surprises, he even gave me a ticket."

There was a long, uncomfortable, no doubt reproachful, silence. "Well, Sam. I certainly will consider the mitigating circumstances when you case comes on the docket, but there's nothing *I* can do to get your Jeep back. Call the chief."

"Call the chief!" She'd rather be horsewhipped. Didn't take much of an imagination to see the chief laughing his fool head off over the Jeep. She wished they'd find a new county attorney. Jeffrey, the former one, had always run interference for her. Now they were farming out the prosecution jobs piecemeal to the town's attorneys in private practice.

"All right, you want my best legal advice?"

"Shoot."

"Pay the tow fee, pick up your vehicle, and forget about it."

"Forget about it! Skip left me to my own devices to get back to the hospital after I'd been paged. Dammit, Stanley. It's the principle of the matter!"

Moots sighed, long and hard. "Sam, pick up your Jeep and find bigger principles." He didn't give her the chance to hang up on him.

She got up and paced the floor. She needed her Jeep back, and she knew only one other person who could waltz into the police station and get the job done with any kind of finesse. She sucked in sharply, and then picked up the phone. She punched in the numbers. The machine answered on the fourth ring. At least she didn't have to listen to his voice, only hers.

"Derek, it's Samantha. The police have impounded my Jeep while it was parked in a handicap space while I was on official business at the high school." Her voice was calm, Academy Award calm. "I'm tied up with these CDC people. Would you mind getting it back for me? Thank you. I love you." Sam hung up very gently. That would go over in a big way with him. Everything was fine and dandy, except that it didn't solve her immediate transportation problem.

"You sure we haven't passed it?" Randy asked as he drove the ambulance at a turtle's pace over the potholes that inevitably pocked the dirt roads after winter. Knowing that her dirt road was not the only neglected one in the county brought only slight solace. It would be summer before the maintenance crews would fill the holes with gravel.

"Might have been the house by the orchard, but I don't

think so. Let's go a little farther." They were looking for a mobile home several miles out on the Little Goose Creek road. The name was supposed to be carved in wood at the end of the lane as well as on the mailbox.

"There's the meat-packing plant." He pointed out a long white building and a Quonset hut. "Charlie at the Texaco station said it was before the plant." The lines on Randy's forehead were permanently set from constant worrying.

"He said he *thought* it was before the plant," Sam reminded him. Charlie knew Frank Gorzalka, Jess's father, intimately through bar conversation.

The orange ball visible behind hazy clouds had managed to climb high in the sky. She wasn't accomplishing much this morning. The lab work was piling up, and she'd put off spot-checking yesterday's Pap smears until today and still hadn't gotten around to them. Letting Eugene go off to Switzerland was the dumbest thing she'd done in a while. Fooling with precursors was the second, especially now that she had CDC doctors crawling all over the lab. She would take everything home tonight.

As they crested a knoll, Sam took in the vast expanse of the snow-laden Big Horn mountains in the west ahead of them, as well as where they curved around to the south. The rugged formations to the south were the more beautiful, to Sam's way of thinking. Especially from the ranch, where the view was unobstructed by rolling foothills or heavy foliage.

The spring runoff, if not the wet winter, had done wonders greening up the valley. Be almost August before the landscape turned a blanched wheat if this cool snap kept up much longer.

"There," Randy said, pointing to a dilapidated red mobile home, camouflaged by overgrown purple lilacs and established evergreens. Junkers and weathered livestock equipment scattered over the acreage could have benefited from some cover.

GORZALKAS was carved and burnt into the wooden plank dangling from one of the two chains on the warped gate, which had been left opened all winter if she could go by the hard mound of dirty snow around its base. The red shale county road was in A1 condition compared to the private narrow lane. They bounced rhythmically within the confines of the seat belts as they traversed the railroad tie bridge over the swift-moving creek. She'd hate to see this place when spring runoff was in full bloom.

They pulled up in the yard in front of the trailer. Smoke was coming out of a pipe on the Gorzalka roof. Most likely the heater, though a couple of cords of pinewood made her question that. An impressive stockpile for this time of year. Her wood pile was gone except for a half cord of green pine they were trying to hold off using until next season.

She looked around for signs of life. Hard telling if the family vehicle was at home with all the junkers about. Sam reached for the door handle. "Wait here until I see if he needs to be transported."

The greening grass between the red flagstones was long and horizontal, as if it had missed a last-chance fall cutting and spent the winter bent under the heavy snow. A hand mower was leaning up against the metal shed, testifying to noble intentions. A three-wheeler took sanctuary in the shed.

No one came to the door. She'd heard the doorbell ring inside all three times she pushed it, so that wasn't the problem. She had a sick feeling she knew what the problem was.

Sam lifted her collar against the chill as she walked around the trailer to the back door. They apparently had a couple of dogs, a large one and a small one. And no one had cleaned up after them for quite some time. The wooden screen was locked, but she took away a splinter as a souvenir.

She ducked under the conifer branches and peeked through the metal slats of a side window. There was nothing remarkable about the bedroom other than its being messy and empty.

The humming heater greeted her as she climbed back into

the ambulance. "Call down to the sheriff's office and ask them to send out a car. We need to get inside, see what's what," she told Randy, then sucked her thumb.

They waited in the back of the ambulance, where Randy, aided by his trusty tweezers, dug a hole in Sam's epidermis as deep as the Grand Canyon to get out the sliver. "Ouch, that hurts." She would not be nominating him for surgeon-of-the-month any time soon.

"Sorry, Dr. Turner, I almost have it," he apologized earnestly as he probed.

Definitely nice guy of the month. He swabbed the thumb with peroxide as the sheriff's outfit rolled over the railway ties. Being nearly as wide as the ties, the brown Bronco didn't have much room to maneuver.

The sheriff pulled to a stop behind the ambulance, slid out from behind the wheel, and then reached in the back for his beige Stetson to cover his thin, graying hair. He was beside the ambulance door in three long strides. The shirt to his starched brown uniform pulled tight across his middle-age spread as he opened the door. His shoulders were not very broad for a man of his height, nor did he wear his height well.

"Sam, haven't seen you in a coon's age. What's up?" He tugged up his brown pants and his gunbelt, both worn at half-mast to accommodate his generous paunch.

"Where's your jacket, Hank?"

He jerked his head to the Bronco. "Finally warming up a little. Betcha we've seen the last of snow"

No one ever said Hank was the brightest man alive, but he was open-minded and always listened to reason, some-thing she couldn't say for the moronic chief of police. "Think we have a sick teenager on our hands. His friend is laid out over at Thaddeus's." Sam glanced at the bandage Randy was wrapping around her thumb. A purple dinosaur. "No one comes to the door. Think you can get us inside?"

Hank tipped his Stetson down in front as he scratched his

head. "Reckon so. Frank Gorzalka can be ornery, but if his kid's sick . . . "

"You know these people?"

"Frank? Sure, everybody knows Frank. He supplies almost everybody hereabouts with wood. Good stuff, never green." Hank nodded to the wood stack. Sam knew whom she'd be calling come summer. "His kid is some kind of a scholar. Always getting Rotary Club awards and stuff."

"And the mom?"

"Died a few years back. Cancer." He started toward the mobile home, made a wide arc, and ended up back at his Bronco. He resumed his trip with a giant ring of keys.

Sam and Randy got out and followed him to the door. Hank wouldn't have made the best cat burglar in the world, but he finally jimmied the lock with a couple of black picks.

"Anybody here?" Hank called as he pushed the door back. "Just wait a minute, Doc," he added as Sam tried to duck under his outstretched arm. "Let's make sure everything's hunky-dory. Don't want anybody getting shot."

Being shot was the last thing on her mind. A teenager with smallpox was the first. She held back, though, because it probably was faster to let him follow procedure than to convince him it wasn't necessary.

"Anybody here?" Hank repeated as he took a hesitant step into the room, his hand on the butt of his firearm. She knew very little about weapons, but she sure knew a .38 hole from a .22. And digging out scattered shot from a shotgun wound was like winning a scavenger hunt.

Hank beckoned them in and motioned for them to stay put while he cautiously went through the rest of the place. The couch and coffee table were littered with newspapers, sports magazines, a filthy glass, and an empty liquor bottle. A giant ashtray was filled with cigar butts. A woman's touch was evident in the lace curtains, figurines, and satin lampshades, but it looked as if no one had dusted since Mrs. Gorzalka's death. The blue carpet was nearly threadbare in foot traffic areas. The kitchen countertops were loaded with small appliances, and the sink was full of dirty dishes.

"Doesn't look like he's here, Doc," Hank said as he returned to the main room. He picked up the bottle. "Canadian Black Velvet. He sure know his whiskey." He chuckled. "That was a good one, huh?"

"I don't get it, Hank."

"Whiskey? Gorzalka?"

She shook her head.

"Gorzalka's the Polish word for whiskey. Everybody knows that."

Except Sam. "You're right, Hank, that was a good one." Sam went down the hall to have a look for herself. The first room was the kid's; she knew from the trigonometry and physics textbooks on the desk. The room was just barely large enough for a single bed, let alone a desk and a dresser.

She scooted between the dresser and unmade bed, and stopped to open one of the bottom drawers just to see how he was able to get anything out of them; it was filled with baseball cards. It piqued her curiosity enough to open the other. She could see a math achievement award and a fat photo album underneath it. Folded T-shirts were in the middle drawer, which opened wide over the bed. The top drawer boasted underwear and rolled socks, a few mismatched socks stuffed along the side.

"This the kid's room, you think?" the sheriff asked.

"Most likely."

He nodded to the bed. "Sis made her bed every morning, but the missus had a heck of a time getting Junior to make his. Boys!"

Something told Sam that his missus made their bed every morning. Sam slid the closet door back to find a half-dozen shirts, a sports jacket, dress pants, and a couple pairs of jeans on hangers. Boxes of comic books filled the rest of the space. The lamp on the TV tray beside the bed was made out of carved pinewood, probably by the same craftsman who had carved the sign on the gate. One library book was Stephen King's latest, the other a Clive Barker. An empty glass and especially the thermometer raised big red flags in her brain. The bedsheets were sweat-stained. She picked up the thermometer. The mercury had reached 102.

The medicine cabinet in the cramped bathroom offered up a tube of Retin-A 0.025 percent and tetracycline 500 mg. prescribed by the dermatologist.

"Find something, Doc?" the sheriff asked as he took the vial out of her hand and rattled the capsules.

"No. That's for zits." The washcloth slipped from the edge of the sink and landed in the wastebasket. Sam fished it out of the trash and draped it over the side of the sink.

"Yeah, that's right. He has a real pizza face, that kid. Tubby with a pizza face."

"Thanks, Hank," she said as she retrieved the tetracycline and put it back into the medicine cabinet. "Appreciate you letting me in."

"What you goin' to do now?"

"Go back to town and call around to the doctors' offices. Someone's seen Jess."

7

Randy dropped her off at the bay doors of the ER. Sam rushed in out of the chilly wind. Connie was sitting at the nursing station reading a book. No one else was in sight. "Honest to goodness. Must take some nerve to cash your paycheck."

"Hi, Sam." Connie held up the book. "It's taken me three weeks to get to page seventy-four."

"Holding down the fort by yourself?"

"Dr. Nguyen is downstairs in the cafeteria, beating the lunch crunch. Dr. Jeffers won't be in until five."

Sam glanced at the clock. Almost noon. She'd have to wait until after lunch to call the doctors' offices. Most of them went home for lunch and a nap. "How are they doing?"

"Dr. Nguyen's a little persnickety. Never worked with the other one." Connie shrugged. "Dr. Jeffers sure can go through the supplies, though. Found enough discarded plaster of Paris in trash to case an entire leg. And I'll take you and Ken in a code over Dr. Nguyen, any day."

"Nice to hear you're cheering for the home team, but do Ken and me a favor and don't let the administrator hear." Sam tapped the counter a couple of times. "Hang in there."

Connie gave her the thumb's-up sign.

Sam started out, then turned back. "By the way, did a Jess Gorzalka come through the emergency room?"

Connie ran a finger down the log. "Last night. Ten-thirty."

So Jess was right here under her nose. "What's his room

number?" Sam asked as she went around the counter to have a look at the log.

"Wasn't admitted."

"Wasn't admitted?" How could that be? Sam took off her jacket and tossed it over the back of the spare chair. "Pull his chart."

"Dr. Turner," Terry called as Sam threaded through the lunch crowd in the basement cafeteria.

As politeness dictated, Sam pivoted and headed to the long table filled with lab and X-ray personnel. What the hell, the table was next to the coffee urn. The star of the show was Tom Polvich. The other two CDC docs were noticeably absent. She'd made the trip downstairs to have a little chat with Dr. Nguyen, who was sitting alone at the back corner table. She'd have it out with him soon enough. "Ah, see you've rounded up the usual suspects, Terry."

"What happened to you?" Kate asked.

Kate had seen her bare-legged earlier, so Sam deduced she meant the purple bandage. Sam held her thumb out like a badge of honor as she rounded the table to the coffee. "Just a splinter, but you know how those ambulance people are. Randy had to doctor it." She tapped Tom on the shoulder. "Hope they're treating you right."

He craned around in his chair. "Like a king."

Sam fished in her pocket for a quarter to throw into the donation basket. "Well, you're so lucky this isn't LA." Sam didn't get the laughs she expected. She poured a cup of coffee. It looked weak but smelled wonderful. "Rodney King?"

The boos, hisses, and cackles were warmly received. As was the sip of coffee.

"That was awful, Dr. Turner," Mindy said with more enthusiasm than she showed when she took X-rays.

"And we were going to ask you to join us," Terry put in.

"Can't," Sam said as she blew on the coffee. "Have to talk to the new ER doc."

"Sam," Kate said, "Derek called. Said to tell you he was waiting for an overseas call, but would take care of the car trouble after that."

Sam hoped the overseas call didn't mean he was about to vanish like her Jeep.

"And Daisy called," Kate went on, "and said she needed you to go down to the office and sign checks for her."

"Will you do me a huge favor and call her back and tell her if she needs the checks signed today, she'll have to bring them to me? I don't have time to run downtown." It was a hassle having the billing office downtown, but the patients who didn't pay their bills by mail found it more convenient to go into an office on Main Street than to drive up the Fifth Street hill to the hospital at the edge of town.

Sam caught the CDC doctor's eye. "Did you find the mortuary?" She hoped he understood what she was really asking. What were they going to do about the smallpox?

He shrugged. "I didn't go with them."

"They're not back?"

"Not yet."

Should she drive over and see what was keeping them? Drive! Maybe they called for reinforcements to inoculate everyone in the county. Maybe Larry took them over to the Holiday Inn for a leisurely meal. "Will you be upstairs after lunch?"

He nodded.

"Good, we'll catch up then." No reason to talk about Jess Gorzalka in front of everyone.

"Oh, and Sam," Kate called as Sam started away. "That DOA Randy brought in this morning wasn't under a doctor's care."

Oh yes, the man transported in the ambulance that had been the answer to her transportation needs. Sam would have a quick look at him in a minute. First she needed to talk with the ER doc.

Dr. Nguyen had done a nice job of cleaning all but the greasy sheen from his plate. If she had stopped to chat with

Terry and the rest any longer, Sam would have had to talk to him over the trash can.

"May I join you?" Sam didn't give him a chance to answer. She pulled out the chair across from him and sat. "I'm Samantha Turner, the pathologist. We met briefly last week."

The small-boned Asian doctor gave her a wry smile. "Yes, of course. The pathologist."

It was nice to be remembered. She took a quick sip of coffee and waved the chart. "Jess Gorzalka, a teenage boy, was seen in the ER last night around ten-thirty. According to his chart, he presented with a one hundred and two temperature and productive cough, complaining of nausea and backache. The orders show that he was advised to purchase an over-the-counter antihistamine for his upper respiratory infection, and then he was sent home."

"Your point?" he asked testily.

Fever, nausea, and backache were the first signs of smallpox, not that any health care expert in the world would have considered smallpox a possibility. Especially if the skin hadn't turned scarlet, or the telltale rash hadn't appeared. She would forgive the doctor that. "Where's the sputum specimen?" They both knew it was more an indictment than anything else.

"May I see?"

Sam slid the folder across the table.

He duly studied it. When he finished, he closed the folder and laced his fingers together over it. "Apparently Dr. Jeffers ruled out a staphylococcal infection without the need for auxiliary diagnostic testing. If you would be so kind as to review the Diagnostic Regulatory Guidelines you will note that unnecessary diagnostic testing is discouraged. Please understand that I sympathize with your plight as a pathologist—"

"Now just a minute. I've not come to you to drum up business, and I'm perfectly aware of the DRGs. However, if this boy had a productive cough, then a sputum culture was mandated." She couldn't have cared less which germ had caused Jess's cold. But had they sent a smear to the lab, Sam could have tested for smallpox. And she needed to make sure he understood that she would expect one if another teenager came through the ER.

"Do you know how many upper respiratory infections presented in the ER this week alone? And according to one of the internists, the number of nosocomial infections among the inpatients—"

She didn't want to talk about infections picked up in hospitals; she wanted to talk smallpox. "Granted, gram-negative organisms are currently the most frequent cause of community-acquired infections, as well as nosocomial infections, but this boy wasn't in the hospital. And, in light of a productive cough, it was vitally important to rule out the possibility of staphylococcal invasion." She couldn't believe they were having this conversation on such a moot point. Characterizing this boy's malady as an upper respiratory infection was like saying jugglers were the only performers in the circus. But she had no intention of telling the pompous ass what she suspected until the CDC could back her up. "This may be the cowboy state, but we don't practice cowboy medicine here. And we don't appreciate a couple of mavericks riding into town and bucking the system."

They stared each other down, until he turned away and had another look at Jess Gorzalka's chart. "I'll look into the matter. May I keep the chart?"

She nodded. She was finished with it. What she really wanted was to find Jess. Where was he? Why wasn't he home in bed if he felt bad enough to go to the ER last night? According to the chart, Bob Wallace was his attending physician. Maybe he would be able to shed some light.

Dr. Jeffers should have sent a sputum specimen to the lab. To think, she was the one who wanted ER docs. An old saw came to mind: Be careful what you wish for, you might just get it.

▽

8

SAM SIGNED HER name to Mr. Hopkins's death certificate, stating the cause of death as a coronary. She hadn't known Mr. Hopkins in life, but in death he had become her fast friend. No only had he been the answer to her transportation prayers but he hadn't required an autopsy.

"He's all yours." She handed the paper to dorky-looking Thaddeus Smith and gave a once-over to his expensive suit, which looked decidedly out of place in the hospital, though a dark suit was an undertaker's calling card. And she knew he'd just come from a funeral at the Baptist Church. "You say the two doctors left before noon? You sure about that?"

"Wouldn't have said it if I hadn't been." Thaddeus stuck the paper in a leather briefcase and then zipped it closed as he gave her a cold gaze and bared his teeth in a sneering grin. She doubted they would be fast friends even in death.

He had been the last county coroner and had not taken his loss to her in the polls gracefully. Most of the coroners in Wyoming were morticians, but after an incident in which she had spent more time convincing him to call an inquiry on a suspicious death of a six-year-old girl than it would have taken her to rule, she decided she'd run against him.

"You wouldn't happen to know where they were going?" It was after four. Sam couldn't imagine where they were.

"Didn't say. And it wasn't any of my business to ask."

"You're absolutely right, Thaddeus. It wasn't your business. I'm the coroner; it was *my* business." Sam showed him her teeth as she gazed into his beady eyes. He was speechless for once, though she suspected he'd find the perfect repartee as he shredded his pillow in the wee hours of the night and would deliver same at his first opportunity. Her not having won the election by a landslide came to mind, not that she would offer the suggestion.

Thaddeus slapped the briefcase to his thigh and turned on the heels of the genuine leather, hand-tooled boots. Business must have been booming. She hoped Mr. Hopkins's funeral wouldn't be too lavish.

Sam had sent Kate across the street to Bob's office for Jess Gorzalka's medical chart, but she wasn't back yet. She tried calling the Gorzalka residence again; still no answer. She went into the lab. Now Tom was gone. So was Terry. She glanced in the general direction of the precursors but decided to wait until after the place was emptied out at five to have a look. She chose going down to Larry's office over spot-checking the Pap smears and calling the ranch. She still hadn't seen hide nor hair of Derek. She dreaded the encounter as much as she looked forward to it. She hated being afoot, and she needed to know about her father.

Everything was coming apart at the seams. Her father needed constant care, but she had to bring him home right away. The clock was ticking on the precursors. Seventy-two hours as of six o'clock last night was all she had. Would Derek manage to find an attendant for her father? Derek sure couldn't take care of him. He already had his hands full with the baby. Not to mention the construction. And what about the overseas call? What would she do if he took off for parts unknown?

Ken's private door was closed so she didn't stop. She could have used a friendly smile to get her up out of the doldrums. Oh, well.

Sam gave Jean, the administrator's secretary, a wave as she walked by her desk. She peeked into Larry's office.

"He's not in." Jean started to roll a piece of paper out of her typewriter but stopped to sneeze.

"Where is he? Out kicking up his heels?"

She blew her nose before she answered. She'd had her cold for some time if Sam could go by the flaming, chapped nostrils. Of course, the cheap, rough tissues the hospital issued could have aggravated the problem.

"Taking the CDC doctors to the airport."

"What! They're leaving?" She slumped in the chair next to Jean's desk. "Did they say anything? Leave me a message? Are they coming back?" What were they going to do about the impending smallpox epidemic?

Jean shrugged as she folded the tissue over and blew her nose again.

"How long ago?" Perhaps she could catch up with them before they left.

"Maybe an hour." Jean wiped her nose.

"An hour?" They'd be long gone by now, plus she didn't have a car. Ten minutes there. Ten minutes back. Forty minutes of good-byes? Where was Larry? It hardly mattered where he was; it mattered where the CDC folks were. She felt as if she were caught in a Kafka story. They couldn't leave. They *wouldn't* leave! Surely she misunderstood what Jean said. "Did he say he was taking them to the airport so they could catch a plane, or pick up more team members?"

Jean leaned around her desk to toss the used tissue into the wastebasket. This sedate pace of hers was killing Sam. "I think they're catching a plane."

Sam opened her mouth to protest but then let it go at that. Jean didn't know any more about it than she, less really. She got to her feet. "Well, when Larry gets back, tell him I'd like to speak with him if he has a minute." Brother, what an understatement!

When Sam got back to the pathology department, Kate held out Jess Gorzalka's medical records folder. Sam skimmed the sheets of the last visit as she crossed to her desk. Bob hadn't seen him since the fall when he referred the boy to the dermatologist for his face. She sat at her desk and browsed through the medical history. The office visits were routine. She scrutinized the well-care immunizations.

A smallpox vaccine was not on the list, nor did she expect it to be.

"Wait a minute!" It hit her like a ton of bricks.

"What?" Kate asked, looking up from her work.

Sam waved her off as she picked up the phone. "Nothing, Kate."

"What do you mean, *nothing*?"

"Something I didn't see at Jess Gorzalka's place. Going to get the sheriff to take me back out."

$\triangledown$

9

SAM AGREED TO whatever Hank was talking about. She was
distracted by looking around the hospital parking lot for her
Jeep. Unless there was a message on her desk from Derek,
she'd give him a call as soon as she settled the score with
this Dr. Jeffers. "You'll let me know if Jess or his father
return home?"

Hank nodded. "Keep the deputy there all night if we have to."

"Thanks, Hank." The night chill rippled through Sam as
she slammed the door to the sheriff's Bronco, went around
the ambulance, and rushed into the ER through the bay
doors.

Dr. Jeffers had to be the fortyish man in the green surgical
scrubs, because she knew the others who were huddled
around examining table number one. Terry took the blood
gases while Dr. Nguyen monitored the EKG strips coming
off the cardiac monitor spool like a runaway train. Gary, the
evening ER nurse, pumped up the blood pressure cuff. Ken
stood at the ready next to the portable X-ray machine.

"Up the oxygen to sixty percent," Jeffers said in a calm,
deliberate voice. He was of medium height and stocky build.
An unruly cowlick at his crown swirled into the mane of
salt-and-pepper hair that swept down his bull neck practically to the collar of his scrubs.

The patient had stolen her thunder. Sam would speak
with Jeffers at a less frantic time She pushed through the
inside doors. The hall in front of the ER was crawling with

distressed friends and relatives of the patient, each having turned to the door when Sam came through, urgency painted on each face. There was nothing unusual in their reaction. They wanted, even expected, news. Good or bad, they needed to know. Pity wrenched her gut. This was universally the least favorite duty of any doctor. She preferred spending her time pursuing academic answers to why death occurred rather than delivering bad news. But this time, delivering news wouldn't fall to her.

Her jacket made them realize that she was a mere interloper. They turned away and returned to their pacing, sobbing, fidgeting, and worrying.

Sam turned on the light in the office and then tossed her jacket to the coat tree. It fell short of its goal, but she would wait to pick it up. She followed the stream of light flowing from the lab. Her heart nearly stopped when she saw Tom Polvich standing over the precursors, a petri dish in hand.

Hearing her unfortunate and untimely squeal, Tom put it down and turned, "So here you are. We've had the hardest time coordinating our schedules."

Her mind was assaulted by a hundred questions and thoughts all at once, but instead of uttering even one, she stood numbly silent.

"What're these?" he asked, motioning to the precursors.

Terry squeezed through the doorway on her way to run the blood gases. Sam was thankful for the distraction. "An experiment," she managed to say as she watched Terry. "Nothing really."

The weak explanation satisfied his curiosity. He crossed to the other side of the lab and beckoned her to follow. He looked at her long and hard, and then pulled her down on the stool next to him. "You're to be congratulated, I fear. Unbelievable."

"How could this have happened?" she asked in a whisper. "I thought the smallpox virus was totally eradicated. For nearly twenty years."

He shrugged. "That's the sixty-four-thousand-dollar

question, isn't it?" He pointed to the three containers of David's innards. "I've gone through these and chosen the specimens most involved. Roger and Kyle have rushed them back to Atlanta to confirm your suspicions, and if what we fear is corroborated, to gather up a team to swoop in here like a swarm of locusts. Nip this thing in the bud."

His words were more soothing than music. "That's great news, but I have some bad. Seems David Crider caught the virus in Washington, D.C., at a Student Congress convention. High schoolers from all over the country were there."

The significance of her words was not wasted on him. "We may be looking at a pandemic as well as an epidemic."

"And I believe we have another case here."

"Here?"

"David Crider's roommate in Washington. He was in the ER last night presenting with symptoms characteristic of poxvirus."

"Exanthema?"

"The report didn't mention skin eruptions. Fever, nausea, backache." She omitted upper respiratory infection, because it was incorrect, and her trip to the Gorzalka residence had proved it.

"Is he on one of the floors?" He got up. "Let's go up and see him."

Sam held up her hand. "He wasn't admitted, and I don't know where he is. I was—"

"Excuse me." Sam turned to see Dr. Jeffers standing in the doorway. He approached. "Excuse me," he said, "I'm sorry to interrupt." To Sam he added, "Dr. Turner?"

"Yes?"

"I'm Earl Jeffers," he said, giving her a warm, lingering handshake. "I wanted to meet you and thank you for catching my error in that young patient's ER report. Jess Gorzalka."

"The error?" she asked, wondering if he would ever release her hand.

"About the productive cough. I meant to dictate it as

nonproductive. Dr. Nguyen said you were the one who caught the mistake."

Sam waved her hand, dismissing her involvement. She wouldn't mention that she'd dragged the poor sheriff out to the trailer to check the wastebaskets for used tissues, which weren't there.

"Please know that I would have cultured the patient if he'd had a productive cough." He pressed her hand between both of his and smiled genuinely. It took a secure doctor to admit an error. Most would have said he *had* dictated it as nonproductive and the typist transcribed it incorrectly.

Sam smiled. "Thank you. Please forgive me for flying off the handle. I'm afraid I owe Dr. Nguyen an apology. I'm so sorry to start our association on such a sour note. Believe me, no one is happier that you're practicing in Sheridan."

He laughed easily. "That's not what Ken Miller told me."

Sam laughed. "All right, no *two* people are happier that you are practicing in Sheridan than Ken Miller and me." She turned to include Tom. "May I present Dr. Polvich from the CDC."

"Earl Jeffers," Earl said, holding Sams hand in his left and extending his right hand to Tom.

"Tom."

When they were finished with pleasantries and Earl had dropped both of their hands, Sam said, "Tom and I were just discussing Jess Gorzalka. It seems he was a close friend of the boy who's laid out at the funeral home. We—"

"Did the patient present with an exanthematous infection?" Tom interrupted.

Earl shook his head. "Are you suspicious of measles?"

"One of the poxviruses. Variola, perhaps."

"Smallpox! You've got to be kidding."

"We wish." Tom sighed. "I understand the patient wasn't admitted. Do you know the boy's location?"

"No, the father was going into the mountains for a few days and said something about taking his son to his sister's house."

"Do you know the sister's name?" Tom asked.

The phone was ringing. Sam left Tom to explain all to Earl "Hello," she said as she straddled the corner of her desk, picked up her messages, and started through them.

"Samantha, did you get my message?" Derek asked.

She was reading it. "About my Jeep having a broken window? A broken window!"She was going to strangle Skip. With her bare hands, she was going to strangle Skip. The message went on to say that they wouldn't be able to get the part from Casper until tomorrow, so she'd be another day without transportation.

"You were to call me and tell me what time you wanted me to pick you up."

Sam bracketed her mouth and receiver with her hand on the slight chance that the two doctors in the room were listening. "Derek, do you have my father?"

"Oh, yes. He's here, all right." Sarcasm was thick in his voice. It must not have gone smoothly. "He's had his dinner and is down for the night. I wish I could say the same for Woody." Poor Derek. He had his hands full.

She would have to take the precursors home with her. "Why don't you send Emil in for me?" Better to send the ranch hand than to have to bundle Woody up to come after her.

"And when might this be?"

"A couple of hours, I guess. I still have a thousand lab reports, and I'm tied up with the CDC folks right now. Have a line on a new case. Derek, are you going out of the country?"

"No, why?"

"You were waiting for an overseas call. I thought—"

"I found a nurse. The daughter of an acquaintance of mine. We'll talk about her when you're home. A new case?"

Thank goodness he wasn't leaving. Thank goodness he found someone to watch her father. And thank goodness that someone wasn't local. "We'll talk about that too, when I get home."

"All right. Emil will be there at seven-thirty. Call if you want him to come for you earlier."

Earlier! She'd have to scramble like the dickens to be done at seven-thirty. "Seven-thirty will be fine." Sam watched as Terry showed Jeffers the blood gases. "And Derek, I love you."

"It's nice to be appreciated. See you when you get home. 'Bye."

Sam cradled the phone and slid off the desk as Terry hurried back to the ER with the blood gas readings. She pulled the Sheridan telephone directory out of her drawer as Tom and Earl came in.

"Nice meeting you, Dr. Turner," Earl said, extending his hand.

"Sam, please. And again, I'm glad you're here and am looking forward to a long, rewarding association."

"So am I . . . Sam." He gave her a smile when he dropped her hand after another marathon shake. "Dr. Polvich"—Earl took Tom's hand—"I hope everything works out."

"As we do."

What Dr. Nguyen lacked in friendliness his partner more than made up.

Sam slumped in her chair and turned to the G's. Tom stood in front of the desk, his hands deep in the pockets of his pleated slacks. "Was the call about the new victim?"

"No, my husband. There're a dozen Gorzalkas. Can you believe that?"

"Is your husband a doctor, too?"

"A journalist. Most likely Mr. Gorzalka's sister has a different last name. But maybe the Gorzalkas are all related and one of them knows where Jess is."

"Sam, I wonder if I could get you to look at something for a minute."

"Sure." She followed him into the lab and leaned over the microscope. She was looking at a low-power view of two foci of pneumonic consolidation. A bronchus filled with exudate. The intervening alveoli contained edema fluid.

"Bronchopneumonia?"

She looked up at Tom and nodded. "Where did it come from?"

He pointed to the container that had held David Crider's lungs. She hadn't noticed any patches of inflammatory consolidation on the lobes during the autopsy.

Sam looked at the label on the container. "Are you certain this came out of that?"

"Prepared the slide myself." He held out a vial of clear liquid. "And smell this."

She sniffed. "Smells like ether." She sniffed again. "What does it smell like to . . . " Tom's face whirled in a circle before her. The entire room oscillated and then turned black.

▽

10

THE COCOON OF sleep ripped apart, and Sam's eyelids spread stringy glue as she labored to see the light on the ceiling. Her jaw was forced open and her throat was sore and raw from the ventilator tube that was jammed down it, doing her breathing for her. An IV line ran along a stainless steel railing into her left arm. Gradually she became aware of the hissing, beeping, whisking, and clicking of life support systems echoing around her like a percussion symphony.

What was she doing here in the intensive care unit? Was she in critical condition? Her father, who was dying, had never made it to the ICU. Was she involved in a car accident? Yes, something about her car. What happened? Why couldn't she remember? Why was her brain so sluggish? Why couldn't she breathe?

Panic hit her like a wall of bricks. She needed to get the fat tube out of her mouth. She tried to free her hand from the restraining terry cloth strapped to the railing guard but was too weak.

"Are you awake?" It was Derek's voice, sounding husky and far away. He cut off the light overhead as he bent over her and stroked her cheek lightly. "Can you hear me?" His blurred features gradually came into focus. His face was ghostly white against the stubble of black whiskers. His lachrymal ducts were tear swollen and his eyes haunted by anxiety. She tried to speak, to assure him that she was fine, but the choking ventilator tube prevented it. She moved her fingers, catching a piece of his hip. He turned and grabbed her hand with an urgency he'd never exhibited before and squeezed her fingers together as if propelling his life forces into her. "You're going to be just fine, Samantha."

Yes, that was what she wanted to assure him. She was fine.

He stroked her arm tenderly, and then ripped loose the Velcro strip in order to lift her hand to his lips. The skin was painkiller numb to his kisses. "Darling, I was so worried."

She willed her finger to caress the side of his nose. He flinched when instead it poked him in the eye. He sucked back tears and then took it to mean she wanted him to take the matted sleep from her eyes. What she really wanted was to know what had happened to her.

"Is she awake?" a nurse asked as she leaned over on the other side of the bed. Sherry; Sam knew her fairly well. She'd been out of nursing school a couple of years. She had always seemed frail when Sam saw her around the hospital. But here in her element, Sherry looked robust and energetic. "You're looking much better today, Dr. Turner," she said as she worked a kink out of the IV line.

Today! How long had she been like this?

"Your urine's flowing nicely now. We won't have to worry about kidney damage." Sherry lifted the urine bag to prove her point. Sam suspected she would have been more impressed if she knew the diagnosis.

Derek squeezed her hand. "Good thing the CDC doctor was here. He recognized your symptoms as hantavirus almost immediately."

Hantavirus. The mystery illness that had victimized American Indians in the Four Corners region of New Mexico and Arizona a couple of years back. If memory served, most victims died of fluid buildup in the lungs. They literally suffocated. She watched her chest rise and fall to the lulling ventilator.

"We have six cases now. Getting real crowded in the ICU."

Six cases? She searched Derek's tired face for answers.

Another person came into her line of vision.

"You remember Dr. Polvich from the CDC, don't you, Samantha?" Derek asked as if her mind were affected as well as her body. Sam gave his hand a weak squeeze, hoping he'd take that as a *yes*. She didn't know if she could manage *no*. One squeeze took half the strength of two.

"There she is," Tom said, a big smile on his face. "You're to be congratulated for calling us in from the very beginning. David Crider will be the sole fatality in this hantavirus epidemic."

David Crider! *No*, she wanted to yell. She squeezed Derek's hand twice. And then again. He stroked the back of her hand. "David Crider didn't die of smallpox, Samantha. The test results came back from the CDC in Atlanta as hantavirus. You and Bob caught it when you performed the autopsy; Thaddeus from preparing him at the funeral home; Terry from the specimens at the lab. And, of course, the Criders."

Sam squeezed his hand twice. No, No, No, No. Hantavirus isn't spread from person to person but by rodent droppings. David Crider couldn't have given her, or anyone else, hantavirus even if he had it. Which he didn't!

Derek squeezed her hand once. "Samantha, you've been very ill. I'm sure you're confused. We shouldn't have upset you with all that's been happening. Try to get some rest. Concentrate on getting well so you can come home to us." He kissed her fingertips and then lowered her hand to her side.

No! She tried to reach his hand, but hers was too heavy.

"I'm giving you something to make you sleep, doctor's orders," Sherry said as she pushed the drug into the IV line. They were all being patronizing, and she hated that.

Who was her doctor? She had an obstetrician, and Woody had a pediatrician. Which of Sheridan's medicine men had been called in to care for her? It made a great deal of difference to her. Not all doctors were created equal. Which drugs had he prescribed? What was Sherry giving her? She didn't want to sleep. She wanted answers. Answers to questions that refused to come out of her mouth.

She tried to contort her fingers around the line to pull the IV out. Sherry moved the line out of her reach. "Now you behave."

Sam looked at Derek imploringly. Don't let them do this, she wanted to say. She wanted him to tell her what all this was about. She wanted to see her chart. She wanted to breathe on her own.

The elephant carried Sam between its yellowed ivory tusks, his trunk down her throat filling her lungs with air. He was decked out in incessantly tinkling yellow bells. The elephant was taking her to Jess, who had all the answers. The earth thundered with each footfall. The sun beat down on them. But they would not be stopped in the quest for truth.

They stomped into the arena. The crowd laughed as the clown jumped off a zebra and wagged his finger, scolding her for bringing an elephant into the center ring at the rodeo. Everyone in the stands got to their feet as the band played the national anthem and the grand entry began. First the color guards—twelve red-velvet-costumed ladies cantered sidesaddle, their hats' feather plumes at the slant in the beastly wind. Then the young cowboys circled round, each of them covered with exploding yellow pustules. Sam shouted through the megaphone trunk that they should disperse, that the yellow pustules were highly contagious, but no one could hear her over the singing.

The crowd fell silent as the clown strode to the center ring, dragging his red cape behind him like a bride's train. He turned his back on the elephant and whirled the red cape in front of him, stamping his feet and yelling, "Toro!" A Brahman bull, with David Crider on top, charged the red cape.

"Can the rider stay on for seventy-two hours?" announcer Ken Miller asked the crowd over the PA system.

At the last instant, the clown pirouetted, whirling the cape in front of Sam. The bull crashed into them, knocking the trunk out of her mouth and sending David somersaulting onto the elephant's back.

The bull had knocked the wind out of her. She struggled to suck air. Someone was above her with a suction bulb, emptying her lungs of fluid. She couldn't catch her breath. She was suffocating. Foaming slobber rolled from the corners of the angry bull's mouth.

Two riders were coming to the rescue. She thought they were on horses, but now she realized they were riding buffaloes. "Don't let your buffalo stir up the dust," she called to the advancing spotters. "The rodent droppings will spread the smallpox."

"Not smallpox," the Asian cowboy corrected as he whirled his lariat high overhead. He rode Curly. Big black stitches, where her murdered buffalo's head had been reattached, ran around his neck like a collar. She was so happy to see him.

"Hantavirus," the cowboy's smiling partner said as he reached out for Sam's hand.

She tried to reach his hand, but hers were tied to the elephant's ivory tusks. She needed to tell Earl to look at the bells on the elephant, to see the yellow pustules for himself. But all she could do was gasp for air.

Earl smiled and shoved the elephant's trunk down her throat. "You don't need to breathe. The elephant is breathing for you."

The elephant has smallpox, and everyone at the rodeo would have smallpox. Unless she could find Jess.

11

Thursday, April 22

As THE CHAUFFER edged right, at a snail's pace, off the highway and onto the Langley exit, which deadheaded at the main gate, Derek wondered how he had ever forgotten Virginia's morning rush-hour traffic. He felt a strange mixture of coming home and being trapped.

He walked down the corridor filled with anxiety and anger at being summoned to CIA headquarters. His wife was fighting for her life, and he wanted to be at her side, but he had been told this meeting was about her.

Derek picked lint from his navy suit. It was fluff from the tail of the bunny appliqué on Woody's yellow sleeper. Somehow he couldn't see the deputy director being impressed with bunny fluff. He flicked it to the floor.

He worried about the baby. It was his first separation from both parents since Samantha and he had brought him home from the hospital. Woody was in good hands, Derek assured himself.

Nicola Sajnovics's plane from Paris to New York had been delayed, causing her to miss her flight to Denver. By the time she arrived in Sheridan, Nicola was exhausted. Not that exhaustion kept her from swooping Woody out of Derek's arms and crooning a Magyar folk song.

It was the same pentatonic tune Nicola's father had sung in soft tones to keep her still as the three of them huddled near the Austrian-Hungarian border, waiting for a military patrol to go by. Twenty years had passed since that dark night when Professor Sajnovics, a revisionist sociologist, and his small daughter escaped the Iron Curtain through the mine fields and barbed wire with only a mine map and a penlight to lead the way. But Derek had no trouble spotting Nicola as she got off the plane—not because she resembled that frightened little girl but because she had inherited her father's height and bulk. Attila the Hun, as he was affectionately called by his students at the Sorbonne.

Derek was escorted into the deputy director's office as soon as he arrived and was taken aback as he realized this was not a private session. Standing in front of their chairs to the right of the deputy director's desk were two men. The pudgy man in a three-piece gray suit pulled at the points of his vest, which didn't quite hide his barrel chest. He bore his weight with a certain dignity, if not a politician's flair. The shorter man wore a department store brown suit that needed a tuck under both arms. To the left was Colin Webster, adviser to the president.

Samantha had outdone herself this time. He only hoped whatever this was wouldn't cost him her life.

"Thank you for coming so quickly. No transportation snags, I trust." The deputy director leaned over his desk, his arm extended.

Derek grasped the outstretched hand firmly. "No, sir."

The deputy director started introductions with the man in the gray suit. "Derek Turner, Dr. Charles Zimmerman, deputy assistant secretary of the Department of Health and Human Services."

"Dr. Zimmerman," Derek repeated as he shook the man's hand.

"And Dr. Maximillian Ross, director of the U.S. Centers for Disease Control."

"Dr. Ross." Derek shook the other doctor's hand. An impressive gathering, to say the least.

"And Colin Webster, adviser to the president of the United States."

"A pleasure, Mr. Webster." Derek finished the handshaking formality, his mind racing with questions he probably wouldn't be able to ask.

The men returned to their seats, leaving the chair in front of the desk for Derek.

After what seemed an eternity, the deputy director cleared his throat. "Derek, it seems we are faced with a delicate situation." He nodded to Dr. Zimmerman, who pushed up his sleeve to give his watch a good look. *The truth shall make you free* was the Company motto. Getting at that truth separated the greats from the would-have-beens.

The doctor adjusted his sleeve just so. "Several weeks ago . . . " He crossed his legs, ankle to knee, and started again. "What do you know about smallpox, Mr. Turner?"

"I know that the boy who supposedly gave my wife hantavirus had smallpox, if that's what you mean."

"Derek," the deputy warned.

"Forgive me. It's a very trying time for my family and myself right now." He had pored over every medical book his wife owned to bone up on smallpox and had been very vocal to the doctors who were caring for Samantha, but he said simply, "I know probably no more than any other layman."

Zimmerman nodded and laced his fingers together over his knee as if settling in for a long lecture. "Smallpox was officially certified as obsolete on May eighth, nineteen eighty. Shortly after that, vaccinations were stopped. The last case of naturally transmitted smallpox was documented in Somalia in nineteen seventy-seven. The last case, however, was in nineteen seventy-eight. A laboratory accident in England exposed and killed a medical photographer, Janet Parker."

"And now?" Derek challenged.

"In a minute, please." Dr. Zimmerman collected his thoughts. "For fear that such an accident might again take place, the world's remaining stocks were consolidated into two collections. A two-hundred-strain collection is in Moscow at the Research Institute for Viral Preparations. The vials have been frozen in liquid nitrogen at a minus ninety-four degrees Fahrenheit, guarded by police around the clock."

"You said two."

Dr. Zimmerman gave Dr. Ross a scornful be-my-guest gesture.

"The other virus specimens are padlocked in a freezer in a tiny room under constant electronic surveillance at the U.S. Centers for Disease Control and Prevention in Atlanta."

"*Were*," Doctor Zimmerman amended.

"Were?"

"The World Health Organization in Geneva has recommended destroying the virus now that U.S. and Russian scientists have finished charting its genetic makeup," Zimmerman explained.

Dr. Ross took over. "Not all virologists agree. Some believe that wiping out a species, even one as despised as smallpox, would set a dangerous precedent. Others fear that despite cracking the genetic code, we may not know all we need to know about the virus. And there are those who question whether there might be some future beneficial use for this virus that we cannot foresee."

"It's a minority opinion. The American Society for Virology and the American Society for Microbiology have voted in favor of destroying the two sets of vials," Dr. Zimmerman assured Derek and reminded Dr. Ross.

Webster stepped to the plate. "Russian leaders have agreed to destroy their sets at the same time we destroy ours."

"How does my wife fit in to all of this?" Derek asked.

Dr. Zimmerman glared at Dr. Ross. "It seems a renegade virologist, who had access to the stock at the CDC in Atlanta, stole a vial."

"His intentions were honorable enough," Ross said defensively. "Not that we condone his action. He was removing the vial to another safekeeping area so there would be one strain of the virus left."

"Needless to say," Webster said, "people would take a dim view of a world power that couldn't manage to hold on to a tiny vial of a virus. We *are* the custodians of a stockpile of weapons."

Derek never ceased to be amazed at the politicians' understatements. "And what happened to the vial?" He addressed the question to the deputy director to cut through the rhetoric.

"His car with the briefcase containing the vial was stolen. The car turned up in Bethesda, Maryland, the briefcase in an alley behind the Hyatt Regency. The vial was in the case, though the seal had been tampered with."

The deputy director consulted the file on his desk before he continued. "Sheridan High School had a block of rooms at the hotel during the time the vial was missing. Our best guess is that David Crider ran across the briefcase with the vial inside, opened the vial, was not impressed, and left it where he found it."

"Smallpox is an airborne virus," Dr. Ross informed him.

"No one else noticed the briefcase? No one else was exposed?"

They shook their heads collectively. It was the one thing they agreed upon.

"What about the carjacker?"

"He must not have opened the vial," Dr. Ross explained.

"All right. Then, Dr. Ross, when the CDC received the call from my wife, a team of doctors went to Sheridan to control the spread of the disease."

"Correct."

"Then why is my wife, not to mention the five other people who came in contact with the boy, fighting for her life?"

"She isn't fighting for her life. None of them are. We needed them out of the way so we could do our work. A muscle-relaxing drug is mimicking respiratory distress."

The memory of her hooked up to life support equipment was enough to make him contemplate killing all four of these sons of bitches. And then slowly torture the one in Sheridan who had been feigning concern for the last seven frightening days and terrifying nights. But this was not the time to let his emotions get the better of him. These men were too powerful to be enemies. He would simmer, long and slow. "Why did you call me here?" he asked, as calmly as he could. "Why are you telling me all this?"

"Three reasons," the deputy director answered. "One, we understand you've been asking a lot of questions. You're one of us, Derek. I wanted to be the one to give you the answers."

His meaning was clear. Remember which side you're on and stop rocking the boat. It's only because we know you will keep our secret that you're not in intensive care with the rest of them. "Thank you, sir."

"Two, all specimens and contamination from the stolen vial have been destroyed, so the matter is closed.

"And lastly, it is time for your wife and the others to make a full recovery. We want you to keep an eye out. Make certain the transition runs smoothly. The patients will be given a memory-suppressant drug, so you shouldn't have *too* much trouble." Their eyes met in shared knowing. The deputy director would not mention in front of strangers—be they coconspirators in *this* operation—Samantha's notorious track record of noncompliance with government agencies.

It was all Derek could do not to leap up, grab the bastard by the collar, and coldcock him. "I understand, sir," he said evenly. The mere thought of Samantha being duped by these men was more than a little unsettling. True, she had a penchant for falling into trouble. Sure, she wasn't the most cooperative person in the world. But it was only because she didn't suffer fools. Period.

Part of Derek understood and appreciated their predicament and the international consequences if this were to get out. The other part felt furious that Samantha was victimized. He was relieved knowing she'd "recover," and hoped he would be able to come up with a credible explanation. But what about her father and his missed chance for a cure? How would he help Samantha deal with that low blow?

He got up to go. He shook hands with the distinguished sons of bitches, and then started to the door. He had his hand on the doorknob before the idea came to him. He walked slowly back, formulating his words. "Sir, I believe I know a way to ensure my wife's cooperation."

∇

12

Sunday, April 25

SHE DIDN'T NEED help getting out of the wheelchair, for petesake. She slapped away John's hand, gripped the arms of the wheelchair, and started to push out. Okay, so this wasn't exactly a bed of roses and Sam knew that just because a person has been discharged doesn't mean they feel like running a marathon, but she wasn't about to worry her husband, John.

"Watch your step, Samantha," John said as the wheelchair rolled backward until the solicitous LPN could brace it.

"Fuck off, John," she said hoarsely. Forget that she was hopelessly shaky, her throat was so sore she could barely swallow, and she had a steel vise squeezing tightly around her chest; she just wished her memory were better. John had to tell her three times the day of the week, Sunday. She'd been in the hospital ten days. She couldn't remember any of it.

"Wow, Sam!" Ken said, laughing. "You called him John."

"What did you expect me to call him—Dr. Turner? I suppose you want to be called Dr. Miller?"

"Sam—" Ken stopped short as the other man shook his head.

"Ha." Why was her brain so fuzzy? She couldn't even remember what she had for breakfast. If she had breakfast. Dr. What's-His-Name said her memory loss was due to the heavy medication they had to give her to resolve her respiratory infection and was not permanent brain damage.

If it were permanent brain damage and this is what she had to look forward to, she hoped John would take her out and shoot her. It was Sunday.

"Watch your head."

"Fuck off, John. I'm perfectly capable of . . . ouch." Her depth perception was on the fritz, too. John's Mercedes was lower-slung than she remembered. Remembered? What a hoot! She collapsed in the seat and rubbed the knot on her forehead. "I can put on my own seat belt!" She wrestled it away. What was wrong with everybody?

Ken leaned in and kissed her cheek. "I'm so glad you're well," he whispered in her ear. "You scared the crap out of us."

"What did I do, Ken?"

Ken and John exchanged cryptic glances, then Ken turned back to her and smiled. "You did good, young lady. You did good."

What did he mean? "What do you mean?"

"I mean I've never seen such an impressive comeback. You fought the beast and won." Ken patted her knee and stepped out of the way as John closed the door.

Fought the beast? What beast? Why couldn't she remember.

John got behind the steering wheel and took off like a bat out of hell. He turned onto the road in front of a pickup. When the driver of the pickup finally laid off his horn, she asked, "What's wrong with you, John? You almost ran that pickup off the road."

He pulled to the shoulder and turned off the motor. The two vertical lines between his eyebrows deepened as he scowled at her. He snapped her seat belt free and pulled her into his arms. "Oh, Samantha. Samantha." He crushed her to him. "I was so afraid I was going to lose you."

Sam savored the warm secure feeling of being wrapped in his arms. Every fiber of her being relished his warmth. "I would never leave you, John. You are my life," she whispered, laboring to breathe. "I knew that first day I walked into your department." The other interns in the orientation group, his staff, everyone else faded away. She stood paralyzed before him, her heart racing out of control.

She felt his tears fall on her neck. That was all it took for her to break down. They sobbed and rocked in each other's arms until the console between them made it too painful.

He leaned across her and pulled the seat belt over her. He searched her eyes for an uncomfortable length of time, as if he wanted to say something. In the end, he brushed her hair away from her face and gave her a tender kiss on the lips. "Let's go home."

The cattle- and horse-dotted landscape was familiar but as wrong as an ill-fitting puzzle piece. She could see John negotiating a winding road into a deep forest and out onto sharp cliffs, not this straight two-lane road running along fenced-off pastures. And instead of the expanse of blue ocean, the road paralleled the high mountains to the west and ran straight toward the southern end, where the mountains dropped off to the eastern plains.

A nagging feeling told her that John and she were out of sync. She was the one out of sync. She was dull-witted. Would her thinking ever clear up or would she be like this the rest of her life? Her brain needed to be a thousand times sharper if she hoped to return to work.

TURNER RANCH hung high over the entrance, erasing some doubts. She was so frustrated. "This is our home, isn't that correct?"

"Yes, this is our home. Yours and mine."

"Yours and mine, and the baby's."

"And the baby's." He found her hand and lifted it to his lips. "Samantha, you have brought me all the happiness I have ever dreamed of." He kissed the tips of her fingers.

"John, you have it backward. It is you who have given me all the happiness I ever dreamed of. My life would be an empty shell without you to share it. I love you with my heart and soul."

John freed her hand so he could downshift. The ruts in the red-shale road were deceptively deep, because they were filled with water. Some were almost too deep for the Mercedes.

"Look," she said, pointing to the south side of the house, "the frame's up." They were building on to the house. It was such a relief to remember something.

"It is indeed. We've been busy bees while you were lollygagging in the hospital. The roof goes on tomorrow, if the cedar shakes arrive."

"The house looks so long. Remember how deep and narrow our beach house was? This house would cost a fortune on the beach."

"Well, if spring runoff gets any worse, the creek's beds will overflow and we'll have beachfront property."

She looked down at the creek as they crossed the bridge. John was right. He always was. The water was way up.

Her Jeep wasn't in sight. There was something about it nagging at her. She hated being so dull-witted! "I was in a car accident, wasn't I?"

"No, you were ill. In respiratory distress," he added as he swung around the north side of the house. Close to the garage there were pockets of snow where the sun never reached. The asphalt pad in front of the garage was icy all winter. Why anyone would build a garage on the north side of a house was a mystery to her. "The diagnosis was hantavirus."

"Really? How odd."

"Odd. How do you mean?" He reached up to the visor to click open the garage door.

Her Jeep was parked in the garage. How clever of him to make room for a second car in their two-car garage. And it wasn't smashed. "It's been so wet. I could see coming in contact with rodent droppings in July, August, or September, but not during the spring."

John pulled into the garage next to the Jeep. "Well, my dear, that's what they told me."

"Told *you*," she said when he came around the car and opened the door for her. "Since when did you ever let anyone tell you anything? You're the one who tells them." Her knees buckled as she tried to get out and straighten up, but John was there to support her. She looked up into his face. "You were satisfied? You looked at the slides yourself?"

He covered her mouth with his and gave her a deep, lingering kiss. "Come on," he said, wrapping his arm around her shoulders, "let's go see the baby."

The family room off the garage seemed chilly. "We should build a fire or two."

"The only wood that's left is green," he said. "Be a while before we can get the truck up the trail for the deadfall. I'll turn up the thermostat."

"Not the two cords at the side of the trailer," she called after him.

He looked at her over his shoulder. "What trailer?"

That was a good question. "I don't know." She pointed to her head. "But I know it's Sunday."

"Sunday it is." He blew her a kiss before he continued his journey to the hall.

The cat rubbed up against her. Its name escaped her.

She followed the cabinet-slamming noise into the kitchen. Her brain fogged up again, and she didn't recognize the woman at the sink. Her shiny dark brown hair was her best feature. Unlike her eyebrows, which practically kissed, her hair was parted down the middle and was cut blunt at the top of her collar. The white lace collar was attached to a dark, flowered cardigan sweater that gapped between each of the buttons, showing rolls of lily white skin. Her black pleated skirt covered her knees but not the tops of her red wool socks. Her moon face was pockmarked, and new acne eruptions were evident.

The Retin-A and tetracycline the dermatologist prescribed weren't working Next time Sam saw him, she would speak to him about starting her on a regimen of Accutane. The twenty-week supply of Accutane was expensive, about a thousand dollars, but it was a one-time treatment, and the result should be well worth the expense. John wouldn't mind paying for it.

Sam hardly recognized the baby in the crook of the meaty arm. Despite the juxtaposition of his lilliputian body against the giant bulk of the young woman, Sam could tell that he'd grown dramatically over the last ten days. The cat's name finally came to her. Kitty Cat.

"Look at you," Sam said as she took Woody. She smothered him with kisses, then just as suddenly stopped as she realized what she had done. John had come into the kitchen at the other end through the hall. "I'm not contagious now, am I?" she asked, a hollowness in her gut at the thought of giving whatever she had to the baby.

He shook his head.

She gave Woody a big juicy smack and held him close. She smiled at the young woman. "Forgive me, my mind's a blank. I can't recall your name."

"Her name is Nicola Sajnovics," John said, as he put one arm around Sam's waist and stroked the baby's hair with the other."You haven't met. Nicola just arrived from Hungary to care for Woody. And you until you're better. Her English isn't good, but I'm certain it's better than your French or Hungarian."

John stepped around her to speak to Nicola. *"Kivanok jo napot."*

"Jo napot," Nicola repeated with a nod.

John pointed to Sam. *"Beszel angolul."*

"Angolul, igen. Ertem."

"I told her you speak only English. She understands," he translated, "and will speak English."

"I speak, ah . . . " It was on the tip of her tongue; she just couldn't remember.

"Trust me, Samantha. You don't speak a second language."

"Latin."

He turned to the woman. *"Hogy va?"*

"Jobb." Nicola shook her head. "Better."

John took Woody out of her hands and into Nicola's.

"Nicola has had some trouble with dysentery, but she tells me she's better now."

"Water," Nicola added.

"She blames our water."

"I understood that," Sam told her English-to-English translator.

He put his hand at the small of Sam's back. "Come on, let's get you upstairs and into bed. You're worn out from the drive home. Please excuse us, Nicola. *Kerem bocsanat.*"

"Welcome to our house, Nicola." As they were going down the hall, she whispered to John, "Where did you find her? In the Amazon?"

"Don't talk that way about Attila the Hun. She's very sweet."

Sam sighed. "Well, we shouldn't have to worry about her running off to marry someone anytime soon and leaving us in a lurch. Maybe we could trim her down some."

"I don't know. Nicola likes to eat."

Why wouldn't she? Food doesn't reject the eater, and it can be rewarding. They would have to find something without calories to reward her. "Maybe she would like horseback riding?"

They hadn't quite gotten to the foot of the stairs when Nicola called after them. "Derek, *hol van a*—"

Sam swung around. They stared at each other as a veil over her memory fell away. Not John, her deceased husband. Derek, his son. Derek, the father of her son. Derek, her husband. "Why didn't you stop me when I was walking down memory lane?" Her tone was harsher, and her voice hoarser, than she had meant it to be. He tried to pull her into his arms, but she pushed away. "Fuck off, Derek." She started up the stairs.

"Don't say that in front of Nicola; she's likely to pick it up." If he was attempting levity, he failed miserably.

Sam squared her shoulders and climbed to the landing, where she stopped because she was out of breath. He was still looking up at her she noticed when she turned to climb the next steps. "You should have corrected me instead of letting me go on hurting you."

Derek took the stairs two at a time. He folded his arms around her, and she cried on his chest until his shirt was soaked. "I know you love me every bit as much as you loved my father." Derek carried her the rest of the way.

▽

13

Monday, April 26

THE POUNDING STARTLED Sam from her frightening dream. The rodeo crowd was laughing at her. She looked down to see that her horse was a zebra. She kept yelling over their grotesque cries, telling them that they needed to disperse before the smallpox epidemic hit them. Then a bull gored her, tossing her into the corral of stampeding elephants. She was happy to be awake and out of her nightmare.

Her head reeled, and even the marrow in her bones screamed in horrifying agony. She looked at the three vials on the nightstand: an antibiotic, a painkiller, and a sleeping potion. She would wrestle with the antibiotic's childproof cap later when she had more strength. Now she had to decide whether or not to kill her pain. Her thinking was so confused, maybe she should suffer the pain and try to clear her head instead of going around in a state of delirium.

Today was Monday. This logical conclusion followed from Derek's—not John's—telling her three times yesterday that it was Sunday. Her body was in worse shape than her mind. Her reward was a fight with the childproof cap. She would take one painkiller in the morning and then try to go the rest of the day without another.

Hammering. That's what had brought her out of sleep. The cedar shakes must have arrived, and now they would have their roof. When the construction was finished, she would bring her father home from the nursing home to live with them.

A little water spilled on the nightstand as she picked up the glass. She didn't bother with the water but concentrated on getting the pill down her throat, which refused to swallow. She coughed and spit, but the pill was down. She was able to get the glass back on the nightstand before she collapsed to the pillow.

She stared at the water spot that would ruin the walnut finish and listened to the whinnying of a horse and the muffled voices beyond the hammering. She recognized one this time: Derek, telling someone that they would discuss it, whatever it might be, when he got back from feeding the buffalo. He and John had the same voice, as well as looking alike. It was little condolence for the overwhelming shame of mistaking Derek for John. Derek had been right, though. She loved him every bit as much as she had loved his father. Maybe even more for giving her the baby and for not dying and leaving her the way John had.

Sam was just about back to sleep when the phone ringing jarred her. She looked at it, but decided to ignore it. There was no one she wanted to talk to right now, and if it were for Derek, she didn't have the energy to take a message. The machine would pick it up on the fourth ring.

The ringing stopped after three.

Heavy footfalls stomped up the stairs. The door opened a crack, and Attila the Hun peeked in.

"Is the phone for me?" Sam asked, happy that she could reach such a conclusion.

The door opened wider, and Nicola answered in apologetic rapid-fire jumbled English. *Kate* was the one word that clicked.

Sam reached over and picked up the receiver. "Yes?" she said hoarsely.

"Is that you, Sam?"

"Yes."

"You don't sound much like yourself. Who was that person who answered the phone? I could hardly understand her. She talked so funny."

"She's our au pair. From Hungary."

"Your what? From Hungary? Isn't that one of those Communist countries?"

"Kate, what was it you called about?"

"Oh, yeah. Sorry to disturb you while you're sick and all, but the co-op just called to say that someone just called them and asked if you still wanted those fertile hen's eggs, because they have some now. I don't know what to tell them."

Sam should have answered the easier Communist question. What in the world did she want with fertile hen's eggs? Herpes simplex was the only reason she could think of, and there were far easier tests these days. "Did you ask Eugene?"

"Dr. Gordon?" Kate asked, in a surprised, if not irritated tone. "He's in Switzerland!"

"Switzerland? What's he doing there?"

There was a long pause on the other end of the line "This is you, isn't it? Dr. Turner?"

"Yes, Kate, it's me. I'm a bit foggy from the painkillers I'm taking." Why Eugene was in Switzerland didn't seem as important as who was minding the store. "Kate, if I'm here and Eugene is in Switzerland, who's there? Who's doing the work?"

"Dr. Polvich was, but he didn't show up this morning."

Who the hell was Dr. Polvich? She hit the side of her skull with the flat of her palm to knock some sense into it. It didn't help but did prove that the painkiller had kicked in. "Did you try calling Dr. Polvich?"

"Of course I did! He's staying at the Holiday Inn, but his room didn't answer."

"Call back out to the Holiday Inn and have them send someone up to his room; make sure he's not ill." Whoever he is.

"Okay, I'll do that right now."

"And Kate—" Sam waited until she was sure Kate still had the phone to her ear and wasn't in the process of disconnecting her—"go ahead and buy the eggs. I'll be in as soon as I can."

Sam hung up and struggled out of bed. Even standing in the shower was a struggle. Soaping up with shaky hands would have been comical were it not so serious. Before, the shower had been a place to do her best thinking. Unfortunately, not today. Understanding, insight—zip. Even clairvoyance would have been welcome. What were the fertile hen's eggs for? Why was Eugene in Switzerland? How had she contacted hantavirus in the wet spring? Who was Dr. Polvich, and why wasn't he covering for her?

Sam wrapped a towel around herself, pulled a green sweater and a pair of clean jeans off the shelf in the closet that connected the bedroom and bathroom, and labored toward the dresser in the bedroom. She rifled through the dregs of her underwear. It didn't take a keen mind to realize that she needed to wash a load of white clothes. She rejected three pairs of panties before she found one with only an excusable small rip. Her white boot socks didn't match, but they were close, and no one would see them anyway.

She sat on the bed to dress. All in all, she'd rather be in Philadelphia. That was another thing. She could recite a quip from W. C. Fields, could remember her childhood like yesterday and most of her adult life *before* her illness, but couldn't remember a blasted thing from when she got sick, until yesterday. She could be thankful that her memory loss was short-term and would bone up on short-term amnesia in the hospital library after she sorted out the lab's problems.

In the kitchen, Sam found Woody conked out in his swing, his head tilted against the blanket wadded up on one side of the canvas seat to fill the empty space and prop him up. Tough work being a little fellow.

She wouldn't disturb him, but it took all of her willpower to keep from pulling him out of the swing and cradling him in her arms. She hoped she wasn't contagious, but even if she were, she'd already exposed him. Iatrogenic disorders, doctor-caused, and nosocomial infections, hospital-produced, were more common than anyone but a malpractice lawyer would care to admit. Derek's reassuring answer to the question about being contagious, which she thought she was asking John, didn't give her much comfort. John would have known that she was asking if she had been afflicted by one of a number of strains of insidious germs that manage to grow under the most sterile conditions and are passed from health-care-worker carriers to defenseless patients.

"Sweet baby," Nicola whispered as she looked at the baby over Sam's shoulder.

Sam smiled. "Yes, isn't he."

"*Nagyon kicsi*"

"Sorry?" She turned to Nicola. The girl showed practically all of her gums when she smiled, making her teeth appear too small for her mouth. And the poor thing needed to tweeze her eyebrows in the worst way. Sam hoped she could get beyond Nicola's looks and get to like her better, though breaking through the language barrier might prove far more difficult.

Nicola pointed to herself and then held her hands wide. "Big." She pointed to the baby and drew her hands almost together. "*Kicsi. Petit.*"

"Petite. Yes, he's petite, all right. Two months premature." The last part may have been lost on the girl. Sam willed her eyes off the baby and helped herself to coffee.

"Breakfast?" Nicola asked not too loudly, following her to the coffeemaker.

Sam shook her head. "Coffee's fine." Coffee wasn't fine, she realized after the first gagging swallow. She turned on the hot-water tap and poured out half the black syrup.

"Bad?" Nicola asked.

Sam shrugged. "A little strong."

"Little! Little. English." She pointed to Woody. "Little."

Nicola was growing on her, and perhaps Nicola and she had something in common after all: the shared frustration of learning a foreign language. "Petite, little." Sam shrugged. "Not big." She filled the cup to the rim with water, wondering if Derek had managed to drink the coffee without complaint.

The keys were in the Jeep. Not so her black bag. She wouldn't go back into the house for it, as she rarely needed it, except for a once-in-a-blue-moon car accident or an on-site investigation as coroner.

She backed out of the garage and was well up the red-shale drive before a quiver betrayed her hand. She was a fool for being out of bed, and she hoped she would find this Dr. Polvich in the lab. She was glad Derek was off with the buffalo, since he would've tried to get her to stay, and wouldn't have taken much to persuade her to go back to bed. She pressed harder on the accelerator until the wheels spun out and the road behind her was nothing more than a cloud of red dust.

▽

14

"I THINK YOU'LL want to take this one." Kate held out the phone.

Nice greeting. Not "I'm glad you're feeling better" or "Glad you're back," only a snide "I think you'll want to take this one." It made her feel needed.

Sam took the phone. "Dr. Turner speaking."

"What did you do with David Crider's body?"

Sam was back in the saddle. She recognized the funeral director's obnoxious wail. But as for answering his question, she was the last person who would know what she had done with the body of a David Crider. "Hello, Thaddeus," she said sweetly. "How are you? Nice spring day, isn't it?"

"Look here, I just got out of the hospital and here I've had to drag myself out of my bed to come down to see what my wife is talking about, and I find she's right."

"You were in the hospital, Thaddeus?"

"In ICU. I almost died."

"Of hantavirus, by any chance?"

"Yes. You already heard, I take it?"

She decided against explaining that she was in ICU with him. "Tell me what's wrong Thaddeus."

"David Crider's uncle came to view the body, but it's not here." He covered the phone to muffle someone's voice in the background. "He wants to know what you did with his nephew's body."

Sam tried to think. She didn't have a clue. She covered the phone. "Kate, who's David Crider?"

"You mean the kid who made all you guys sick?"

"Us guys? Thaddeus and me?"

"And Doc Wallace, his parents, and Terry."

"Is his corpse here in the hospital for some reason?"

Kate shook her head, setting her dangling earrings in motion. "Doubt it. Where would we've put it?"

Sam uncovered the phone. "I'll be right over."

Sam parked the Jeep in the space in front of the funeral home that was reserved for the hearse. Thaddeus wouldn't be needing the space since he didn't have a corpse to go in the hearse.

She'd taken the time to read the CDC report before she had left the hospital. Apparently, she had called in the CDC after her autopsy of seventeen-year-old David Crider uncovered an unexplained respiratory distress syndrome, or URDS. The CDC recognized the URDS as another outbreak of hantavirus and did so in time to treat her and everyone else who had come in contact with the boy. She could be thankful that she'd called them in early enough and that they were familiar enough with the symptoms to know what they were dealing with. She would never have suspected hantavirus in this wet climate. She shuddered to think whose body might have been laid out in Thaddeus's hearse had the CDC not been here.

Her logbook was missing, and she couldn't imagine what she had done with it, but a note in the CDC report mentioned that it was missing. She hoped she came across it soon or she'd be taking twelve chicks to the ranch.

Thaddeus, sweating bullets, met her at the door. He was a little frayed around the edges, mirroring her appearance. No one said recovery was a bed of roses. "I don't understand this at all," he said.

"Nor do I, Thaddeus. Just settle down while we try to piece it together."

"Don't expect me to help piece this together. I can't remember a thing and I should be in bed. My wife is worried sick, do you understand that? I practically died, you know." Boy, that would have been a real bummer. He provided such a great service to the community, and white-collar grave diggers were probably hard to find. She doubted even big-town newspapers had a subindex in their want ads for white-collar grave diggers.

"I'm sure she is worried." Sam refrained from asking him if he had prearranged plans for his own funeral. Would his be the grandest of all funerals or the least of the lot? She was just happy that they weren't doing a double funeral together.

"Is David Crider's uncle still here?" she asked.

"In my office, waiting for you."

Sam followed Thaddeus to his office across the hall from the empty viewing room. The man politely rose as soon as they entered the room. He was tall and thin, with a generous aquiline nose, and was gripping a worn black Bible with both hands. His dark brown eyes bored through her with enormous intensity, making her uncomfortable in a way painkillers couldn't correct.

"Mr. Crider, may I introduce Dr. Turner. Dr. Turner, may I introduce Isaac Crider."

Sam offered her hand. "May I extend my condolences to you and your family?"

Mr. Crider shifted his Bible to his left hand and duly took her unsteady one and gave it a weak shake, his eyes never leaving hers. "Thank you." He turned and looked at Thaddeus with an unspoken question. It was pretty obvious, under the circumstances, what that question was.

"Please sit down, gentlemen." Sam sat in the chair next to Crider, leaving the one behind the desk available for Thaddeus. The best defense was a strong offense. "Thaddeus," Sam said, "you said something over the phone about Mr. Crider's nephew. Could you elaborate?"

Thaddeus opened his mouth, but nothing fell out. He took in a breath, a sigh in reverse. He threw up his hands as he rounded his desk and sat.

"Mr. Crider?"

Their eyes locked, and Sam wasn't about to be the first to look away. In the end, he cast his eyes on his Bible.

"My brother called on April fourteenth to tell us not to come to Sheridan for David's funeral that following Saturday because the coroner—you, I now realize"—he looked at her—"were holding his body until you could determine the cause of death." He rubbed his index finger back and forth over the spine of the Bible.

"When did you next hear from the Criders?"

He looked at her as if he could see through her eyes to her soul. "I didn't. A disciple in my brother's congregation of the Church of Divine Light called to say that both my brother and my sister-in-law had been taken away in an ambulance." He motioned to his Bible. "The Bible teaches us that God is the only true healer. And by faith are true believers healed. My brother and his wife would not have gone in the ambulance of their free will."

"No, it hit them pretty hard, I suspect," Sam assured him. "Who called the ambulance for them?"

Mr. Crider stared at her in disbelief. "Dr. Turner, I've come here for David. Where is his body?"

If she were holding the remains pending an investigation, it would be in the mortuary's vault. Sam looked at Thaddeus, who was dabbing at his sweat-drenched face and neck with his handkerchief. His face became exceedingly pale. "In the vault."

Thaddeus fainted dead away.

Sam rounded the desk before Thaddeus tumbled to the floor. Sam broke his fall but was caught under him when he landed. Isaac separated their twisted limbs and positioned Thaddeus on his back.

Fatigue, illness, or hunger increases the susceptibility of loss of consciousness, but Sam feared that this syncopal attack had more to do with the anxiety over David's body that was supposed to be in the vault. His muscles were utterly flaccid and motionless, his breathing shallow. She had to work at finding a pulse.

The Good Samaritan stood over them, his head uplifted and his eyes shut tightly in divine concentration. He gripped his Bible mightily as his lips moved in silent, but intense, prayer.

Sam monitored Thaddeus's pulse for a minute or more before it became palpable and accelerated. She was thoroughly impressed that it took such a short time for the Healer to hear and answer Isaac's prayer. Thaddeus's breathing deepened and quickened; his eyelids fluttered and his face pinkened. And then he was back among the living . . . as well as the unburied dead.

Thaddeus, aware of his embarrassing predicament, tried to get up. Sam forced him into horizontal stillness. Isaac looked as if he had disconnected the line of communication to the great ER in the sky, and besides her humble earthly medical training had taught her that her patient's muscles were still in a weakened condition and that rising prematurely would induce another attack. Not to mention pain if he should happen to fall on her again. "Take it easy, Thaddeus. You're fine. Just a bit weak from your hospital stay."

His frightened eyes searched her face for hope. It was not altogether a pleasant realization that her archenemy was lying in her arms like a helpless baby. Her opinion of Thaddeus had turned 180 degrees, but she assured herself that she would learn to dislike him all over again as soon as he was feeling better.

"Is he all right?" Isaac asked.

"He'll be just fine," she answered, to reassure both men.

Isaac paced in giant steps. Now that she had the time to take a good look, she noticed how tastefully the office was decorated. Deep reddish mahogany built-in shelves matched the massive carved desk and the frame of the upholstered chairs. The backs and seats of the two chairs were done in a delicate pink-flower-design needlepoint. The lime carpet picked up the darker green leaves in the needlepoint, as well as the wreath on the door. A mortician would always have cause for a wreath at the door; someone was always in mourning, and it was the mortician's place to comfort them, as well as separate them from a nice chunk of change.

That thought was enough for Sam to push Thaddeus into a sitting position and scramble to her feet. Her left foot had fallen asleep, thanks to the weight of Thaddeus's head. "Just stay like that for a minute or two, and then it should be fine for you to get up."

"Where are you going?" Thaddeus called, as if he were a little boy who was afraid that his mother was abandoning him.

Sam didn't bother to answer as she left the office and headed for the vault. Isaac caught up with her in quick time and insisted on opening every door for her until they were standing in front of the vault.

She opened the stainless steel door. Despite being assaulted by the 40-degree temperature, she was relieved to see the sheet-draped body in the cavernous vault. Relief flooded through her as she caught a glimpse of the toe tag with David's name written on it. She tucked the foot under the white sheet out of respect for the grieving relative's feelings. She pulled the gurney all the way out for better viewing, and then walked to the head on the left as Isaac went up the right side. She took hold of the corners of the sheet and, with all solemnity, made a nice rectangular fold so only the head and neck showed.

Isaac's intense eyes were on her. He made no attempt to look at his nephew's body. Not so much as a cursory peek. She looked suspiciously down at the face and knew instantly why Thaddeus had fainted. The body was that of a man who appeared to be in his seventh decade.

"This isn't your nephew, I take it?"

"No, that's Charles Hopkins," he answered with the patience of a saint, though he looked a bit hot under the collar.

"You know this man?'

He shook his head very, very slowly. "No, Charles Hopkins was the name on another death certificate you signed." Oh, so *she* knew this man. "And the name on the receipt Mrs. Thaddeus Smith has from the crematory in Billings."

Sam turned to the wall and knocked her head against it.

15

Her Jeep was gone! Sam was certain she had left it in the hearse parking space. What a joke! She wasn't certain about anything anymore. Her steel-trap mind was a free-flowing sieve. She looked up and down the street, wondering where she'd parked.

"What do you think they'll do?" Thaddeus asked, wringing his hands like Pontius Pilate and helping her pace back and forth along the cracked sidewalk. (Spring had a way of showing off all the damage winter had caused. And winter in Wyoming was rarely kind.) What did she think David Crider's family would do? Isaac had left them with only the smallest indication that the wrath of God would soon be on their shoulders, but he might have been right. Her Jeep and she were separated, and no amount of concentration could make her remember where she had left it.

She went around the corner and looked all the way down the hill. No brown Jeep with red interior was anywhere to be seen. "You should have this one fixed." Sam stopped and pointed to the block of concrete that was standing on its ear. "Someone's going to trip and sue you."

"Don't say that word." He buried his face in his shaky hands.

"Sue? Is that the word I'm not supposed to say?" she asked with a good deal less reserve than Isaac had shown. She felt like putting Thaddeus back into the ICU. How could he have married such a stupid woman? "How could your wife

not tell the difference between a seventeen-year-old boy and
a seventy-year-old man?"

"I don't know. Maybe the casket was closed." He threw
up his hands. "How could she let them have a seven-
thousand-dollar casket?"

She felt like screaming. And why shouldn't she? She held
her hands over her ears and screamed until her lungs were
empty and her throat was too sore to scream again. She dug
into her pocket and pulled out a shredded tissue for the
phlegm.

A patrol car pulled up. "Is there a problem?"

No-chin Skip. He was the last person on earth she would
tell if she had a problem, which she did. She had two. "No,
Officer, everything's fine."

Thaddeus waved and parroted her words about everything
being fine. Skip looked disappointed that they didn't have a
problem they wanted to share with him. He could just wait
and read all about it in the front page of the local newspaper
when Thaddeus and she got their butts hauled into court
and had their asses sued off for cremating the wrong
remains.

Cremains.

They cremated the remains of a boy whose parents were
such religious fanatics that they didn't believe in medical
treatment. Cremated, for heaven's sake! The irony was more
than she could stand. She had no doubt, even if Isaac hadn't
spelled it out for her, that she would share the blame because
she hadn't released the body for the scheduled burial.

Thaddeus and she watched the patrol car pull away at a
good one mile per hour. No doubt so they could get a good
whiff of his exhaust fumes.

"What do you think the Criders will do?"

Sue your butt off, you fool. And mine, too! "Thaddeus, I
can't talk to you now."

"We don't know for sure that they cremated David
Crider's remains."

"You're absolutely correct, Thaddeus." She led him to the wrought-iron staircase that would take him to his apartment over the funeral home. "Why don't you just go on up to bed and try not to worry about any of this. It's all likely to clear up all by itself. Be just a nightmare we'll all wake up from."

"Pinch me, Sam," Thaddeus said wringing his hands, "see if I'll wake up." It was the closest she'd ever heard him come to humor, but the juxtaposition of humor and this mortician was more than she could stand, so instead of pinching him she gave him a shove up the first step.

Sam waited well out of the way as he climbed. She wasn't about to cushion his fall a second time. When he disappeared inside, Sam rounded the corner to Main Street and resumed her Jeep search. The keys were in her pocket, so she knew no one took it for a joy ride. Well, if they did, they would have had to go to the trouble of hot-wiring it. And why bother when most parked cars in Sheridan had keys in the ignition. She'd lived in San Francisco too long ever to adopt that local custom.

Her office was five blocks down Main Street. Maybe she'd parked there and walked up. Bob Wallace's house was a block and a half up the hill on Main Street, just before it dead-ended. More likely she'd parked there and walked down the hill, intending to visit Bob on the way back. She started up the hill.

Sam was pooped by the time she climbed the stairs of the Wallaces' porch. She rang the doorbell and then slumped down on the double swing to catch her breath. She was wrong about leaving her Jeep up the hill. Now she'd have six and a half blocks to walk to the office, but at least it was downhill.

Betty opened the door and then pushed out the screen door and looked around to see where her company had disappeared to. "Well, I declare," she said, genuinely happy to see Sam; then her smile faded as she remembered the bad blood between them. "Sam, you look all tuckered out," she added politely.

The best Sam could do was nod.

Betty sat down beside her. "You look a great deal better than you did in intensive care, I must say," she said kindly. "I dropped by to say hello to Derek . . . after I left Bob's room one night," she added, lest Sam misunderstood that she made the trip to the hospital solely to visit her.

Sam knew better. She had exposed Betty's son as a murderer but had mixed feelings over the role she'd played. Little Bob had needed to be brought to justice, but she was sorry so many innocent people had been hurt.

"How's Bob doing?"

Betty nodded. "Better. Dr. Jeffers assured me that he would make a full recovery."

"Who's Dr. Jeffers?" Sam could tell from the expression on Betty's face that she should have known Dr. Jeffers. "Please forgive me, Betty, whatever they were giving me to resolve my respiratory infection has left me with a sketchy memory."

"You, too?" Betty sighed. "I've been so worried about Bob. He can't remember a blasted thing." She put her arms around Sam and gave her a big hug. "You poor dear."

One thing about Betty—she couldn't hold a grudge long. "Bob will be fine, Betty. It's only a temporary affliction." She didn't add, *I hope.*

"That's what Dr. Jeffers said, but you know how doctors are, sometimes they tell the patients' families what they want to hear."

The rusty chain creaked for mercy as Betty pumped the swing with her stubby legs. They shared the swing quietly, each taking in the signs of spring on the quiet end of Main Street. A robin pulled a slick worm out of the wet greening grass, two preschoolers on the other side of Main Street fought over a tricycle, a runt of a dug—the kind her yellow Labs would make a quick appetizer out of—yapped behind a fence somewhere in the neighborhood.

"Refresh my memory, Betty. Who's Dr. Jeffers?"

"Earl Jeffers and Lee Nguyen are the newest members of the Sheridan medical community. They're covering the ER, but Dr. Jeffers is board certified in internal medicine and infectious disease, so he was called in for a consultation. Then Ken assured both Derek and me that you and Bob would want him to be your attending physician."

In other words, Clarence, the most inept doctor on the face of the earth, was on call when they were admitted, so he won them as if they had been part of a lottery, and Ken politely replaced him. She would give Ken a big kiss when she saw him next. He probably saved her life. "What about Roger Ryder, the Centers for Disease Control regional director? I read the report he filed. Did you meet him?"

"No," Betty said, letting the swing's rhythmic motion slow to a near stop when her foot hesitated, as if all the parts of her body had to pull together while she concentrated on the question. She resumed pumping, vigorously this time. "I met Tom Polvich from the CDC."

So that's who Tom Polvich was. Good, he would have all the answers. If they ever found him.

"I like Earl a great deal, but that Lee Nguyen is something else. Like he has a chip on his shoulder. Don't know why Earl partnered up with the likes of him."

"Lee Nguyen. He's Asian, I take it. Maybe he's a little uneasy here. We don't have many—"

Betty laughed. "I can't believe you of all people are defending him."

"Why?"

"The way I heard it through the grapevine, you were the first to come to blows with him."

"Know why?"

Betty shook her head. "Heard you told him you didn't need a couple of cowboys coming into town like they owned the place."

"Couple? I didn't like Jeffers, either? Guess I owe at least Jeffers an apology. He did save my life, after all." She'd have to find Ken and ask him what her beef was with the two new doctors. "Betty, there's one thing I don't understand." She didn't understand *anything*. "Isaac Crider, the uncle of the boy who exposed us to the hantavirus, said the family didn't believe in doctors. But Bob was his attending?"

"No, no, no. You called Bob a week ago last Wednesday and asked him if he would stop by Thaddeus's because there was something you wanted him to see. I know, because by the time he got here his noon meal was cold."

"I'm sorry, Betty."

"Two minutes in the microwave." She dismissed it with a wave of her hand. "Anyway, that's when he started losing it." She tapped her forehead. "He could hardly eat, kept saying Sheridan was going to have an epidemic of smallpox right in time for the college rodeo."

"Smallpox?"

Betty tapped her forehead again. "Silly ol' coot."

$\triangledown$

16

Sam TRUDGED UP the steep staircase in the Cady Building, wondering how she'd gotten into this sad state of affairs. Her pain pills were on the nightstand, and she was out of breath, and her legs screamed to be amputated. The only thing keeping her going was the knowledge that she could collapse in a chair, put her head down on the spare desk, and that Daisy wouldn't call the mortician to come for her body until four-thirty when she closed up the billing office.

Daisy had worked for Sam for five years and she had seen more than one little old lady in complete exhaustion by the time she reached the second-floor office at the end of the long hall to pay her lab bill in person. Sam didn't know how far her patients were willing to walk to reach her billing office, but she knew how far she'd walked. Seven and a half blocks. She'd miscounted; the block Woolworth was on was twice as long as the others and should really count for two blocks. Eight and a half blocks.

The two women in the insurance office at the head of the stairs were gaily chatting. Sam waved as she passed their open door, hoping they wouldn't think her too rude for not saying hi. Truth be told, she couldn't breathe and talk at the same time, and she needed to breathe if she intended to get to her office at the end of the hall so she could collapse in the chair and put her head down on the desk and wait for the mortician to come for her.

Someone had to come for her; her Jeep was nowhere in sight and she hadn't passed it between here and Bob's house.

She was completely mystified and was beginning to think somebody had stolen it.

Fertile hen's eggs and smallpox went together like a horse and carriage. A chick embryo chorioallantoic membrane culture, an antiquated test for an obsolete disease. Or was it obsolete? A smallpox epidemic had been the driving force behind her rodeo dream. Was it merely an amazing coincidence that Bob would tell Betty the same silliness she herself would dream nearly two weeks later?

She'd gone up to Bob's room and talked to him for a few minutes, but he was even more in the dark about the last week than she was. He didn't remember the visit to the funeral home, let alone what she wanted him to see. He only shrugged when she asked about smallpox and said that he saw a case once when he was an intern.

Sam would give anything right now to crawl into bed and die with her head on a pillow. She'd made it down the hall. Sam rested her hand a nanosecond on the hundred-year-old brass doorknob that proved to be more a crutch than a reminder of the palatial history of the landmark building. She turned the knob and walked through the door, into the cramped office, and straightaway to the other desk.

Daisy took her stocking feet off her desk and slipped the romance paperback she was enthralled with into the drawer. "Good morning, Sam."

Sam mumbled a greeting and collapsed in the chair. She thumped her head on the desk with a metallic clank and rejoiced in her wait for the grim reaper.

She felt Daisy pushing papers under her elbow. "I have some Medicare forms for you to sign."

"Not now Daisy. I want to die first."

"Derek called looking for you."

Boy, that was a big surprise. "What did he say?"

"He said you should be home in bed."

Sam had half a notion to have Daisy call him and tell him to come and get her and carry her to her bed. If he did, she would promise never to get out of it again.

"Have I ever mentioned smallpox to you?" Sam asked, her head molding into the metal desktop.

"No."

"When did you see me last?"

It took Daisy a while to remember. She rustled through her daily calendar, turning pages backward. "Thursday two weeks ago; to sign reimbursements. Never understand it. Medicare patients send in their checks practically the day they get their bill, then Medicare sends them a check, and then they turn around and send the check to us, and then we have to turn around and send them a check because they overpaid."

"They were alive during the Depression, they don't want to owe anyone." They had this conversation once a month, so it didn't take a lot out of Sam to reiterate the hypothesis.

"Well, you can't say that for the new generation of adults." Daisy went to the filing cabinet to pull out the thick computer printout of their deadbeat file. Not that Sam could see any of this activity, but it had become a ritual. Sam drifted off during Daisy's tirade about how young people thought society owed them everything their parents had taken years to acquire. She especially liked fanning the pages of the thick printout that moved the stuffy air around her. The windows had been permanently sealed by a rainbow of layered paint, and they had to rely on the central air-conditioning in the summer and central heating in the winter. This time of the year it was hard to judge which was needed, but that was one of Daisy's duties, and Sam was a mere interloper whose job description included listening to complaints.

When Sam was satisfied that Daisy had had her say, she asked, "Did I tell you what I wanted with fertile hen's eggs?"

"Fertile hen's eggs? You going to raise chickens now?"

Sam sighed. "I don't think so."

Daisy returned the deadbeat printout to the filing cabinet. "Don't send a bill for David Crider."

Daisy started rustling papers. "A post?"

"Yes."

"Too late."

"Well, don't send another one." The desk wasn't as soft as it had been when Sam first got there. She lifted her throbbing head and rummaged through the middle drawer, scribbling on a scrap of paper until she found a pen that worked. She signed her name to the first Medicare form in the stack. "Have you seen my Jeep?"

"No, but I paid the bill for the broken window."

"What broken window?"

"The window that was broken by vandals when it was at the police station."

"What was it doing at the police station?"

"The bill I paid to Texaco Towing said it was impounded by the police department."

"Why was it impounded by the police?"

"The ticket Derek gave me to pay said that it was parked in a handicap space at the high school."

"What was it doing at the high school?"

"I don't know."

"When was all this?"

"Week ago last Thursday. The day I had to close up the office and drive to the hospital to get you to sign the checks. You were too busy to come down."

Sam clenched her fist and pounded the desk as illumination struck. "Goddammit, that's what Skip was doing."

"What?"

"Oh, Skip was cruising by the funeral home and asked if there was a problem. He was taunting me. I bet anything in the world he towed my Jeep away when I was inside talking to Thaddeus. No wonder I couldn't find it. Bet they're all sitting around the police station laughing their fool heads off at my expense."

Sam got to her feet, adrenaline skating through her body. "Could you give me a ride to the hospital?"

17

Daisy DROPPED Sam at the front door of the hospital just before noon, and she hurried through the halls so she could catch Kate before she left the lab for lunch. She didn't have the energy to traipse down to the cafeteria looking for her.

"Kate!" Sam called as she saw Kate about to go down the stairs. It must have been noon straight up; Kate was nothing if not prompt.

"There you are," Kate said as she met Sam more than halfway. "Derek's around somewhere, and he's not at all happy. Think he said he was going downstairs to the doctor's library. Want me to find him and tell him that you're back?"

Sam wondered what he was doing in the library. Medical journals weren't high on his list of reading material. He was more the Tom Clancy type. "No, but thanks for the warning."

"He said you should be home in bed."

Sam put up her hand to tell Kate to stop. "I know. Did you get hold of Tom Polvich?"

"No. When I called the hotel back they said he'd checked out."

"Checked out? Just checked out without so much as a good-bye, it was nice knowing all of you, and I hope Sam doesn't mind me leaving a pile of work for her?"

Kate rolled it over in her mind. "That's odd, huh?"

"Yeah, that's odd." Sam took a deep breath, hoping to get a grip on her frustration. "When's Eugene coming back?"

"Tomorrow. On the late plane, so he won't be back to work until Wednesday."

Sam shrugged. "That's fine, I'll put off my recovery until Wednesday so I can work a couple of days."

"Can you do that?" Kate smiled and nodded. "Oh, I gotcha. You're kidding."

Sam returned Kate's smile and nod. "Yeah, it's a joke, all right. And I'm the butt." She waved her on. "Go eat, I'll see you after lunch."

Ken Miller was next on her agenda. Sam turned around and headed back toward the main entrance and then slipped down the back corridor so she wouldn't have to go by the pathology department, just in case Derek was finished in the library and was loitering around the lab.

She found Ken in the reading room, looking at a series of skull X-rays hanging across the top of the light box like clothes on a line. She walked softly toward him as he dictated his impression, because she did not want the recorder picking up her clicking boot heels. Transcribers had it tough enough with doctors coughing, clearing their throats, mumbling, chewing gum, or eating sandwiches as Ken was doing.

Sam put a hand on his shoulder. He patted it as he finished up. Didn't take a radiologist to see the skull fracture on this one. Nor the tissue swelling. Looked like this patient had been in a grisly accident.

Ken turned off his recorder and then pulled her down onto his lap.

"Don't, my husband's around." She put up a token resistance, but not enough to free herself.

"Tell me about it. He's been looking in every nook and cranny for you."

"So I hear."

"Now, young lady," Ken hugged her tight enough to shoot pain through every organ in her chest, "why are you out of your sickbed?"

"Because no one's here to do my work . . . not that I've been here long enough to do it." She leaned back on his shoulder, happy that someone else was supporting her weight. He offered her a bite of his sandwich; she pointed to the Styrofoam cup.

"Has a cigarette butt in it," he cautioned.

"No one's supposed to be smoking in the hospital."

"Tell that to your husband."

Sam wished Derek would stop smoking. Didn't he want to be around to watch Woody graduate from high school? She took a bite of the turkey sandwich. Swallowing was a chore. She'd have to chew long and gulp less for a while. "My turn to ask questions."

"Have at it. Nothing I could say or do would keep you from your purpose."

"You make me sound like the postman."

"Given your track record and the postal service's, I'll bet on you."

"Don't be too sure. My Jeep's been arrested twice in the span of, let's see—"

"Again?" he asked, saving her the trouble of counting.

"Yep, again. What's the saw? If you can't remember your mistakes, you're destined to relive them."

"I think it's if you can't *learn* from your mistakes, you're destined to relive them."

"Remember is more appropriate in my case, since I can't remember anything that's happened to me in the last two weeks."

"Take my word for it, you're better off not knowing."

Sam hoisted herself up far enough to plant a big smacker on his cheek. "That's for holding Clarence off with a baseball bat."

"You would have done the same for me."

They fell into silence, she trying to build bridges in her weary mind, he reviewing the films along the light box.

"Did I mention anything to you about smallpox, Ken?"

"*You* didn't." He reached around her and ripped two of the films off and threw them on top of one of the many manila envelopes spread out over the long counter under the light box, narrowly missing the last morsel of the sandwich

she was eyeing. He noticed and popped it into her mouth.
"Bob did, though. Said you thought you had a case. You
didn't. I asked Tom . . .Tom Polvich. He's been covering for
you."

"Not anymore. He's disappeared into the great unknown."

"Tom? That doesn't sound like him. He's AOA." Alpha
Omega Alpha was an honorary fraternity that tapped only
the top medical students. Ken's point was that Tom was the
crème de la crème, the salt of the earth, not a flake. Besides,
Ken and she were AOA, so that made the three of them
family.

"So where is he?"

"Maybe some big epidemic hit in a Third World country
and every CDC doc under the sun has lit out."

"I'll buy that. Wish he'd said so, though." She sighed,
adding one more chore to her mental list. "I'll call Atlanta
and make sure he didn't come down with this. If I ever
muster the energy to get up."

Ken's attention went to the remaining films. She was
clearly in the way. "I should go."

"No, no, you're fine." He squeezed her. "Stay and keep
me company."

"It's funny about the smallpox, though," she said after a
bit. "I apparently ordered some fertile hen's eggs."

"You'll have to do better than that if you want me to
understand what you're talking about."

"Incubated eggs were used for isolating and identifying
the viruses of variola, vaccinia, and most known strains of
human monkeypox. It must be the reason I ordered the
eggs." She sighed long and hard, and he gave her a reassuring
hug. "I can't believe I ordered fertile hen's eggs!"

"Maybe you were coming down with the hantavirus and
were confused?"

"It makes a nice excuse."

They looked at each other and laughed.

She twisted around on her right hip to get more comfort-

able and to help him look at the films. She should be over
in the lab working, and she'd get up in a minute, as soon as
she regained some strength. "But why would I ask Bob to
meet me at the funeral home? Betty said that Bob told her
that I'd asked him to meet me at Thaddeus's to show him
something, apparently a case of smallpox."

"Betty said that Bob said . . . now that's reliable, prime-
source information."

"I know, but the strange part is that I had a dream last
night about smallpox. I didn't learn about smallpox until
today from Betty, and yet I had a dream about it last night."

"That's not true." Sam and Ken spun around to see Derek
leaning against the door frame, combing his fingers through
his hair.

Ken waved him in. "Come on in, I've captured your
woman for you."

"Good. Thought for a minute there you were making time
with my gal."

Ken patted her hip. "You need to feed her more, she's
pretty bony."

Sam interrupted the bonding males. "What do you mean,
'that's not true'?"

"I told you at the hospital yesterday morning that Bob had
been jabbering about smallpox. Don't you remember telling
me that he saw you going into the funeral home and went in
with you because he thought you might know the hematocrit
for one of his patients he'd sent over to the lab?"

"No, I'd forgotten." It was strange that he'd think *she*
would know the count; the techs ran hematocrit tests. Bob
usually had someone in his office call the lab. Besides, he'd
been avoiding her like the plague. And rightfully so, since
she had given it to him. "That explains the dream, anyway."
Now if she could only figure out why she wanted the fertile
hen's eggs.

18

"YOU COULD HAVE given me ten minutes to clean up some work!" Sam slammed the door of the Mercedes for all she was worth.

Derek seethed.

Too bad. Slamming the damned door once in a while wasn't gong to hurt anything. And who the hell did he think he was, dragging her away from her work?

"Samantha, simply go up to bed. I don't want you having a relapse." Derek said in his calm, deep, and collected voice that made her more angry than she already was.

"You don't want? Since when do you make my decisions for me?" She grabbed her throat to constrict the pain of yelling. She wanted him to fight like a man instead of being so damned solicitous. She hated that.

"Since you can't think sensibly enough to make them for yourself," he explained, oh, so quietly.

She hurled around before she got to the door. "And just what the hell does that mean?"

"It means that you're ill and you need to be in bed and you're too stubborn to admit it."

"No one is covering for me. What was I supposed to do? Just let patients die because their doctors couldn't get the results of various tests because there was no pathologist to interpret said tests?"

"I don't care about the other patients' lives. I care about yours. I don't want Woody growing up without his mother."

"And what about you?" she yelled. "What about your smoking? Want Woody to grow up without his father?"

Nicola, with Woody in her arms, was standing in the middle of the family room staring at them as they came through the door. She'd been frightened by Sam's shouting, if Sam could go by the horrified look on her face.

"Sorry," she said sweetly to Nicola as she took Woody's fist out of his mouth and held his tiny arm. Bubbling coos came out of his cupid lips. The top lip had a clear blister from sucking, and his ear a scratch mark from his sharp little fingernails.

The fist went back into his mouth the moment she released it. He'd be wearing braces in his teen years, that was a given. It was hard staying mad at the man who had fathered this wondrous little fellow, but she was going to try.

Adrenaline gave her the power to march down the hall, up the stairs, and to slam the bedroom door. She collapsed across the bed. Except for the white cotton comforter that had found its way into her nose and mouth, restricting her breathing, the bed was a thousand times better than the metal desk in the billing office.

The door creaked open and then closed again before she really had a good chance to turn her head to the side and catch her breath. She could hear Derek working his way across the carpet. He stopped at the nightstand to get her glass, and then went into the bathroom and ran the water.

The bed gave under his weight as he sat on the edge. He busied himself untwisting the childproof caps on her medicine. She was thankful he was doing it, because she didn't have the energy. Probably the only people who had both the energy and the inclination, and were really good at lining up the arrows, were children.

"Here," he said as he held out a sleeping pill, a painkiller, and an antibiotic in the palm of one hand and a glass of water in the other.

She was too exhausted to need the sleeping pill and wasn't so sure she wanted to take the Percodan, but she was behind on the antibiotic. "I don't want the sleeping pill. I'll be waking up about time to go to bed for the night."

"Than you can take another one to get you through the night."

She was too tired to argue with his peculiar logic and let him put the pills into her sweaty palm. He motioned to her to start putting them in her mouth as he held the glass of water out like a carrot on a stick. She obliged him. It was obvious her jailer wouldn't allow her back to work today; she might as well dope up and take a good nap.

"Will you get my Jeep back?" she asked as he pulled off her boots. For half a second she pondered asking about her radio, if they'd fixed it with the broken window, but she really didn't care enough to expend the energy.

"Emil and I'll drive in and get it as soon as you fall asleep."

"Are you going to hold me until I fall asleep?" she asked as he worked at getting her out of her jeans.

"Yes, my darling, I'm going to hold you and comfort you and thank God for giving me another chance."

"Don't talk to me about God."

He pulled her sweater over her head, nearly twisting her arm off. "You mad at God, too?"

She couldn't help but smile, and she was quickly losing her resolve to stay mad at him. "No, just one of his disciples. I'm about to be sued because the wrong body was cremated while I was ill."

Derek pulled the covers out from under her and managed to get them over her, tucking them under her chin. She pushed them down to free her arms. He squatted down on his impressive haunches so they were eye to eye. "Don't worry about it, Samantha. It wasn't your fault. No jury in the land would convict you of something that happened while you were fighting for your life in the ICU."

"I wish I could be so certain, Derek," She searched his eyes. He looked as if he wanted to say something but didn't know how to begin. "What is it?"

He gave a slight shake of his head to tell her it was nothing, and then added, "Everything will work out, Samantha. Please don't worry."

"Are you going to hold me from there?"

He gave her a roguish grin as he stripped down to his shorts. He crawled over her and flopped down on his side of the bed, rustling the covers until he was under them. He gathered her into his arms and pulled her close. She could feel him harden against her backside as his tender fingers traced the line of her body. "Do you have any idea how much I love you, Samantha?"

"Well, if that boner's any indication . . . "

He shifted so he wasn't as close. "Don't tease me, I can't help it." He leaned over her to kiss her cheek. "Now take your nap."

"All right," she said magnanimously, since the sleeping pill had kicked in with more power than a stubborn mule. "Then I'm going to go back to town to see my dad," she added halfheartedly.

Derek brushed her hair back and then nibbled on her earlobe. He was sending mixed messages. Did he want her to go to sleep or turn over and pay some attention to him? She only had energy for the former; he had to know that. "We'll talk about it later."

She turned over, but she wasn't going to pay him the kind of attention he'd like. "Nothing to talk about, Derek," she said, clumsily raising herself up on an elbow. "I'm going."

"Now don't bristle, Samantha." He tried to pull her down, but anger forced her out of bed. "Samantha, be reasonable," he said as he stretched the length of the bed and caught her at the foot.

"I'm just going to the bathroom. Or do I need your permission for that, too?"

When she dragged herself back from the bathroom Derek was still in bed, the pillows propped up behind him. He patted the bed invitingly. "Come here. There's something I need to tell you about your father."

Sam froze in her tracks, her heart pounding furiously against her ribs. "He's dead?"

"No, he's fine." He patted the bed again. "Good news, not bad."

She could use some good news. She crawled under the covers and curled up beside him. Her will to stay awake was losing the battle against the chemicals she'd swallowed, and it wouldn't take much to drift off.

"Do you remember why you let Eugene go to Switzerland?"

"I don't even know why he went, let alone that I had a say in the matter."

"He's a delegate to a WHO conference."

"Eugene?"

"His name was picked at random."

"I've never heard of such a thing." The slow pounding of his heart stopped reverberating in her ear as she lifted her wobbly head from his chest to face him. "Picked at random from what? The telephone book?"

He settled here against the pillows. "The AMA roster, I would imagine. I don't know and I don't care. That's immaterial. What *is* important is that you let him go because you wanted him out of the way."

She idly wondered why Derek phrased it like that, that she'd let him go. Eugene made his own decisions. If he wanted a couple of weeks off, she'd take an equal amount at some later date. But that wasn't important enough to ask. "Why did I want him out of the way?" Her speech was becoming slurred.

"You were making precursors."

She raised up in utter astonishment. "What?"

He settled her back onto the pillow. She yawned as she concentrated on keeping her heavy eyes open. Her senses and brain were turning to mush.

"Patrick performed a hysterectomy with the ovaries attached. You had me fertilize them. After you were taken ill and knowing what those precursors meant to you, I arranged for your father to go to a research facility."

She felt as if she'd been attacked by a band of renegade Indians, a hundred arrows coming from all directions at the same time. Her father was too confused to be off somewhere by himself; he'd be frightened in new surroundings without her. She was going to treat her father's condition with precursors? She didn't know she even knew how to go about it.

She couldn't think straight. She was going to treat her father? What of the legal ramifications? Had she learned the process? Something else she'd forgotten. She hoped it would come back to her. Gene therapy had a good shot at revolutionizing medicine, at restoring quality of life. Her father was a fine candidate. She hadn't thought of him—in a very long time—as the jolly businessman he used to be, only as a helpless, confused old man.

"You're just now telling me this?" The pills had put her at a disadvantage, and she had to work hard to get the words out, as well as choose adequate words to express her bewildered thoughts.

"I didn't want to worry you."

"You didn't want to worry me?" She was so weary, outrage was the only thing keeping her going. "What about my father? He's in unknown surroundings with no one—"

"Sharon's with him. You know he can't tell you and your sister apart. He probably isn't aware that he's not at the nursing home. Probably thinks they transferred him to a new room, if he noticed even that."

Her faculties were becoming numb; that was the only reason she was getting sucked into buying his argument. "And the precursors are working?"

"Well . . . no. Tom Polvich said they'd been sitting too long. He found the ones you froze, but then someone had a miscarriage. Tom gave me the fetus's ovaries to take to the clinic. I'm not sure which they used, but I know the clinic had a private rest room and nicer specimen cups."

In other words, Derek donated the seminal fluid again. What facility? Who was doing this kind of research? And what of the medical ethics of using fetal ovaries? Of course, they were being used for precursors, not procreation. In vitro pregnancies using the ovaries from an aborted fetus. It was now possible for a being who had never been born to be the biological mother of a healthy baby. She fell asleep considering the possibility of a twelve-year-old-girl having an abortion so as not to be a mother and becoming a grandmother instead.

$\triangledown$

19

Tuesday, April 27

Sᴀᴍ ᴡᴏᴋᴇ ɢᴀꜱᴘɪɴɢ. There was a whiskey barrel on her chest and everyone was stepping on her to get at the tap. No, she gradually realized, it was a dream. Derek was the only one in the room with her, and he was sleeping soundly beside her. She turned on her side and closed her eyes. She had on her bra and pants, not her usual nightshirt. Oh, yes, she'd been down for a nap. Curiosity got the better of her, and she turned her head to see the green digital numbers on the clock on the nightstand: 2:43.

That was some nap.

She'd missed another amoxicillin. She got out of bed, groped the three vials, and wandered into the bathroom. She was through with the sleeping pills and the painkillers; she needed to clear her system of chemicals. But she took the antibiotic and then made room for the vials in the medicine cabinet. She stood staring at the shelves, trying to work through the image. She closed the cabinet, turned off the light, and then turned it back on so she would have enough light to find her robe in the closet. She ripped it off the hanger and then turned off the light in the bathroom. She tiptoed across the floor and out of the door. The cat got in and raced to the bed. That would go over in a big way with Derek.

She padded down the dark stairway and passed the library, where Nicola was snoring softly on the hideaway. She waited until the door was closed to turn on the light in the second bathroom. That's what she thought. The medicine cabinet held neither a tube of Retin-A nor a vial of tetracycline. They couldn't have been Nicola's because she was meeting her for the first time.

Where had she seen them? Whose medicine cabinet had she been looking through? What name had been on the prescription? Why couldn't she remember?

A scraping noise took her to the nursery. The night-light in the wall outlet was enough to see by. The circus mobile over the crib was magically swaying and drifting. Woody was controlling the magic. He cooed at the animals.

"You little dickens," she whispered. "You're supposed to be asleep."

She thought he favored her with a smile. She rewarded him by picking him up. His blue jumper looked as fresh as he smelled, leading her to believe that Nicola had been up with him not too long ago. She held him close, wondering how she had ever managed to live without him. She had managed because she was ignorant of the great joy that came with having children.

The scraping was at the window. A confused squirrel wanted in. A flash of headlights illuminated the side of the house. The truck was weaving up the path toward the barn. She and Woody went to the window in the kitchen to follow its progress. The dogs were chasing the truck. Emil stumbled out of the truck, made a swiping attempt at petting one of the dogs; and then they all disappeared into his shack. Drunk again. She missed the old, reliable days with Jake. She hoped Jake would come back soon. Maybe he would have some influence over his nephew. She turned away from the window when the light in the shack went out.

Woody's eyes were heavy. It was a one-way street with her son. He wanted someone up and paying court to him when he was hungry or dirty or fussy, but with a full stomach and a clean diaper he'd just as soon go back to sleep and leave his mother to her own devices.

She put him in his crib, and then rummaged through the refrigerator. Gnawing on a chicken leg only reminded her of her work; swallowing it reminded her of her sore throat. She chewed each piece much longer than her growling stomach would ordinarily have allowed. She chose a soft slice of bread instead of another piece of chicken and gobbled it down before she reached the stairs. She reraided the refrigerator for another couple slices of bread, but after the first her hunger was not as demanding, and she only halfheartedly ate the second while she pulled on her jeans.

Her Jeep had returned to the garage like a runaway horse to its stable. Even now that she knew about it, she couldn't tell which window had been replaced. The black bag she always left on the floor behind the driver's seat was missing. She wasn't going back into the house to look for it, nor was she going to wake Derek to ask about it.

The trip to town was dark and lonely. Main Street was rolled up, and the lights were dim at the hospital. She rang the bell at the ER entrance and waited as old Bertha, the registered nurse on duty, left her patient's side and came to the door to unlock it and let Sam in.

A fretful baby about three times Woody's size was the center of attention at examining table number one. Clarence's sport coat didn't quite disguise the pajama top under it as a dress shirt. A tie might have done the trick by covering the large buttons. The baby's worried parents most likely didn't care what the doctor had on.

Sam slipped out and headed for the lab and a mountain of work. Radiology was lit up like a Christmas tree. Sam wandered through the department and found Ken and the X-ray technologist in the reading room. The baby's chest films were spread across the light box. The lungs were cloudy with infiltrate. Anyone could have read these films.

"Pneumonia," Ken said to the tech. The tech took off to deliver the message to Clarence.

"Clarence called you in to read those?"

"You know Clarence. Didn't know whether it was pneumonia or bronchitis."

"Same treatment either way. He could have waited. Why's

he here? Thought that was what the new ER docs are for?"

"Not after eleven or on weekends if the patient has an attending."

"Pretty good work if you can get it."

"Plenty of time for fishing. We won't keep them long if Flash has anything to do with it, though. Heard he took Jeffers up to Sibley Lake to do some ice fishing and they just about drowned. Flash is such a loser."

Sam slapped his arm. "Don't say that about Eugene; he's my partner."

"Don't know how you put up with him."

"He's okay."

"Yeah? See you've never responded to a code with him."

In fact, Sam and Eugene had responded to the same code in the ER more than once. And Ken was right. Eugene either froze in an emergency and they had to stumble around him, or he inappropriately ran the show. He'd order Isuprel when atropine should have been given and became arrogant when his orders were questioned. She was happy the two ER docs were doing all that now. Or most of it, anyway.

"What are you doing here at this hour, Sam? You're supposed to be home in bed. In your sickbed, I might add."

"I've had all the sleep I can stand. And if you call Derek to tell him I'm here, I'll never speak to you again as long as I live."

"Wouldn't dream of it. I wish I were. Dreaming of it, I mean. Wish I were dreaming of anything."

"You can have mine. The animals on my son's circus mobile have been terrorizing me."

"Thank your lucky stars they aren't sheep that keep you awake counting." He took the top envelope from the films that had accumulated during the evening and night and rammed two views of an ankle under the rim of the light box. "Might as well get these out of the way as long as I'm here."

"Me, too. See you later."

Sam was having trouble feeling a sense of place in the lonely lab. Usually she worked to the background noise of patients coming and going and techs hopscotching between work centers. Now she heard only the various mechanical noises the equipment gave off periodically and the central heating system as it kicked on and turned off.

A red wedge of light was visible through the eastern window by the time Sam finished up in the lab. She read and initialed Tom Polvich's reports that had been left on her desk, and then looked up the phone number for the Centers for Disease Control in Atlanta. They were two hours ahead, but she'd give Tom another hour so as not to be confused should the operator, or whoever, tell her he wasn't in yet.

She picked up the phone and called her sister's number in New Orleans. Maybe she could catch her brother-in-law before he left for the office. After the fourth ring, the machine picked up. She was about to leave a message when Jack answered.

"Yeah?"

"Jack, Sam."

"Hello, doll. Hang on a sec." She heard a clang, a bounce, and a second clang, hurried footsteps getting fainter, silence, hurried footsteps growing stronger, a clang. "Sorry, sweetie, had to turn off the shower. Don't want to use up all the hot water. You're better, I take it?"

"Much. Listen Jack, I'm calling to see about Dad."

Jack laughed. "That's a switch."

"Derek said he's with Sharon."

"He's doing fine." he said as compassionately as a lawyer could. "Sharon called last night. Everything is going swimmingly."

"Swimmingly?"

"A little humor. Sharon was watching the sunbathers on the beach from your father's window when she was talking to me."

"Where are they?"

"The Caribbean. St. Thomas. Let's see, the—"

"Blanca Institute," Sam said flatly, her world screeching to a halt.

"Right."

A tremor took her hand. She had never been so frightened in her entire life as when she was there. She hoped her voice didn't betray her horror. "That's all I wanted to know," Sam said with more conviction than she felt. "I'll let you get back to your shower."

"Nice to hear your voice, doll."

"Yours, too. Bye-bye."

Emptiness hit her square in the gut. Why had Derek deceived her? The clinic was supposed to have been shut down. Now her father was there?

Anger eclipsed the fear. How could Derek do this to her? How could he have done this to her father? And what about her sister?

No, no. She had to get a grip. Just because the Institute was open didn't mean Blanca was there. They were simply continuing his good work; otherwise Derek wouldn't have sent her father there. The Blanca Institute was on the cutting edge of medical technology; she'd seen the wondrous results for herself. Derek's people had stepped in and ridded the place of the atrocities. Derek had said that she herself had provided the precursors; everything was aboveboard—well, sort of aboveboard. Derek was giving her father a chance to recapture his life.

Sam thought of her father playing the baby grand, with she, her mom, and her sister standing around it singing Christmas carols. Maybe next Christmas he'd be playing carols for Woody. Science fiction meets modern medicine.

She changed her mind about waiting to call Tom. She picked up the phone and dialed the CDC's number.

20

Sam's TIMING LEFT a good deal to be desired. Between the runaround in almost every department at the CDC and dodging Derek's phone calls, she'd managed to hit the high school parking lot at about the same time as the students. This time she found a space to park on the back forty off the blacktop. She dodged cars in training for the Indy 500 and then followed students through some doors. She didn't have the foggiest idea where she was or how to get to the principal's office but was carried on the tide.

"Dr. Turner," said the petite woman as they crossed paths at a busy intersection.

Sam held out her hand. "Hello," she said, wondering where the hell she knew this person from. She assumed the woman was a teacher, not a student. She was young, wore her black, curly hair almost to her waist, her denim skirt to the ankles of her turquoise boots, but she was too fashionable to be one of the students. They wore jeans, baggy sweaters, and high-top sneakers without laces. To tell the sexes apart, the boys wore laces that flopped about as they walked. Sam wondered about the broken ankle Ken was reading on the light box last night. Dangling laces might be the mainstay of the orthopeds' workload these days.

"I'm glad I ran into you, Dr. Turner. We've been worried about Jess. He hasn't been to school since you were here, and we haven't been able to reach him. Is he . . .very ill?"

"Jess?"

"Jess Gorzalka. Does he have—" She interrupted herself

to look around the crowded hallway. "You know, being David's roommate in Washington." She must have meant David Crider. Washington?

"Is there a quiet place where we could talk?"

"I have a first-period class." She glanced at her watch and grimaced. "Maybe I could—"

"Ms. Norton, will you sign this?" A girl thrust a paper in her face.

She pushed it away. "Not right this minute."

"I have to have it back to the office by fifth period or I can't help set up the concession stand Friday for the rodeo. I need the DECA hours or I won't get my school letter, and my mom's already bought my letterman's jacket."

Ms. Norton duly scribbled her name between two other signatures, as she said, "Have someone turn in Friday's assignment for you."

"Yes, ma'am," the girl replied as she took back the paper and hurried away.

"Sorry."

"You were asking me about Jess Gorzalka. I'd like—"

The warning buzz sent students screeching every which way. Lockers slammed up one side of the hall and down the other, and the race was on.

Ms. Norton looked nervously up the hall. "I have to unlock my door."

Wasn't much left for Sam to say except, "I'll come back."

There was something oddly familiar about the Gorzalka place, from the wooden plank dangling form one chain to the purple lilacs framing the red mobile home. Sam pulled the Jeep up to the truck trailer filled with logs. She realized she'd been there when she saw the stack of wood along the trailer.

"Morning," she called to the scrungy-looking man chopping wood.

He drove the ax solidly through the thick log, splitting it as easily as if it had been a twig. He picked up the two pieces and pitched them toward the split stack. He finally gave her his attention. "What can I do for you?" he asked, taking off his cowhide gloves.

"Do you know who I am?"

"Should I?"

"Are you Jess Gorzalka's father?"

"Why?"

She extended her hand. He didn't make a move to take it, instead running his hand over a good week's growth of beard. "I'm Dr. Turner," she said, sticking her hands in her pockets, "the medical examiner for Sheridan County. I need to talk to your son about David Crider, a friend of his."

"I don't know all his friends."

And he wasn't ever going to get to know this one. She motioned toward the trailer. "May I go in and speak with him?"

"He's not here. He's at school."

"When did you last see your son?"

"Not since last night. I got home late, slept in late this morning."

Closed the bars and woke up with a hangover, she thought, taking a careful breath. "Is your wife at home?"

"My wife's dead."

"I'm sorry, I didn't know." She wasn't sure what to tell him. She wasn't the truant officer. "Mr. Gorzalka, your son isn't at school and hasn't been for two weeks."

"I don't believe that. He likes school."

That was the wrong answer, and knowing that he was exposed to hantavirus worried her that much more. He would not survive hantavirus untreated. "Has he been ill?"

"Not that I know of."

"Wouldn't you have known? You live with him, don't you?"

"I've been in the Big Horns." He nodded at the timber. "Didn't get back until late last night."

"What about last night? How did he look?"

"He was asleep."

"Did you see him in bed?"

"His door was closed."

"So you really haven't seen him since when?"

He had to think. "I don't know. The day before I left, I suppose."

Sam motioned to all of the cars in the yard. "Is his car gone?"

He nodded.

"Do you mind if I go inside and look around his bedroom?"

"Do you have a warrant?"

"Mr. Gorzalka, I'm not the police. I'm concerned about your son's well-being. I thought we might find something that would help us locate him."

"Like what?'

"Phone numbers of friends."

"Maybe he's with his girlfriend. Or she might know where he's at."

"What's her name?"

"Debbie . . . Debbie something or other." He rolled his hand as if trying to pull the name out of his mouth. She certainly knew the helpless feeling.

"Do you know where I can find her?"

"At school. Or at McDonald's."

"You don't mind if I use your bathroom, do you? Long way back to town." She wanted to satisfy her curiosity and see if the medicine cabinet held tetracycline and Retin-A.

▽

21

Sam REACHED THE ranch by eleven, Derek running to the Jeep and opening the door for her, saving her the trouble of looking for him. He gave her his customary stern look as he helped her out.

"Shall I tell you what it felt like to reach over to pull you close, to hold you," he asked as he reined her in and kissed her, "only to find empty sheets?" He closed the door behind her with his foot.

"I wish I'd been there to feel for myself." She returned his kiss. "You lied to me," she said and captured his lips again. "I talked to Jack this morning."

The roofers whistled and cheered as Derek picked her up and carried her the rest of the way to the house. "And what did Jack have to say?"

"Sharon and Dad are in St. Thomas at the Blanca Institute."

He pushed through the doorway, kicked the door closed, and kissed her again. She felt vibrantly alive.

"Where's Nicola?" she whispered breathlessly against the warm flesh of his neck.

"I don't know," he said, "but she's not in our bedroom. And if she is, she'd better hustle out fast or she'll be getting the show of her life."

"What about the Blanca Institute?" Sam asked as she spread her fingers over the back of his head, gripping his hair and yanking back to align their lips.

"Save that question. Let's make up first and quarrel later."

*   *   *

"What about the Blanca Institute?" she asked later as she curled up against Derek's side and snuggled close.

He wrapped his arm around her lethargically. "Shh, let's rest a minute or two."

Male hormones! "You can rest all you want when I leave."

Derek tightened his grip. "No, don't leave," he whispered so as not to wake himself. His arm fell away, his meager protest aborted, as she crawled out of bed. He rolled away, burying his face in his pillow.

Sam took an amoxicillin and a shower. She leaned up against the wet tile and let the warm water pulsate against her weary flesh. She had so many things to do. Jess Gorzalka and his girlfriend Debbie, Tom Polvich, meet Eugene's plane and find out what he knew about hen's eggs, check on Terry to see how she was making out. Sam might even consider doing a little work.

Derek opened the shower door and stepped in, cutting off the cascading water momentarily. He pulled her in under the nozzle and supported her weight.

"Recovered?"

He lowered his head to attack her neck.

She pushed him away. "Now, don't start up with me again. I have to go back to town."

"Please don't go back. Stay and rest." He took the bar of soap out of her hand and turned her around and lathered her back.

"And have my days and nights mixed up even more? I'm feeling much better than yesterday. A zillion times better than the day before. And no one's covering for me."

"Where's Tom Polvich?"

"That's the sixty-four-thousand-dollar question." His scowl wasn't nearly as menacing when it was directed at someone else's actions and not hers. "Tell me about Dad."

"Not much to tell. Figured I'd better do something about his condition before it was too late. Made a few discreet calls."

"How come the Blanca Institute opened again?"

"Blanca's lawyers are even better than the Danes'."

"I thought the Americans owned St. Thomas and the Danes were our landlords. Or something."

"Blanca's lawyers are the best then. Isn't the rule two better, three best?"

"Blanca as an Institute or Blanca as in Ponce?"

"Does it matter?"

"It matters to me. Ponce Blanca was responsible for the premature birth of our son. Woody's been struggling for four months now to make up the eight weeks he missed growing in my womb. And it might take him years to catch up."

"Settle down, Samantha. Woody's fine. Alan Martin was responsible, not Ponce Blanca."

"You should have seen what Ponce did to Tiffany. That wasn't exactly fair play."

"All right, you win. We can't always be choosy about our political bedfellows in such volatile times."

"What does politics have to do with my father?

"Nothing. Nothing to do with your father. The Blanca Institute is at the cutting edge of gene therapy. Controversial, if not unethical, by current U.S. standards. But should that mean that lives that they have the technology to save should be lost while the morality is being debated? And why am I taking this side of the argument when two weeks ago you were?"

It did sound like something she would have said. She offered up a kiss. "Thank you, Derek. How's he doing?"

"It's a little early to tell. We'll simply have to wait and see."

Sam lifted her arm to show him a rough spot. "Look at this. What is it?"

"It's fine. A scab where they gave you an injection."

"An injection! I had an IV line. Why give me an intermuscular injection?"

"They gave them to everyone in the hospital as a precaution." He pointed to his.

Pounding on the bathroom door startled them. Derek

opened the shower door enough to call out. Nicola slid the bathroom door back so Derek and she could exchange loud foreign words. Everything was steamy and Sam doubted Nicola could see much, but still Sam burrowed her head in Derek's back in sheer embarrassment at being caught in the shower with her husband. Having a stranger in the house had its downside.

Derek closed the door and got back under the tap. "Hank's come for you. They have a floater."

Interstate 90 going north was smooth sailing to Ranchester. Ditto Route 14 between Ranchester and Dayton, and even up the foothills of the Big Horns. But the twisting mountain road to Lake Sibley in the sheriff's Bronco had knocked Sam out. They were deep into the evergreens on a snow-packed single-lane path when Hank's voice woke Sam. He was getting directions from the forest ranger.

The ranger backed his truck up ten feet and into a campsite to let them pass. The ambulance was in the parking lot between the deputy's Bronco and a Volvo station wagon with New Jersey license plates and a ski rack. Two young women, bundled up for cross-country skiing, sat at the picnic table in the sun. The other table, in the shade of pine trees, was still covered with snow.

The south shore of Sibley—the one nearest Sam—was ice free, but a big chunk was floating near the north end by Route 14. She had been asleep when they drove by the lake, so she didn't know about the west side.

Four men, two skiers and two in uniform, huddled at the edge of the boat dock, watching two frogmen in thick black wetsuits paddling a yellow rubber boat. Two volunteers sat on the tailgate of the Blazer, while another two were warming up in the cab of the Dayton fire department rescue truck.

"Let me out here," Sam said as they passed the two outhouses. "I'll catch up." The one-holer was slick with melting snow coming in off the screened-in roof by day and freezing at night. Keeping flies out in the summer months took priority over dripping water in the spring when almost no one was around to use the outhouse. Sam wished she'd heeded her mother's warnings about not sitting on public toilet seats as soon as she touched the icy plank. Of course there was no paper, and she had to take off her gloves to dig around in her parka for a tissue. She came up with a shredded, used one. Good enough for government work.

She trudged across the parking lot, snow-packed and mud-caked, to the knot of men surrounding the floater and crouched down beside the body. The body was fresh and wasn't dressed for fishing. He wore khaki pants and a polo dress shirt, no jacket.

This one hadn't been in the water more than a couple of days. It would have taken months for enough gas to form within the tissues to raise a sunken body to the surface in such cold water. Sam looked at the fingernails. They hadn't started loosening up. He was covered with cuts and abrasions. A piece of gravel was caught in his nose.

Sam twisted the corpse around to get into his pockets. Nothing. Picked clean.

She got to her feet. "Who found the body?"

The deputy thumbed to the two skiers. "They did."

"Where did you find the body?"

The taller of the two pointed across the lake, closer to the northern end. "He was over there by the shore."

"Caught between the ice and some driftwood," the other one added.

Most likely an exposed root of one of the forty-foot conifers that circled the lake. Sam had no desire to go around to find out. It was marshy all along the south bank, and she wasn't keen for a ride in the yellow dinghy. She watched the ripples. The victim probably fell, was pushed, or was dumped from the side of the road; rolled down the steep gravel incline, and drifted along the eastern shoreline.

Sam pulled Hank to the side. "Hank, why don't you send a couple of men up to the road and see if they can get some tire imprints between those two railings."

Hank surveyed the area while he worked the notion through his mind. Sam sat on a dry boulder as Hank gave orders and finished up. She got off the boulder after the body was loaded onto a gurney.

"Randy, run by the hospital and see if Dr. Miller can ID the corpse before you take it to the mortuary. And ask him to run the usual gamut of X-rays."

"You think Ken knows him?" Hank asked.

"If this is Tom Polvich, yes."

22

THE GOLDEN ARCHES of McDonald's loomed up as they headed back to town from the north. "Buy you a hamburger, Hank," Sam said, giving a perfunctory glance at her watch. It was after three and she was starving. If Debbie Something-or-other was there, so much the better.

"Best offer I've had in a heck of a long time. Sarah's got me on a fat-free diet. Haven't had french fries since I don't know when. And the fresh air up in the mountains really makes a body hungry."

So does missing lunch. "I said I'd buy you a hamburger. I didn't say anything about fries. But I'll throw in a salad for good measure."

"Gee thanks, Sam," he said with as much enthusiasm as a child about to sit through a Sunday church sermon. Church!

David Crider's body was missing. Jess Gorzalka was missing. Tom Polvich was missing, or on his way to the hospital in the ambulance ahead of them.

"What do you know about David Crider or the Church of Divine Light, Hank?"

"Don't know much about the kid, but I heard Bill talking about a Hell's Angel some members of the congregation took in who robbed them blind. That's about all I know, Sam."

She'd have to ask the illustrious police chief himself about the Hell's Angel incident when she went in to see if they just happened to be holding her black bag. And if they weren't, she'd be happy to tell them that it was stolen from her Jeep under their very noses in the impound lot. "You know Jess Gorzalka?"

"Course I know him. Don't you remember?"

"Sorry, Hank. Whatever they were giving me to resolve the fluid in my lungs has caused a temporary memory lapse. Refresh my memory."

"Yeah? You can't remember things? What's that like? Did they have to tell you your name and stuff?"

"Knew my name. Had trouble with Derek's for awhile. Mainly, I've lost track of two weeks in my life."

"Once we picked up this suspect out at Bradford Brinton who thought he lived there. Said he didn't know who he was or where he came from, all that. But we knew he was lying. Turned out he was an ex-con. Served time for grand theft. Casing the museum, going to steal the Remingtons, betcha."

The Bradford Brinton Memorial wasn't too far from her ranch, and she'd been there often enough to look at the art collection, but as interesting as a big-time art heist might have been, it wasn't helping her learn about Jess Gorzalka. "What should I remember about Jess Gorzalka?"

"Oh, yeah, let's see. You called me out to the Gorzalka place because you thought he was sick or dead or something. Left a deputy out there until Frank got back."

"When was that?"

"Friday. No, Saturday. Yeah, had vouchers for two nights."

Gorzalka had lied to her.

They followed the ambulance off I-90 at the Main Street exit, but turned in to McDonald's. The place was nearly empty. Only two people were working the counter: one counted and rearranged the hamburgers in the warming bin, the other pulled a wire basket from the deep bubbling grease and turned it out onto a steel rack under warming lamps.

After arm-wrestling over wallets, Sam ended up paying for the tray of food, including Hank's fries. "Is Debbie here now?" Sam asked as she wadded up her change and stuck it in her jeans pocket.

"Debbie Schrieber or Debbie Freeman?" the middle-aged cashier asked, eyeing the sheriff.

"The one in high school."

"They're both in high school. But Debbie Freeman's the only one here." She pointed to the big-haired blond at the drive-through window.

Hoping her fifty-fifty chance was a winner, Sam said, "Could I speak with her for a minute?"

The woman conferred with the man who had been rearranging the hamburger bin and who was now testing the carbonation in the soda machine. He looked at Hank and then went over and relieved Debbie. Debbie looked a little confused as she took off her headset and the transmitter around her waist to give to him. He pointed to the sheriff.

"Why don't you find a place, Hank? I'll be right there," Sam said.

"Debbie, I'm Dr. Turner. Do you know Jess Gorzalka?"

Color drained from her face. That was answer enough.

Sam looked around the room and then pointed to the empty booths under the windows. "Why don't we sit over there?"

As the girl was coming around the counter, Sam crossed the room to where Hank was sitting and grabbed her coffee. "Go ahead and eat. I need to talk with her for a moment."

Sam sat down across from the girl. "I'm looking for Jess. When was the last time you saw him?"

"Wednesday night, two weeks ago." She started crying. "I should have made him use a condom."

"I'm sorry. What did you say?"

Debbie hid her face in her hands and wailed. Sam got up, pulled some napkins from the dispenser, and then slid into the booth next to the girl to comfort her and to hand her the napkins.

"Tell me what happened."

"That's what my friend Lisa said, that I should have made him use a condom. You know, because of AIDS and stuff. Lisa said they don't like to wear them, but they will if that's the only way they'll get any. I should have made him use one." Debbie's wet eyes turned to her. "He has AIDS, doesn't he? That's why you're looking for him, isn't it, doctor?"

"No, it's not. But your friend's right," Sam answered, "you should always insist that he wear a condom." Building a latex wall between lovers seemed somehow incongruous. In an ideal world, everyone would be monogamous. Supplementing the male hormone vasopressin in those vasopressin-deprived men who stray would solve the polygamy problem.

"Thank God he doesn't have AIDS. I thought he had AIDS. I didn't know how I was going to tell my mom that I was going to die."

"You know, Debbie, condoms aren't a hundred-percent effective." She sounded like the school nurse, for chrissake, and had the girl in tears, but she kept on going. "Sometimes they break, leak, aren't applied correctly. Before I'd let a boy touch me, I'd ask myself if I loved him enough to die for him. Because that's the kind of risk people are taking these days."

Now she had the girl howling. Everyone was looking at them. Hank held her cheeseburger up to his mouth and pointed to her, indicating something or other. Probably that it was getting cold and did she want him to bring it to her so she could eat it. She shook her head and tried to get across the notion that he should eat it and she'd get a fresh one by flapping her hand uselessly in the air. From his expression, he didn't get it. She flapped both hands toward him, to double his confusion.

"I do love him enough to die for him. But he doesn't love me the way I love him." More tears.

"Do you know where he is?"

"At his aunt and uncle's, I bet." She blew her nose in the rough napkin. "He hasn't called since he told me he'd decided to go to Notre Dame." She cried all the harder.

"Notre Dame is a good school."

Debbie looked at her as if seeing her for the first time and then wailed. "So's UW. If he really loved me, he'd go down to Laramie with me. He could get every bit as good a scholarship to UW as he's getting to Notre Dame." She made Notre Dame sound like a couple of distasteful words.

Sam wasn't going to win this one. "I need to talk to him about his friend David Crider. Who's his uncle?"

"He had lots of them. He's going to die? Like David did?"

"You knew David, too?"

"Not really. A little. Jess roomed with David when we were in Washington."

"You went to Washington with them?"

"Sure. We were delegates to the National Student Congress before spring break." Debbie flipped around on the seat so they were face to face. "Oh, you're here about the man."

"What man?"

"The man David was telling Jess about. After David died, Jess said he thought he should go to the police."

"And tell them what?"

"Tell them about the man."

"What about the man?"

"How he asked all these strange questions about where David was from, how big the town was, where the nearest hospital was. What kind of perfume survey was that?"

"A perfume survey? What do you mean?"

"David was always going off by himself. You know, taking walks, that kinda thing. And one of those people like you see up in Billings at the Rimrock Mall said he'd give David ten dollars to test a perfume."

"This was in Washington? In the street?"

"Around the hotel somewhere. The guy gave him ten dollars for smelling some perfume for a survey, but David couldn't smell it. The man said that it was a light fragrance and that only some people could smell it. But he still gave him the money. That's weird, don't you think? I mean, like, if he couldn't smell the perfume from the test tube, why would he pay him when he couldn't answer the questions on the survey? And ten dollars! They only pay fifty cents in Billings, if they pay at all."

"Who'd wear a perfume that only some people could smell?"

"Yeah, I didn't think of that. We thought maybe it was some sort of drug. You hear about people in the big cities like New York and Los Angeles getting stuck with AIDS needles by crazy people. Maybe that's what this man was doing." She furrowed her brows. "But why would he pay ten dollars?"

23

Sᴀᴍ ᴡᴀꜱ ꜱᴄʀᴀᴘɪɴɢ bottom now. Hank held open the door for her. It was the last courtesy she could expect here.

"Ladies," Hank called to the police dispatchers.

Sam stared at the floor as she followed Hank through the door for authorized personnel to the policemen's sanctuary, matching Hank's long, light footfalls with her shorter, ominous ones. The lion was in his den.

"Howdy," Hank said from the door. The chief stood up, rounded his desk, and met Hank halfway with open arms. "Doc here needs a word with you. We've been up to Sibley. Got a floater. Gonna run her up to the hospital when she's through here. Give me a call. Be in my office."

"I'll come get you," Sam said. It wasn't much of an imposition; the sheriff's office and the police department were housed in the same building. Different entrances was all. And if she were willing to walk through the jail block, she didn't have to go around the building. Hank waved and was off.

"You're afoot, Dr. Turner?" The chief's tone was somewhere between counterfeit concern and obnoxious buffoonery.

"My Jeep's at home in the garage, being punished for going off with strangers." She sat down in the chair in front of the desk and waited for the chief to take his place behind it. She ran a finger over his genuine marbled plastic name plate. "William Johnston, Police Chief. Great name plate, Bill. Wonder if Woolworth's can make me one like it?"

He moved it out of her reach. "Hear tell you've been sick."

"Sicker than a dog, Bill. How 'bout yourself?"

"Healthy as a horse."

"Keep taking those steroids, Bill. Keeps your testosterone level up." She noticed him clawing at his collar and decided enough small talk. "Bill, did Jess Gorzalka come in here?"

"In jail, you mean?" he asked, all business.

"No, no. With an accusation. A suspicion about the wrongful death of a friend of his. David Crider."

"Oh, the kid who died of that virus epidemic we had."

Seven cases was a few cases shy of the epidemic they could have had if the CDC hadn't been johnny-on-the-spot. "Right. Did he? Jess Gorzalka? Did he come to you? Is there a report?" Sam asked in as many one-syllable words as possible.

He picked up the phone and pressed the intercom button. He asked a person named Susie the same questions but managed to do so in even smaller words. Sam took a gander at the desk between them. Looked like Sheridan was having a regular crime wave, with the hurricane touching down on Bill's desk first. She leaned forward and caressed the name plate again, liking the way Bill's neck blotched red. He eyed her as he uttered his big-shot grunt into the phone. She was too impressed to breathe. Blowing her nose might help. She poked around in her pockets for a tissue but came up short. The outhouse must have gotten her last one.

"Guess not," Bill said with chief-of-police finality as he hung up.

"Guess not?" she mimicked. "Is that an unequivocal guess not, or a tentative guess not?"

"Huh?"

"Is Susie going to go through these files?" Sam ruffled the papers in his OUT basket.

"These aren't anything important."

Sam leaned back in her chair, relieved that nothing important had been left in his care. "I need to find Jess Gorzalka. He's been missing two weeks and his father practically wanted a search warrant for me to use the bathroom in his trailer. What do you know about these people?"

He shrugged.

"Okay, Bill, here's an easy one. Where's my black bag? It was in my Jeep when one of your men hauled it away."

He shrugged again.

"Okay, Bill, here's an easier one. How did my window get broken while you had it in protective custody?"

He scratched his head as if it helped him think.

"Okay, Bill, here's a real easy one. Whoever has my black bag has a rather impressive collection of narcotics. What do you think the street value might be here in Sheridan?"

"Hi," Sam said as she caught Ken inspecting a film at the small light box in the hall outside the processor. He held his gloved fingers up and close to his chest so the blood would drip into the palms or down the front of his green scrubs. "Busy?"

"In the middle of an arteriogram. I ID'ed Tom Polvich for you. Haven't had time to look at his bone survey films yet. What's going on?"

"I haven't a clue." But her apprehensions had not proven groundless. "Come find me when you're finished."

The coffeepot in the lab had been emptied and cleaned for the night. Sam found the #1 MOM mug Woody, by way of Derek, gave her for Christmas and headed for the radiology department, hoping she'd have better luck there. She and a mug of coffee returned to pathology to find Kate looking weepy. She must have heard about Tom Polvich.

"Any messages?"

Kate was covering her typewriter with its plastic case. It was only half past four, not quarter to five when she habitually covered her typewriter; she must have been stressed to the max. "You have a couple of call reports. Your eggs arrived and are in the incubator. And Derek said to tell you to call when you're ready to come home." Sam had no idea what to do about the eggs but would have to look at the call reports pronto if she intended to call the doctors' offices before they closed at five. "And here." Kate reached for a shoe box and handed it over. Looked like everyone and his mother had called. There had to be a hundred messages. Too many to contemplate. She put the lid on and set the box on her desk.

"I'm sorry Kate, I know it's late, but I wonder if you could go downstairs to records and pull some charts for me before they close up."

Kate nodded, and then popped a tissue from the box on her immaculate desk and dabbed at her eyes. Sam took the next tissue and stuck it in her pocket, then another and blew her nose.

"I'd like mine, Thaddeus's, any Criders' you can find, Terry's, Dr. Wallace's, and see what they have on Jess Gorzalka."

Sam headed into the lab to see about the call reports as Kate finished writing out her list.

Kate threw the charts on Sam's desk as Sam was reporting some preliminary good news to the surgeon's office about a frozen tissue section. Sam rifled through the files as she hung up. She pulled Jess's out of the stack. The phone was ringing. Kate seemed more interested in putting her jacket on than in answering the phone. No wonder, it was after five. Just as Sam reached for her phone, Kate picked up hers.

"Pathology," she said as she laid her purse down, rounded her desk, and took a pen out of her drawer. "Dr. Turner isn't in."

Sam looked up.

"She's gone for the day." Kate was filling in a while-you-were-out slip. "I'll give her that message." Kate hung up.

"I'm not in?" Sam asked as she brought the message to her.

"Good night, Dr. Turner."

Sam watched her leave. Mystified. Corrine Miller was the name on the message. She turned the contents of the shoe box out on to the files. She didn't recognize any of the names. The phone rang.

"Dr. Turner speaking."

"This is Dr. Turner?"

"Yes."

"The archangel's apostle who ordered the burning of one of God's chosen children?"

Sam hung up, gathered up the messages, put them back in the shoe box, and threw the box in the wastebasket. After the tenth ring of the next phone call, Sam pulled the telephone cord out of the wall.

What had become of Jess? According to the outpatient report from his visit to the ER, he wasn't nearly as ill as the rest of the hantavirus victims had been. Could he be in one of the Billings hospitals? Or in Casper? And what about the addendum to the outpatient report? Why would Dr. Jeffers dictate another report to change *productive cough* to *nonproductive cough*? If it had been hers, she would have changed it with a ballpoint pen before she signed the report. Idle curiosity, nothing she'd ask him about. "Fever, nausea, backache . . . and a nonproductive cough." Not much to go on.

She drew her chart out of the pile. It proved too painful to read. Brushing up against one's own mortality wasn't easy. She read Bob's instead, and still fought a pang of despair. She compared Bob's to Jess's. Nothing to indicate the life-threatening illness the rest of them suffered.

Sam closed the charts with a heavy sigh. She didn't know whether to wait for Ken or go to the mortuary and post Tom Polvich. Yes, she did. Having no transportation made the decision easier.

She ripped sheets from her yellow legal tablet until she was down to a clean one and started writing.

> fertile hen's eggs
> Jess Gorzalka missing
> father wants search warrant

Tom Polvich's suspicious death
Eugene picked at random
perfume that doesn't smell
wrong remains cremated
missing black bag
smallpox, Bob says
six people recover from a dry-weather illness
amnesia—Bob, Thaddeus, Sam
Jeffers, Sibley

"What a day!" Ken exclaimed as he came in and wheeled Kate's chair over to Sam's desk.

"Tell me about it."

"Lordy, you look haggard." He put the back of his hand to her forehead. He sat down instead of announcing a fever.

She held the inside of her wrist to her forehead for a second opinion. No fever that she could tell. A wonder—she was so far behind on her antibiotic treatment that, at the rate she was going, she'd still be trying to take her pills in the next century. "Short of dragging me down to the ER and hooking me up to a bottle of Ringer's lactate, I don't think there's much to be done."

He nodded to her coffee. "Plenty of liquids and a jolt of caffeine can't hurt."

Sam took a sip of coffee.

"What ya doing?"

She held out the yellow legal tablet for him to take. "Looking for the zebra."

Ken studied the list. "Negative for fractures on the bone survey, by the way."

"What was Tom like?"

"Nice guy. Friendly."

"What about the ER docs?"

He shrugged. "Jeffers is warm. Nguyen cold. Why's Jeffers on the list?"

"Because he's an outsider who's been to Sibley." Sam took back the list. "What do you think's going on?"

"I'm at a complete loss."

"Listen to this," she said as she shuffled paper to pull Bob's chart. She couldn't find the note she was looking for. "Anyway," she said, tossing the chart on the mound, "it said something like 'experimental drug X.' That's a big help."

"Actually, it was a big help. Resolved the pulmonary edema, and I have the pictures to prove it. Talk with Jeffers."

"You know what I meant." She tapped her temple. "The amnesia. And don't be so quick to defend our good Dr. Jeffers. Don't you think it's a little strange that everyone who came in contact with David . . ." She stopped. That's not what she meant. They'd supposedly contracted their illness from him. She didn't have words to express her feeling. "I smell a conspiracy."

"Conspiracy? You think Jeffers made you ill to get you out of the way? Isn't that a bit far-fetched?"

"That was the result, wasn't it? I was out of the way. The brand new, overqualified ER doc becomes my attending. Cures me of a virus I shouldn't have caught in this climate and leaves my mind with a two-week hole in it." She tapped her temple again for good measure. "Oh, my dream to close down the rodeo." She added it to the list.

She drew an arrow from *fertile hen's eggs* to *smallpox, Bob says*. And an arrow from *rodeo dream* to *smallpox*. Wrote *the source* beside *perfume*. Wrote *C* (for conspiracy) in front of *Jess, father, Tom, Eugene, wrong, six, amnesia, Jeffers*. That left only the black bag out of her smallpox theory, and probably that was a random theft to obtain drugs.

"The zebra keeps coming up smallpox."

"Wow, Sam, that's a quantum leap."

"Just listen for a minute. Fertile hen's eggs. A test for smallpox. I gather I called Bob because I thought I'd found a case of smallpox and I wanted him to verify it. And I had been dreaming about smallpox and the rodeo."

"Haven't you forgotten something, Sam?"

"Probably. What?"

"Derek explained about Bob and your dream."

"You're right," she admitted dejectedly. She crossed Bob and her rodeo dream off the list. She leaned back in her chair. "Oh, Ken, I've never known such fatigue. Both physical and mental. Why can't I think straight?" She sighed until her lungs were empty, and then sucked the sigh back in. "I need to go over to the mortuary and post Tom. See if I can determine the cause of death. We need some evidence, not more suppositions."

"You think he was murdered?"

"I don't know what to think." She propped her head up in her hands and sighed again. "Maybe he realized there was a conspiracy going on. Did he say anything to you?"

"He didn't seem concerned about anything. Quite the contrary. Wished all his fieldwork were this manageable."

"How did he get along with Jeffers?"

"I don't know that he had any dealings with either of the two ER docs, other than at the staff meeting when he singled them out and reminded them of the hantavirus symptoms to watch for."

Sam stared at the ceiling until her eyes began closing of their own accord. Then she got to her feet by sheer willpower. "I need to get to the mortuary. Will you give me a ride?"

"I'll give you a ride home. Tom's body will keep. Yours won't."

▽

24

THE SKY WAS still light when she got home; a couple of months from now the sun wouldn't go down until after ten. Light or dark, it was after seven, and they'd waited dinner. The scowl on Derek's face was for her. Nicola was busy dishing up the meal and setting the serving plates on the kitchen table.

"Eugene will be back tonight," Sam said as she sat in the chair Derek pulled out for her. "I won't have to go to the hospital tomorrow," she added as she scooted closer to the table.

"Good." Derek went around the table and pulled out a chair for Nicola.

Nicola smiled with a hint of embarrassment, bared only the smallest glint of pink gums, and sat down more gracefully than Sam had expected for a person of such bulk.

They were all nicely seated, and Derek's scowl had softened to merely intense. Sam reached for the mashed potatoes but Derek took her hand, then Nicola's. Nicola reached across the table, and Sam's other hand met hers over the chicken platter. They bowed their heads for grace, which Nicola offered in Hungarian.

"It's our new family tradition," Derek mumbled as he handed Sam the potatoes.

"Yes, I see," Sam mumbled back, realizing she knew less about the people of the Communist bloc than she thought. Come Sunday they'd probably be squeezing into the Jeep and heading off to church. She would draw the line at membership in the Church of Divine Light. Hell, she'd be black-balled there. "Woody's asleep?" Sam asked.

Nicola showed two inches worth of gum as she beamed ear to ear. "Sweet baby sleeping."

Derek and Sam exchanged less distinct smiles; she hoped they could protect Woody from the evils in life forever. Sam gobbled her potatoes. Derek had made them. Not so the chicken, she realized as she grabbed for a glass of water.

"Much paprika?"

"It's fine," Sam managed to say, mouth aflame and throat raw. "Cleared my sinus passages." She looked at Derek. "Paprika? An interesting word to know."

"We took inventory of the kitchen supplies this morning. They grow paprika in Hungary, in Szeged it seems."

"Alsovaros," Nicola said with a firm nod.

"That's the south end of cosmopolitan Szeged."

"Thank you," Sam said to both of them for the geography and agriculture lessons. Sam took another helping of potatoes.

"Would you like more peas to go with the half dozen you took earlier?" Derek offered her the bowl, knowing full well she hated canned peas. Frozen peas were bad enough, but at least they were dark green. Not puke green.

"No, thank you. I'll eat these first."

"There's ice cream for dessert," he said invitingly, tempting her with the vegetables.

"In that case, I won't eat the peas I have and save room." Sam smiled. Nicola returned her smile and took a goodly helping of peas from her host.

"Nicola went riding with Emil this afternoon." He added something to her in what sounded like French and bounced on his chair to tease her.

She put her face in her hands and giggled.

"And how was your afternoon?" Derek asked seriously after the conversation died of inertia.

"The floater wasn't the fisherman we've been waiting for. It was Tom Polvich."

Derek gave her a disconcerting stare. A hard, long one. "How did he die?"

"Drowning comes to mind."

He shot her a disapproving frown. "I take it your apparent capriciousness means that he didn't drown."

"I was hoping you'd extend me a professional courtesy and listen to a madwoman's hypothesis."

"Let's talk about it after dinner."

At Derek's insistence, Sam left the two of them to clean up the dishes and went upstairs to get ready for bed. She'd heard a plane overhead a bit ago but figured she had time to wash her face, brush her teeth, and take her amoxicillin before Eugene could kiss his wife, claim his luggage, and drive home. She pulled her 49ers nightshirt out of the clothes hamper, wondering if it meant the honeymoon was over when the bride would rather wear a crumpled, dirty, warm shirt to bed than a frilly silk nightie. Though she didn't know why she wondered. She didn't have a silk nightie and not much of a honeymoon.

The sheets were cold, and she shivered when she climbed into bed. She dialed Eugene's number. The answering machine picked up after the fourth ring. She endured his message about not being home unless a burglar was calling, in which case they were in the backyard. "You'd better be at the airport, you—"

The beep interrupted her.

"Eugene, Sam. Give me a call ASAP. Don't even put down your suitcase. I'm at the ranch," she added as an afterthought so he had no excuse for missing her. "No matter how late it is." Actually, it did matter how late. She wanted him to call right away. She hated the jumbled state she was in and wanted answers.

And there was the man to help work out the deadly jigsaw puzzle. The bed sagged as he sat on the edge to take off his boots. He carried them to the closet, picking up hers along the way so they could keep each other company in tidy alignment under the long line of neatly organized suits, sport jackets, and dress shirts to the left and a short, disarrayed assortment of skirts and blouses to the right.

She held out the yellow sheet of paper after she recovered from the ten-point somersault landing Derek scored easily to get into bed beside her. "Nothing like having an acrobat in bed."

Derek did a double take, thought better of outquipping her, and then concentrated on the sheet of paper. "What's this?"

"My Christmas list. A partridge in a pear tree has been replaced this year with fertile hen's eggs."

He pulled her close and kissed her forehead. "This is some list. Perfume that doesn't smell?"

Sam told him about the ten-dollar survey. Telling a five-year-old that there was no Santa Claus could not have produced more disbelief.

"How about this one? 'Father wants search warrant.' "

"I went out to the Gorzalka place out on Little Big Goose. I asked if I could go through the trailer and look around. He asked if I had a search warrant." Sam could tell from his casual shrug that he didn't think that was of any significance. But he seemed plenty unnerved about the rest. This was odd, because he usually masked his emotions well. "Besides, he lied to me. Said Jess hadn't been ill that he knew of and that he'd been in the Big Horns until last night. But the sheriff said he came back a week ago Saturday."

"Maybe he was gone twice. What do the C's mean?"

She cleared phlegm from her throat. "Conspiracy."

"Why did you cross out these two? The smallpox and the rodeo dream."

"Because you explained about those. But I'd forgotten until Ken reminded me."

"I take it Jeffers is your prime suspect for Tom Polvich's murder?" He signed quotes as he said the word *murder* to let her know he wasn't certain.

"He is an outsider. Eugene took him ice fishing at Sibley."

Derek folded the paper and stuck it in his shirt pocket.

"No, you don't," she said, pulling the paper out. "I'm the one with the faulty memory. I'll just keep this."

He got up and went to the window and looked out into the darkness. His profile was etched with overwhelming seriousness; slowly, he inched into the ghostly shadows. His behavior frightened her more than reading her chart had. A draw, anyway. The sounds of her harsh breathing and his grinding teeth broke the silence every now and again.

Finally she shattered the foreboding quiet, unable to endure the torment even a moment longer. "What are you thinking about, Derek?"

Another uncomfortable silence followed. The curtains wafted as he let go and turned to her. "I was wondering how much trouble you're in and how much more we can get into."

She took in a steadying breath. "What does *that* mean?"

"If you want my help," he answered without missing a beat, "you'll have to give me twenty-four hours."

"What are you talking about?"

"Take it on blind faith. No questions." He came to her, squatted down beside the bed, and took both her hands in his. "You know I love you with all my heart and that you and Woody come first in my life. I would make any sacrifice for the two of you."

"You're frightening me, Derek." She searched his eyes for the answers he couldn't or wouldn't give her. "What are you talking about?"

"Give me twenty-four hours to straighten this thing out," he pleaded. "And don't talk to Jeffers while I'm gone."

"Straighten what out? Do you know what this is about?"

He rose and paced the floor. All she wanted was the truth. How hard could telling the truth be? How terrifying could the truth be? He stopped pacing in order to look at his wristwatch. He went into the closet and came back with his duffel bag.

"Derek, what are you doing?" she asked as she shot across the bed to take the duffel bag away from him. "Don't run off and leave me like this. I need you here. I need you to tell me what's going on."

"Give me twenty-four hours and I'll explain all."

"No, I want answers now."

"I don't have the answers you want to hear."

They both turned to the ringing phone. Eugene? Talking to him now seemed inconsequential, but she was afraid not to answer for fear Nicola would. Then she'd come upstairs, and Derek would make a fast getaway. Sam threw herself across the bed to the phone, picked it up, and put it down again, silencing it. "Where are you going?"

"Samantha, don't do this to me. Please, give me twenty-four hours."

"Tell me why I should." Sam was paralyzed with fright as she watched Derek pull his 9mm Ruger out of his nightstand drawer. She jumped as the phone rang. He checked to make sure the handgun was loaded, and then rounded the bed and picked up the phone on the third ring.

"Hello." He dropped the Ruger into Sam's purse. "We're glad you're back. Samantha called to say that she won't be in tomorrow. She's been ill."

Sam sighed with relief as she realized the gun was for her protection and not something he was packing.

Derek wrapped himself in cord as he twisted around to watch her while listening to Eugene. "She's asleep now. If you have a question or two after you've checked with the personnel at the hospital, I'm certain she wouldn't mind if you called her tomorrow. Good night." He cradled the phone.

"Where are you going, Derek?"

"I'm going to see if I can change the rules, and if not, bring in the pawns before this powder keg blows up in our faces."

25

Wednesday, April 28

Sam TURNED OVER and picked up the ringing phone. She must have dozed off. She'd tossed and turned all night trying to decipher the meaning of Derek's words. And was still awake to watch a shaft of light work its way across the wallpaper. Still awake when the rat-tat-tat of hammers started.

"Hell—" She cleared her throat and tried again. "Hello."

"Sam?"

She didn't recognize the whispering voice. "Yes?"

"It's Ken," he whispered again. "I need to talk to you."

Sam lifted up, bracing herself on her elbow. "Where are you?" she whispered back before she realized the gesture illogical.

"At the hospital."

"I'll come in," she said in a normal tone.

"No!" He paused, and then whispered. "Meet me at the city park. By the bridge."

There were two foot bridges in Kendrick Park, one on the south side near the seasonal concession stand and the other that crossed Little Goose on the northeast close to the YMCA and, more importantly, the general and orthopedic surgeons' office building. If Ken and she met there, their colleagues might misinterpret the meeting. Better casual acquaintances thought they were having an illicit affair. The south bridge was surely the one he meant.

She pulled up next to the boarded-up concession stand and looked around for Ken's car.

The mild, sunny spring day had drawn a number of preschoolers and parents to the park. She watched a small boy come down the monstrously large slide practically on his back once the gravitational force got him. His mother caught him at the muddy bottom. An older preschooler called to the boy to watch as he flopped on his stomach and glided down the slide headfirst. The show-off overshot and landed with a splash into the puddle.

A tap of a horn drew her attention behind her. Ken had parked on a residential side street on the other side of the bridge. Outside the park.

Sam got out of the Jeep and locked it. She crossed the street on the diagonal, hopping over the speed dip. Her actions seemed casual enough, she hoped. This despite her world being turned on its head. Nothing was as it seemed. Ken, her cheerful cohort across the hall in radiology, was suddenly her coconspirator in a deadly game for which they didn't know the rules. The calm, confident man who knew the rules, as well as the name of the game, had raced out of their house last night like a lunatic to catch a chartered plane. She'd worried and racked her brain throughout the stressful night for answers, but none came. "Bring in the pawns." Could her father and sister be the pawns? She was mystified. Concerned. Hurt. Terrified. And a thousand other emotions she couldn't express in words.

She started across the bridge as Ken came from the other side. She glanced through the chinks in the wood planks at the roiling water running through the obstacle course of smooth granite boulders. She was simply an intruder teetering on the brink.

Ken wore a windbreaker, instead of a spy's trench coat. *She* wore a trench coat. The one with ripped-out lining in both pockets, and she'd worn the denim skirt that had no pockets and left her purse in the car. She held on to her keys for dear life.

"I think I found something you'll want to read." Ken looked around to make certain no one was watching and then slipped a clipping into her hand. It was slick like the pages in most medical journals.

"What is it?" She didn't have her reading glass and from what she could tell the print was small, bordering on fine.

"An article about smallpox."

She handed it back. "Read it to me."

He looked around again, then unfolded the clipping. "The heading reads: 'A race against time to wipe out a scourge of millions.' And then, 'Smallpox, variola major, the only disease ever eradicated by man, has run out of time. In its monumental decision the World Health Organization in Geneva has recommended destroying the last two sets of smallpox vials, the legacy of one of the most remarkable accomplishments in the annals of medicine. The vials at the U.S. Centers for Disease Control and Russia's Research Institute for Viral Preparations contain the only known specimens of a virus that killed untold millions through the centuries. Destruction of the remnants of this dreadful disease is the culmination of man's efforts to stamp out this scourge from the face of the earth, and will mark the first time that man has intentionally rendered a species extinct.'

"But listen to this, Sam." He scanned down to the paragraph he wanted her to hear. " 'Not all scientists in the virology community agree that smallpox should be destroyed. Some argue that wiping out any species sets a dangerous precedent, while other researchers believe that killing smallpox might mean burying important scientific secrets forever. Still others suggest that some beneficial, and as yet unknown, use for the virus might be discovered.

" ' "Smallpox thus far has done nothing for the good of humanity, but it would be shortsighted to assume that this virus will forever be our enemy. We are only beginning to understand the functions of the virus's genes." Dr. Lee Nguyen, the dissenting—' "

Sam grabbed his arm. "Our Dr. Lee Nguyen?"

" '—virologist on the ad hoc committee of the World Health Organization, went on to say—' "

"World Health Organization?"

" ' "What if British physician Edward Jenner in seventeen ninety-six had discovered a cure for cowpox instead of observing that English milkmaids who had been exposed to cowpox seemed to be protected against smallpox? Can we afford to forever lose access to a virus that might have some beneficial use that we cannot foresee?" ' "

"Dr. Lee Nguyen and the World Health Organization." Sam nodded slowly as a couple of the pieces slipped into the jigsaw puzzle in her mind. "Nguyen and Jeffers. And we're the country bumpkins with their cowpox of the future. They really . . . " Sam stopped to choose her words, but then realized she didn't have any worth expressing.

"Put one over on us?"

"They really put one over on us. Exposed one of our children to smallpox, came out here, and sat back and waited for the boy to show up in the hospital." Sam laughed. "They sure picked the wrong boy to turn up in the ER."

"Because of his religion, you mean?"

"Yes," she said absently. Sam wondered how they were planning to keep it quiet. Chances were fifty-fifty that the boy would have shown up in the ER, not at a doctor's office. Were they always planning to run the hantavirus scam on everyone who ventured too close? Did they believe no one would think to call in the CDC? Why kill Tom Polvich? Why not give him the same amnesia? Why send Eugene to the WHO conference instead of putting him in ICU? What was Derek's involvement? Why would he go along with the two of them?

"So now we know the motive."

Sam pursed her lips and watched the water rush under the bridge. "Motive? It's not enough. These virologists"— she motioned to the clipping—"are opposed to killing an organism that has ravaged this planet for centuries. Why would they kill innocent people to save something like that?"

"Does seem to be a contradiction. Like killing the hangman to protest capital punishment."

"Greed or passion are the two most common reasons for committing a murder. And although our good friend Lee Nguyen sounds passionate enough about the plight of this little creature, I'll bet on greed."

"Greed. Like what? Selling it to an unfriendly nation? Terrorists?"

"That does sound far-fetched. Though we haven't given smallpox vaccinations on a routine basis since . . . I don't know when."

Ken looked at the article. "Since nineteen seventy-six, according to this."

Derek was unnerved. That was atypical behavior for him. Maybe this *was* something big. Maybe it wasn't as far-fetched as they thought. She wished Derek had confided in her. She was hurt that he hadn't. She wished he were back with the promised answers.

"What are you going to tell the CDC about Tom?"

"Amnesia has its benefits." She shrugged.

26

SAM DROVE BY Thaddeus's place and kept on going. The notion of sweeping in and posting Tom Polvich disappeared when she saw the mob out front. She had a pretty good idea about the identity of the congregation without reading the waving signs. " 'The flame of the fire slew those men that took up Shadrach, Meshach, and Abednego.' Daniel 3:22."

She didn't think Tom's corpse would tell her much—his virologist killer had access to the most insidious of all the nasty little bugs—but she had hoped for a careless or hasty instrument of death. The body disposal was tacky; maybe a toxicological examination would come up with something.

But what difference did it make whether she could prove murder if she couldn't pin it on Nguyen and Jeffers? She sure couldn't tie them to David's death. And she didn't have a body for Jess Gorzalka. Pretty obvious that he was dead. She'd have Hank bring in the father and interrogate him. His behavior was too bizarre to be dismissed as lightly as Derek had.

More pickets greeted her at the hospital. She particularly liked the sign that read: " 'In vain shalt thou use many medicines; for thou shalt not be cured.' Jeremiah 46:11." That seemed appropriate for a march on the hospital.

She passed up the doctors-only parking spaces next to the front door and drove around back, looking longer for a parking place than she cared to admit. Even the handicap spots were occupied. She would appreciate her privileged parking space from now on, or at least for a good long time.

Finally, she saw backup lights on a Honda. She backed up and waited for it to come out, then squeezed in and parked incognito between a Ford pickup and a Suburban.

Kate looked up as Sam came into the office. "I see you got in in one piece."

"Came through the back by the kitchen." Sam slumped into her chair. "Whatever happened to 'love one another'?" Or "thou shalt not kill," she thought.

Kate didn't bother to answer.

Sam took out her telephone directory to find the number of the ambulance; 911 wasn't appropriate for this occasion. "Kate, is the ambulance under city or county?" She ran her finger down the Sheridan page. "Never mind, it's city government."

Kate was busy typing and probably hadn't heard a word she said, which was just as well, because Sam was one step above babbling.

"Sam!" Eugene exclaimed as he walked in with a can of Pepsi in hand. "God, I can't believe it!"

She covered her ear to listen to the dispatcher. "Yes, this is Dr. Turner. If the ambulance is available, will you send it to the mortuary to transfer the remains of one Tom Polvich to the VA hospital?"

Sam waved at Eugene while she waited for the dispatcher to write everything down and repeat it back to her. Eugene didn't look the worse for his two-week vacation. She wished the virologists had sent her to Switzerland and let Eugene breathe through a ventilator in ICU.

"Yes, that's correct. Thanks." She hung up the phone. "Glad to see you back."

"Glad to see *you*. They told me you were in ICU, for heaven's sake. You look amazingly healthy, considering."

"Amazing, that's the word for it." She got up. "Come on, I'll buy you a cup of coffee downstairs and we can swap stories." She draped her arm over his shoulders. "Of course, my mind's a blank, so you can do all the talking."

He did. Sam listened with waning interest to his tales of

$6,000 leather coats that were as pliable as kid gloves, one jewelry store after another with million-dollar chess sets to tempt the most choosy of the Arabian oil barons.

"You should have seen this one set of diamond necklaces. Muslims can have up to four wives as long as they treat them equally, you understand?"

She stopped stirring her coffee and looked across the table. "Yes, I understand. My amnesia is limited to the last two weeks. I can still tie my shoes."

He laughed nervously. "Anyway, the display window had four identical diamond necklaces, except for the colored stone in the middle. One was an emerald, another ruby, a sapphire, and a topaz. That's the one I'd give to my least favorite wife," he added as an aside. "I mean, the center stone alone would choke a horse. Had to be twenty carats, I don't know, fifty maybe."

"Big," Sam helped out.

"And that was only the colored stone in the middle. There had to be hundreds of diamonds around it in kind of a tear-drop arrangement and then at least three rows of diamonds that went around the neck." He used his hands a lot in describing it. Sam got the impression it looked like the one Audrey Hepburn wore to the ball in *My Fair Lady*. "Can you imagine what kind of wealth we're talking about if someone has enough money to throw away on four of those little baubles?"

"Amazing wealth." Sam took a sip of coffee, her eyes straying to the cooks setting up for lunch. She'd eat at the VA instead. They had great milkshakes.

"And, I mean, you don't get away with just that, I bet. Throw in a bracelet, a ring or two, a tiara."

"No tiaras. We'll draw the line at tiaras," Sam told him.

"Fur coats, and dresses fit to be worn with a necklace like those. Shoes, purses. Gucci. Saw a lot of Gucci purses there."

A couple of friends had given Sam a Gucci purse and even a matching wallet, but they were still in the signature box on a shelf in the closet. When the one she was using gave out, she'd have to get the Gucci out to impress Eugene. "Tell me, Eugene, did you see anyone actually wearing jewelry like that?"

"No, but I didn't get to the theater or anything. Oh, and the prices of food. They had two Wendy's, one on each side of the bridge. And I mean to tell you it cost me an equivalent of twenty dollars to eat lunch there. And the meat was the pits." He leaned his chair back on its hind legs as he polished off his can of Pepsi.

"Eugene, not to change the subject, but what kind of meetings were you attending?"

"AIDS. Usual stuff. Oh, this is fascinating. In Kenya there's a group of twenty-five prostitutes who have been constantly exposed to HIV . . . try to guess how they were exposed," he said in a husky voice.

"I think I've got that one figured out, Eugene." She gave him a wink.

"Anyway, the virus can't be found in these women. They seem to have a natural immunity to AIDS."

"Like milkmaids to smallpox." She thought this a mere coincidence that had nothing to do with their Sheridan problems. But she'd pursue the topic a little longer. If nothing else, she was happy to hear this news. It could spur efforts to develop a vaccine for AIDS.

He stared at her, as if trying to bridge the parable. "Yeah, like milkmaids to smallpox."

"So, Eugene, how many other delegates were there in these meetings?"

Eugene snapped his fingers. "Of course, Nguyen mentioned something like that."

"What? Nguyen? What are you talking about?"

"Milkmaids and cowpox and how smallpox may one day help us cure even more deadly diseases. What a weirdo!"

Sam sipped her coffee as she gathered her thoughts. "When was this?"

"Three weeks or so. Right after they arrived. Don't like him much. Sneaky. Don't know how Earl puts up with him.

He doesn't fit into our medical community."

"What did you say to him when he told you all that?"

"I told him he was full of shit."

"Was that before you were invited to Switzerland?"

He thought back. "Yeah, but what does that have to do with the price of tea in China?"

"Absolutely nothing, Eugene." Sam smiled. And his reward for not wanting to be recruited to the case was a trip to Switzerland. "I've got to get over to the VA for a postmortem." Sam got to her feet. But first she'd call Hank.

27

SAM SWUNG BY the sheriff's office on her way back from the VA; a technician had given her a message from Hank asking her to call. She decided to come calling instead.

She found him in his office talking to Frank Gorzalka, who didn't look a bit happy to see her. He'd shaved since yesterday, but only once. He wouldn't have had a chance to grow a five-o'clock shadow otherwise. He hadn't bothered to dress up to come to town. She'd worn clean clothes. She had Tom's blood on them now, but they were clean when she came into town this morning.

"Sam, come on in." Hank rounded his desk and came to greet her. He pulled her under his long arm and closed the door solidly. "Frank here and I've been having a nice little chat and I think we can clear this little misunderstanding up with a spit and a promise."

He took a stack of papers and periodicals off a folding chair, dumped them on the floor in the corner, and pulled the chair around in front of the desk for her. She sat.

Hank returned to his seat behind his desk, leaned back, laced his fingers together, and nodded to Frank.

Gorzalka gave her a forced smile. "I'm sorry about yesterday."

She waited for him to continue. He didn't. She glanced at Hank.

Hank brought his tipped chair forward. "Frank's wife died of cancer," he said as if that explained it all.

Sam gave a what's-your-point shrug. She didn't see the
need of offering condolences a second time.

"He doesn't trust doctors."

And women doctors even less. Sam measured her words.
"Mr. Gorzalka, please understand that Jess's welfare . . . "
No that wasn't going to cut it. Jess was surely dead, and she
didn't want to hold out unlikely hope. "Have you seen Jess
since our meeting yesterday, Mr. Gorzalka?"

He masked his anxiety poorly as he shook his head.

"Jess hasn't been to school in two weeks."

The father swallowed hard.

"Do you have any idea where he might be?"

He started to say something but changed his mind.

"Mr. Gorzalka, you understand that I need to find Jess to
ask him some questions about a friend of his who died of a
contagious illness. I need to assure myself that Jess hasn't
been contaminated himself." Or murdered.

"I called my sister-in-law . . ." He broke off in favor of
shaking his head.

"She hadn't seen him?"

He shook his head in response to her question. "Maybe
he drove back to . . . " He broke off again.

This meeting wasn't productive. He didn't like doctors
and wasn't going to tell her anything. Hank stood a better
chance of getting the answers. She had a box filled with
containers of tissues to take to the lab; she needed to get
going anyway. Then it hit her. Why hadn't she realized?
"Hank." She motioned to the door.

Hank followed her out into the hall and closed the door
behind him.

"Get a list of all Jess's relatives. And try to find his car."

"Frank's okay, Sam. It's just, you know."

"Yeah," Sam replied, her mind distracted, "I know."

Sam dropped the box on the counter near Eugene and went
in search of David's innards. How had she not thought of it
earlier? She would have taken the organs back to the hospital

after she'd posted the boy. She had the answers to his death right under her nose. She looked from one shelf to another like a cook after chicken noodle soup.

"Anyone know where the David Crider specimens are?"

"I boxed them up for Dr. Polvich," Vivian called over her shoulder as she drew blood from an outpatient.

"For the CDC?"

Vivian nodded. "Said toxicology needed more specimens."

Now they were getting somewhere. She hurried to her desk to put in a call to Atlanta. Why hadn't she thought of this sooner? Her mind was scrambled by the wonderful Dr. Jeffers, that's why.

"Sam," Kate called as she put down the phone. "That was the ER. They want you down there. And there was some weird-acting guy in here earlier looking for you."

"Weird how?"

"Had on a three piece suit. Big guy, bigger vocabulary. Lawyer, I betcha."

The lawsuit over David's cremation, Sam suspected. "Did the ER say why they want me?" Code blues came over the public address system.

"Someone's in hysterics asking for you. They can't understand her."

Nicola. Something's happened to Woody! She ran; the ER wasn't that far away, but every childhood illness and accident flashed through her mind before she pushed through the bay doors.

She breathed a sigh of relief when she saw Debbie Freeman, Jess's girlfriend, sitting up on the corner of the examining table, struggling with a woman in orange polyester pants pulled tight across wide buttocks that the tail of her plaid shirt couldn't conceal. Connie was on the other side of the table trying to get a blood pressure cuff around Debbie's arm.

Dr. Nguyen was in the chair next to the examining table taking her history. Sam wouldn't have expected him actually to dirty his hands touching the patient now that she knew him to be a virologist masquerading as an ER doctor. What she didn't understand was why he and Jeffers were still here. Unless they were afraid they'd blow their cover by pulling out too soon. Or wanted to stay around to make certain the smallpox was eradicated. She'd give them points for that.

"No, Mom, let me go. I have to go throw up." Apparently Debbie had complained of nausea, as Connie had provided a metal basin for the girl to retch into to her heart's content, but it was clean.

"Debbie?"

The girl stopped battling and looked up expectantly to Sam. Nice feeling being someone's hero. "I feel so bad." Debbie reached out to her, the cuff pulling away from Connie. Connie rolled her eyes and threw up her hands in disgust.

Sam sidestepped the orange whale, held the girl in her arms, and tried not to breathe in the direction the girl was exhaling. Her skin was hot to the touch. "What's wrong, Debbie?" Sam asked, tucking a strand of hair gently behind her ear. "Why don't you lie back for a minute and let me have a look at you?"

She sobbed into Sam's blouse. "I'm going to die," she wailed. "I'm going to die."

"You're not going to die, Debbie," Sam reassured her as she eased her flat to the table. "We're going to examine you to find out what's wrong and then we're going to spiff you up."

Sam focused on the teenager's eyes. Her pupils looked a bit dilated. "May I?" Sam asked as she pointed to the penlight in Nguyen's breast pocket.

He handed it to her.

Fortunately, Debbie's pupils constricted rapidly and without disparity to the light stimulation.

"My head hurts."

Sam palpated it for hematomas, and then palpated her neck as Connie cuffed her. "Is this tender?" She palpated the trachea while Debbie was deciding if her neck was tender.

"No, not really. It's my back and stomach that hurt."

Connie called out the blood pressure reading. A little high but not unexpected, taking into account her heightened state of anxiety.

Sam palpated the chest and then took Connie's stethoscope. She put the damned thing in her ears backward, ripped it out, turned it around, and tried again. It didn't make that much difference in the hearing, but she didn't want Dr. Nguyen to think her a fool. Bad enough to be thought of as a country hick. "Take a couple of deep breaths." No subcutaneous air that she could tell, heart sounded fine. She switched the valve on the Sprague stethoscope from the bell to the diaphragm receiver and listened again. "That's good. Breathe normally." The quiet respiration produced a whooshing noise, longer during the inspiratory phase, shorter during the expiratory phase.

Connie slipped a disposable sheath over the thermometer and shoveled it between the girl's lips. "Hold it under your tongue."

"Your stomach hurts or you just feel nauseated?" Sam palpated the abdomen as the girl nodded and mumbled "nauseated" around the thermometer. "Is it tender here? Here?" she asked, moving to the lower-right quadrant.

The girl muttered again, but Sam wouldn't be impressed unless the girl jumped out of her skin. She unbuckled Debbie's belt and unzipped her jeans. They were stiff and tight, but she managed to get her hands at the girl's abdomen. "Tell me if it's tender anywhere."

Debbie whimpered. Sam palpated the area a second time but was unimpressed. She palpated the extremities. Connie showed her the thermometer. One hundred and two.

Fever, headache, nausea and backache. Except for the nonproductive cough notation in Jess's record, the complaints were identical. Not that she trusted this virologist bastard or his partner.

"Who's her attending physician?" she asked the frightened-looking mother as she helped Debbie sit up.

"I used to take the kids to the pediatrician when they were little, for their shots and stuff. But Bobby was sick that time last winter, no, the winter before, and the pediatricians were filled up and the lady on the phone said that unless it was an emergency . . ." She was wringing her hands an angry red. "It wasn't an emergency really so I got an appointment for the next day, but then I called my husband's black lung doctor and they could see Bobby that afternoon. So I started taking the kids there. But I couldn't get hold of his office today and the operator said that it was because it was closed on Wednesday afternoon, so I brought her here."

Gave new meaning to obtaining the family medical history. Bob Wallace had the federal contract for the coal miners' black lung program. "That's fine," Sam reassured her. "We'll call Dr. Wallace and tell him Debbie's here." She turned to Dr. Nguyen. "If that's all right with you."

"Fine." He gave a be-my-guest gesture. Sam wondered if he suspected what she did. Smallpox. Was the girl in danger at his hands? Probably not. He surely knew they'd found Tom Polvich. Two suspicious deaths and a missing boy. Nguyen couldn't afford to do anything to the girl, except help heal her. She hoped.

She took Debbie's hand. "You have a fever. Probably just the flu, but we're going to admit you for observation."

Debbie wailed.

Sam patted her back as she caught Connie's eye. "Isolation."

28

By the time she'd gotten back to pathology and called the CDC in Atlanta, where it was two hours later, they'd all gone home for the evening. She left a message for someone to call her with the toxicology report on David Crider. She called both hospitals in Billings, the one in Casper and the Gillette Hospital. Neither Jess Gorzalka nor a John Doe fitting his description turned up. Hank wasn't in his office when she called for the list of Jess's relatives, nor did anyone know where Hank or the list was. She'd called two Gorzalkas before she found someone who could give her Jess's family tree. She spoke to his mother's brother, a Benson, but no one had seen hide nor hair of Jess. She did learn that he was leaning toward turning down Notre Dame and accepting University of Wyoming. She called Laramie and spoke with admissions. He'd done neither, and the deadline had passed. Ditto Notre Dame. He was dead. She knew it to her marrow. She also knew that he hadn't been cremated, because she called the crematory to make certain.

The call to the crematory didn't relieve her anxiety over the mistaken identity of David. Being a corespondent in a lawsuit with Thaddeus and the crematory owner would be the icing on the cake. She believed the smooth-talking undertaker about Jess, and she could understand why he couldn't discuss David's case without consulting his attorney first, but why was he so adamant that David wasn't brought to the crematory in the missing casket? Probably because he sold it to a Billings mortuary to sell to some unsuspecting grieving family who would never know that old Uncle Charley was being laid to rest on secondhand satin cushions. Cunning devils, undertakers. And the crystal ball showed her sitting between them at the defendants' table.

But one disaster at a time. Jess. She had exhausted all known sources but one. And he was standing in the doorway, looking into the storage closet behind the nursing station and talking to Gary, the evening RN, who was coming down a ladder, a box of gloves under one arm. The emergency room was deserted except for these two.

"Dr. Jeffers?"

Jeffers turned around, then smiled warmly. "Well, look at you," he said, swinging around the counter and coming to her, his hand outstretched. Instead of shaking her hand, he held it. The other one went around her shoulders and became a hug. Then he stepped back but continued to hold her hand. "What, may I ask, are you doing here? You are supposed to be home in bed. Need I remind you that you were gravely ill?"

This is the man she suspected of murdering Tom Polvich? "I wanted to thank you for saving my life."

He squeezed her hand. "Next week would have been soon enough." Jeffers smiled. "But I'm so happy to see you up and about." The smile slipped away as his eyes trailed down her body, performing a cursory examination, and then returned to her face to scrutinize it further. "You blush easily, I see."

"I prefer to be the doctor."

Jeffers squeezed her hand again before releasing it. "Don't we all."

"Would you let me buy you a cup of coffee to thank you?"

Jeffers turned to Gary. "I'll be downstairs. Page me if you need me."

"Yes, boss."

Jeffers took her elbow and felt it. "Ice cream for you, and that's your doctor's order."

"Will ruin my appetite for dinner."

He bought her a chocolate-covered ice cream bar out of the machine in the basement hall. She would have preferred an ice cream sandwich, but apparently so had everyone else in the hospital. He dug around in his pockets looking for change for the coffee.

"No, no. I invited you." She handed him a dollar bill. The tired, crumpled dollar was rejected over and over. She juggled her ice cream bar to find another one, which didn't look much better. The machine liked the kind kept in wallets, not wadded up in pockets.

"I'll tell you what," he said, sticking the dollar bills into her pocket with the hand not fishing in his own. "I'll buy my own coffee and bill your insurance company."

"Now you're talking." She liked Jeffers and was having a hard time sorting out her feelings, or remembering her purpose. "Why are you working in the ER?" The whole damned chocolate covering on the bottom broke away when she bit into the bar. She slid it back in place, her hands in need of a good licking. "You're an internist—a good one; I'm living proof of that."

"Let's ask some personal questions, shall we?"

Sam laughed. "Don't you think I deserve to know about the man who saved my life?"

"Don't give me a swollen head. You need to thank Roger Ryder and Kyle Wells for saving your life. I only monitored their good work."

Roger Ryder was the CDC regional director, Sam knew from his report. "Kyle Wells?"

"Of the CDC. Roger Ryder's assistant. I take it you know Roger."

"Read his report. If I met these men, I don't remember."

Jeffers opened the door to the doctors' lounge. No one was there. Sam found a napkin on one of the tables and put it to good use.

"What was in the experimental medicine that's wiped out my memory?" she asked when he was seated across the table from her.

He shrugged. "Temporary memory loss seems little enough price to pay."

If it were on the up and up. "So why did you?"

"Why did I what?"

"Become an ER doctor."

"My wife became ill and I wanted to spend whatever time she had left with her. Then after she passed away I didn't want to return to the practice, so my partners bought me out."

She felt like an unfeeling bastard. "How did you get to Sheridan?"

"Answered an ad."

"The hospital placed an ad?!"

He laughed. "You should see your face."

"I simply couldn't believe *our* administrator placed an ad. I've been after him for years to get some ER coverage. It's been like talking to a brick wall."

"No, it was Lee's ad. He wanted a partner."

Oh yes. That made some sense. Jeffers unsuspectingly and unwittingly became party to Lee's plan the same way Sheridan had. She liked that scenario a whole lot better than trying to believe that this nice man was involved. "Did you hear about the other CDC doctor?"

"Dr. Polvich, you mean?"

She nodded as she caught ice cream drips in the palm of her free hand. She ate faster.

"Yes," he said with all due solemnity. "So very sad. I liked him a great deal." He rolled his coffee cup in his hands. "I'm somewhat surprised to hear he went up to Sibley after hearing about my experience."

"What was that?"

"You must be the only one who hasn't heard about it."

If everyone knew about the Sibley escapade, maybe Nguyen dumped the body at Sibley to throw suspicion on Jeffers, and it worked. "I'd hate to be the only one who doesn't know."

He winked. "Someone took me up there to do some ice

fishing. We were able to get out onto the ice, but by the end of the day the ice around the bank had melted so much we were stuck on a floe."

Eugene, of course, was the someone he was so chivalrously protecting. "How did you get off?"

He shook his head. "You do have a way with frank questions." He took a sip of coffee, his eyes on hers. "Well, we walked around the edge until we found a fallen log we could use as a bridge. That was fine, but unfortunately it led to marshland, which bogged us down. I never did find one of my boots."

They looked at each other and burst out laughing; Sam had to cover her mouth to keep from losing ice cream.

"Dr. Jeffers to ER. Dr. Jeffers to ER." The page from the public address speaker in the hall was so faint that they barely heard it over their laughter.

"That's for me," he said, getting up. He pushed in his chair and picked up the coffee, and then smiled down at her. "I'm glad you're well. I prefer you as a doctor to a patient. We'll have to do this again." He hurried out.

She caught up with him at the stairwell. "I have another question. A patient by the name of Jess Gorzalka presented in the ER a couple of weeks ago. Do you remember him?"

He took her arm as they started up the stairs. "I don't remember the name."

"A high schooler. Headache, fever, nausea—"

"Yes, the boy whose father is a woodcutter."

"His father was with him?"

"No, he was on the mountain when the boy came in."

"Do you know where the boy went after that?"

"He said something about staying with an aunt."

"No one's seen him."

Jeffers stopped. He looked at her. "How could that be?"

A question she wished she could answer.

29

Sᴀᴍ ᴡᴀs ʜᴏᴍᴇ before dark. She parked in the garage for no other reason than to see if Derek's car was there. It wasn't. Derek's twenty-four hours were almost up. She wanted some straight answers. And he'd better cough them up if he wanted to crawl back into her bed anytime soon. They still had the couch in the family room that wasn't in use.

Emil's back greeted her as she walked in from the garage. He was on the phone in the kitchen. He hung up, and it immediately rang again. So now the protesters were hounding her home.

Sam took the phone out of his hand and hung it up. Nicola was at the kitchen table, giving Woody a bottle.

"Nicola couldn't understand the people, so I came in to talk to them," Emil said as a joint explanation and apology.

"Thank you, Emil, I appreciate your help. They've been calling the hospital, too."

"What's it all about?" he asked.

Emil wasn't like his Uncle Jake. Jake, an observer of traditional Indian ways, wouldn't have asked. Asking would have been an aggressive act, and aggression was directed toward enemies only. "A body was erroneously cremated. His church's congregation believes, also erroneously, that I'm to blame."

The phone rang again. Sam answered it.

"Dr. Turner here."

"Defiler of—"

"Please don't keep calling. There is nothing I can do to

restore David's remains. And I'm every bit as upset about it as you are."

"Dust to dust—"

"Good-bye." Sam hung up. Her hand rested on the phone as she tried to work it through. She was going to have Derek put up a gate down by the road first thing. "Emil, could you block off the entrance down by the road with some bales of hay? Or something Derek can move to get his car in."

Nicola looked frightened, probably because she caught only a few words but all of the emotion. Emil noticed too and rested a hand on Nicola's shoulder. Emil wasn't the most reliable ranch hand, and his drinking was a sore subject, but that gesture went a long way in earning Sam's respect.

Sam picked up the phone before it stopped ringing. "Dr. Turner."

"Is that you, Sam?" It was her sister's voice. A frantic voice. A frantic, faraway voice.

"Sharon? Where are you?"

"I'm in Miami. I've been trying to call you for hours but your phone's been busy."

"Is Dad with you?"

"No, Derek decided to leave him. He—"

"Derek? Is Derek with you?" Sam rounded the corner into the family room for a little privacy.

"No, that's why I'm calling."

Sam's knees buckled. She slid down the wall to the carpet. "What happened?" she managed to say, trying not to jump to any conclusions. She saw him laid out on a stainless steel table, a tag around his toe.

"He was detained."

Sam exhaled. "Detained?" she asked after she'd recovered from the imaginary disaster and realized the real one.

"In St. Thomas. Something about his passport."

"Tell me from the beginning."

"Derek came to the clinic. Said he wanted me to go with him. First he wanted to take both of us, but Dad was in surgery. He'd started to respond to the graft. Sam, he was

like his old self until last night. And then this morning he
was so . . . " Her voice was filled with disappointment. "Dr.
Gentry conferred with Dr. Blanca and decided they'd try
another graft this afternoon."

"Dr. Blanca?" Sam whispered into the phone. How could
Derek have taken her father there, knowing Ponce Blanca
was back? Or was that the reason he went for them? How
did hearing that Tom Polvich was dead make him realize that
Blanca was at the clinic and that he had to get them out?
How was Blanca tied to Tom Polvich's death?

"The head of the clinic."

"What, Sharon?"

"Dr. Blanca is the head of the clinic."

"Go on about Dad and Derek."

"Derek didn't tell me what it was all about, just that I had
to go with him. He said he'd come back for Dad . . . go back
for Dad . . . when Dad could travel. Derek started throwing
my things in my bag and hustled me out of there so fast I
couldn't think straight. Dad was in the operating suite, and
Derek wouldn't even wait until the doctor came out to talk
to us. It was just so confusing. I didn't know what to do."

"What about Derek?"

"Well, we had to stop at this stand to show our passports
to some official. So I went through all that rigmarole first.
But when it was Derek's turn, the man picked up the phone
and called someone. Derek turned away from the official and
whispered 'go' and shoved me toward the metal detector. He
didn't make the plane. I didn't know what to do, so I got on
the plane by myself and flew here."

"I don't suppose he gave you a message for me or
anything?"

"Just said 'go.' " She sighed. "I caught his eye when I was
on the other side, but he turned away and ignored me. The
couple in the line way behind us asked me at the gate what
had happened. I told them I didn't know. They said Derek
was talking to another official when they went through. She
asked me if I was really going to go on without him. But her

husband said it was easier to get one seat on another flight than two."

"Do you think Derek took another flight?"

"I don't know. Do you want me to check at the airline counters?"

"Yes . . . no. I don't know."

"I missed my first flight to New Orleans, and the new one is about to board, but I could take the next one instead. It wouldn't be a problem."

"No, don't miss your plane."

"Then I'd better hurry. I'll call you when I get home. 'Bye."

" 'Bye, Sharon." Sam hesitated to hang up the phone. It had been the only link to Derek. Emil, Nicola, and even Woody were staring at her. She hung up. "Derek isn't coming home tonight." The phone rang. "Block the entrance with the truck."

Emil went out through the sliding patio door.

"Dr. Turner," she said, answering the phone.

"The Heavenly Father—"

"Will forgive you for making these nuisance calls a hell of a lot sooner than I will." She slammed down the phone.

Woody cried. Nicola, unnerved, got up and paced the kitchen floor, trying to soothe the baby.

The doorbell rang an instant before the phone. "Hello," Sam said.

"Our—"

She could name that sermon in one note now. She hung up. "I'll get the door," she said, stopping Nicola as she brushed by. They hadn't gotten the roadblock up in time.

The man at the door was tall and broad and distinguished looking. He wore a lawyer's three-piece suit. If he started spouting fifty-cent words, he'd be Kate's mystery visitor. "Mrs. Turner?"

"Yes?"

He reached into his inside breast pocket and extracted a leather folder. He flipped the cover to reveal identification. Sam took it out of his indifferent hand and studied it.

Central Intelligence Agency. Harrison Ribet, Deputy Director of Operations, European Section. Derek's superior? Her insides were jelly. She gave the ID back with a hand that no longer seemed a part of her body. Fright made her feel completely detached, in slow motion, Ribet flipped the protective cover back in place and returned it to his inside breast pocket.

"Derek's been detained in St. Thomas," she said in as steady a voice as possible.

"No, not detained. He's on assignment," he said with what could pass as a smile.

Then he was all right. This wasn't one of those we-came-to-tell-you-of-your-husband's-death-in-person visits. Wait a minute. Just what in the hell was it then? Derek's not being detained, he's on assignment? She believed her sister over this well-pedigreed stranger. And now that she was thinking clearly, Harrison Ribet had uttered his words with just the right mixture of surprise and candor. The deputy director of operations was a better liar than Derek. They must advance through the ranks on that quality alone.

She'd been an ignorant fool to blurt that out about Derek's being detained. Now she'd played her hand.

He waited for her to let him in.

She did.

The phone was ringing again. It wasn't her sister or Derek, she assured herself. Only the protesters. She heard Nicola's hello and then after a moment, a string of Hungarian in a harsh tone before a crash of the receiver to its base.

Harrison Ribet followed her noiselessly through the hall and into the library. He pulled the glass doors together, leaving a sweeping design on the carpet in front of the right door. She'd mention it to the carpenters one of these days when she didn't have anything more important to worry about.

The ringing hadn't finished before Nicola answered the phone this time. The deputy director walked to the extension phone, picked up the receiver, listened, spoke a couple of sentences of fluent French, apparently to Nicola, waited, depressed the button, listened, and then set it on the desktop.

He motioned to the couch as if *she* were the guest in his home. She sat in the rocker. He took the couch.

"Derek's a very lucky man. He said you were beautiful. I didn't take him as seriously as I should have. Sometimes my men say that and then I'm disappointed when I see for myself. In your case, I must say, the opposite is true."

The operative words from the deputy director of operations were *my men*. She was being told her place, she suspected. "How very kind of you to come all the way out her to flatter me."

"Another surprise. He didn't mention how charming you are."

"But he did mention that I have a brain, didn't he?"

The deputy director of operations smiled. "Your father is doing quite nicely. Derek asked me to pass along that message."

Two pawns. "Well, Mr. Ribet—"

"Harrison."

"Harrison. I'm not very good at games to which I don't know the rules. Why don't we just cut through the bullshit? You tell me what I have to do to get my husband and father back."

"I had hoped, Mrs. Turner—"

"Please, Harrison, don't be so formal. Call me Dr. Turner."

He burst out laughing. "Now I see how you earned your reputation, Dr. Turner."

The man was not without a sense of humor, but she didn't think she should be all that flattered.

"All right, Dr. Turner. We went to a great deal of trouble, at Derek's insistence, to provide your father with a very controversial medical treatment. We did this because you're family."

"At Derek's insistence, you say. Would you care to elaborate?"

"I'll be candid with you, Dr. Turner. A patient of yours was infected from a vial of smallpox stolen from the U. S. Centers for Disease Control and Prevention in Atlanta. We are *very* interested in keeping this a secret. It wouldn't do much for the United States' reputation. Nor do we wish to alarm anyone. Derek promised your cooperation in keeping this under wraps in exchange for helping your father. We went to a great deal of trouble to reopen a clinic in St. Thomas for your father's welfare. He's part of your family, and you're part of our family. It's as simple as that."

Now that was an Academy Award performance. But who in his right mind would believe such a cockamamy story? She believed the part about Derek promising her cooperation in exchange for her father's treatment. And she would worry about how she felt about that later. But the United States asking the CIA for help to protect its reputation! *Give her a break*. The CIA worked outside of the United States, not in Wyoming. And the United States already had a terrible reputation; burglary in the CDC building wasn't going to make it any worse.

What she *did* believe was that this had something to do with greed. Maybe even terrorists spreading an epidemic in a Third World nation. *That* would be under the CIA's domain. And it was typical of the spooks not to confide in her. They might tell her she's family, but she wasn't, and she knew it.

"Why are you detaining Derek then?"

"No one is detaining Derek. He's on his way to Europe. To Geneva. He asked if I would send someone out to explain it to you. I have a meeting in California early in the morning. It was simple enough to stop myself. I'm happy I did." He had a friendly smile. She wondered how long it had taken him to cultivate it.

"If I called the Geneva hotels, would I be able to get hold

of him?"

"I doubt he'll be staying long enough. Perhaps it would be better if you waited to hear from him."

A very convenient answer. They had her father and her husband. That was enough to secure anyone's cooperation. That Nguyen would sell the virus to terrorists and kill untold numbers of innocent children was an even better reason. "What is it you want from me?"

"Derek and I met early this morning. He told me that he suspected this problem wasn't as simple as we first supposed. He believes the boy who died was intentionally exposed and that someone might have acquired the smallpox virus through the current episode here in Sheridan."

"And what did you say to that?"

"I told him that I agreed with him that we should confiscate the stolen property. *If* we could do it quietly."

"What if you can't do it quietly?"

He shrugged. "Then we'd better hope *they* can keep *their* vial in a safer place than we did."

An idiot wouldn't buy this story. And she was insulted that he even tried it on her. "There's one little point that I don't understand. What reason would anyone have to intentionally expose the boy?"

"To acquire the virus without our knowing about it. They knew we'd be able to trace the vial; only a limited number of people had access. They knew that eventually they would have to give it up."

"Then tell me this. Why didn't they take the virus out of the vial and grow a culture?"

"Because we knew where to look for it. The CDC and FBI conducted a thorough search of the thief's home and all laboratories to which he had access. He hid it in the boy's body."

Why did that make some sense? All right, it makes a degree of sense using the scenario that the virologist simply wanted to protect the species. *But* Tom Polvich was murdered. Something else was going on. "What can I do to help?"

"It is *imperative* that the stealing of the smallpox vial remain secret. The local authorities have jurisdiction over the deaths that have occurred here. Make certain that your investigation remains separate from ours."

30

Thursday, April 29

Sᴀᴍ sʟɪᴘᴘᴇᴅ ɪɴ through the back door, the blood-bank door, in the lab, but instead of going through to the offices, she headed toward Terry, who was at a work station. Sam had meant to check on her at home, but good intentions and all . . .

"Feeling better?" Sam asked as she laid a hand on Terry's back.

The girl nodded.

"Amazing how the physiological process works." Not to mention the modern medicine of corrupt doctors.

Terry pulled down her mask and let it hang around her neck. She was taking precautions against another laboratory "accident." "And you? They said you were in the ICU also."

"Fine." Except for the idiopathic crying that crept over her in the wee hours of the night alone in her lonely bed. But it was not idiopathic; Sam knew precisely what had caused her heart to ache. An accumulation of the horrible last two weeks, some of which she could only imagine, her helpless father, and Derek. She didn't know whether to be upset with Derek or frightened for him. She wanted to be furious with him for his deceit and for placing her father in harm's way, if only to vent her own frustrations. But she believed his intentions honorable in seeking out medical treatment for her father and trying to rescue her father and sister from the clutches of . . . of whom? Unethical medical researchers and government men. Monsters.

"They said the pickets out front are for you."

"Oh, yes. These are mine, but Thaddeus over at the mortuary has another set. It's our coroner-mortician thing."

Terry took off her safety glasses and looked up questioningly at her.

"You know, like a mother-daughter or a father-son thing. Only one heck of a lot more fun."

"But why?"

"A corpse I had on ice was cremated in place of the one that was supposed to have been. You wouldn't remember anything about David Crider by any chance?"

Terry shook her head and slipped the used blood lancet into the slot of the red plastic disposal container.

"Do you remember Tom Polvich?"

"The one who was supposed to be cremated?" Terry shook her head. "I don't think so."

"No, the pathologist who covered for me while I was ill."

She shook her head. "Must have come after I came down with hantavirus."

Sam patted the girl's shoulder. "Glad you're back."

Terry repositioned her safety glasses and mask and returned to her work.

Eugene was hunched over a microscope. Sam got by him without being noticed.

"Sam?"

She *almost* got by him without being noticed. She retraced her steps.

"Eugene."

He didn't look up but continued to peer into the microscope. "Working today?"

"No, wearing my coroner's hat."

Eugene repositioned the slide. "Can't you do something about those pickets outside?"

"I'm open to suggestions."

"Call the police," he said as he refocused.

"Why, so they can get in on the coffee concession?"

"Larry's not at all happy. Said—"

"Fuck Larry."

"I don't have the anatomically correct equipment." He looked up at her for the first time, a smirk ear to ear.

Sam returned his smirk.

His interest returned to the microscope, and she started off. "What are those eggs for?"

Sam turned around. "My Four-H project. I'll get rid of them."

"I take it the test tube of whiskey in the freezer is part of a Four-H project, too?"

"That you can't blame on me," she said as she hurried off. She'd ask Kate where the eggs came from and see if they'd take them back. No refund necessary. She would even pay them for their trouble.

Kate wasn't at her desk. She must have been running around doing something or other, because it was too early for her ten o'clock coffee break. Sam dropped her purse on the floor behind her desk, too tired to put it in her bottom drawer, and threw her trench coat over the coat tree.

Sam looked at the messages on Kate's desk. The only one that interested her was the one from the CDC. The toxicology report on David Crider was consistent with hantavirus. What!

She slumped against the edge of Kate's desk as she read the message again. She went back into the lab. "Eugene, did you see this?"

Eugene took the message and read it. "What's wrong with it? Didn't you realize you'd caught it from him?"

She stared at him, her mind a million miles away. Tom Polvich had to be in on it with Nguyen. That would explain why the CDC doctor would stay on to cover for her after the others left. He carefully selected tissues that showed no variola involvement, infected them with hantavirus, and shipped them to the CDC for a toxicology analysis. Then the two had a falling out and Tom ended up facedown in Sibley Lake.

"Sam, did you hear me?"

"What?"

Eugene got up and waved his hand in her face, back and forth, back and forth. She grabbed his hand, immobilizing it. What about the initial report by Roger Ryder, regional director for the Centers for Disease Control? It was consistent with URDS, an unexplained respiratory distress syndrome . . . hantavirus. How many conspirators were there?

Bob Wallace, like all the other real doctors, had made his rounds between seven and eight, and was across the street in his office seeing to patients not ill enough to need hospitalization. She would have missed him even had she not spent the last hour in the hospital library cranking up on caffeine and familiarizing herself with smallpox.

Sam pulled Debbie's chart out of the carousel on the counter of the nursing station and read the orders Bob had written. Tylenol every three hours. The working diagnosis was influenza. Rule out infectious disease. He was being a good sport, and she'd pay a visit to his office to explain why she'd put Debbie in the hospital before he came looking for answers.

Sam wondered how Harrison Ribet, deputy director of operations, European Section, would take the news of Sheridan's new outbreak of smallpox. Harrison being family and all, Sam would go ahead and take care of the problem without involving outsiders.

Wasn't that the prime directive? Render unto Caesar what was Caesar's, and deal with local problems without causing embarrassment to Caesar. That seemed fair enough. For family and Caesar.

Except for one smallpox problem, for example an outbreak in some remote area of the world where sluggish mules transport the sick and dying to understaffed medical centers where vaccines arrive sporadically, on the backs of more sluggish mules, from faraway places where it is said that buildings are as tall as mountains and every family owns a box that keeps food and medicine from spoiling.

And what of the World Health Organization and the United States Centers for Disease Control and Prevention and their dedicated medical staff who work tirelessly to rid the planet of scourges? Didn't Sam owe it to them to cut out the cancer that had grown in their own bodies?

Dr. Nguyen, of the WHO, she knew almost certainly was part of the conspiracy. Dr. Ryder, regional director of CDC, had to be involved to write out the report. Tom Polvich must have been killed for what he knew. But how was she to be certain of their involvement? How many others were involved? How could she possibly find out? And what would she do if she did find out? The CIA would rather the cancer grow than have a scar.

The immediate problem was in room 308. Sam ignored the gowns and masks at the door and walked on in. Debbie's eyes were fever-glazed, her skin scarlet and scorching to the touch.

Sam studied the mother, who was suited up and looked every inch a surgeon. "Mrs. Freeman, would you mind stepping out for a moment while I examine your daughter?"

Mrs. Freeman was more than happy to comply. Sam followed, closing the door after the woman was in the hall. Sam returned to the bed and sat in the chair Mrs. Freeman had warmed. "Debbie, you saw David Crider the week he died, didn't you?"

"No! My parents would have a cow if I'd gone over there. We're Catholic."

"And David is"—Sam said as she groped for David's church denomination—"not Catholic."

"They're not even Protestants! Don't tell them," she said, suddenly crying irrationally. "Please don't tell my parents."

"Tell them what? That you didn't see David?"

"About sleeping with Jess," she answered, wiping her nose with the back of her hand. "They'll kill me."

"I've missed something." Sam leaned over to pull a tissue

out of the box on the stand beside the bed.

"I should have made him use a condom. Lisa said—" Debbie whisked the tissue from Sam as she broke into racking sobs.

"That boys don't like to wear them but will if that's the only way they'll get any." Sam repeated what Debbie had attributed to her friend Lisa at McDonald's.

"No, that he probably had a real bad case of herpes." Her shoulders heaved as she looked pleadingly at Sam. "He just had a bad zit breakout. His skin is real bad," Debbie asked more than stated.

"Did Jess have big yellow pustules . . . pimples or blisters all over him?"

Debbie nodded, her eyes wide with fear. "It was more like a rash when we did it, though. He didn't break out until the next day."

"When was this? That he had the pimples, I mean."

"A couple of weeks ago. Wednesday night. I got off work early because we weren't busy, and I drove out to his place because we'd had a fight about colleges and I wanted to tell him . . . " she broke off.

"And when you saw him?"

"He didn't look very good. I called my mom and told her that he'd come in to McDonald's so she wouldn't know I was out there. She said he should see a doctor and told me to take him to the hospital."

He had the pustules when he presented in the ER. Jeffers faked the report. His nice-guy persona sure had her fooled. And now he knew she was asking questions about Jess. Why hadn't she listened when Derek told her not to talk to Jeffers? "Jess visited David when he was home ill, I take it?"

"Yeah, his dad didn't care what he did. I didn't go with him. Well, I sat in the car. Honest."

"When was this?"

"A couple of days after David didn't come to school. Jess took him his homework. But I didn't go in. Honest."

"I believe you." Sam straightened out the girl's IV line. "When you were in the emergency room with Jess did the doctor say anything to you about Jess?"

Debbie shook her head. "Just that everyone in our families would have to have a gamma something shot. Jess's dad was already up on the mountain, though. Do you think he got his shot?"

Sam looked at her arm for signs of intradermal scarification. The telltale mark was in the posterior axillary fold, the same place Sam herself had a scab. The hyperimmune vaccinia gamma globulin may have been given with the smallpox vaccination, but the true motive for giving the vaccination was prophylactic. A primary vaccination given within three to four days of exposure to smallpox gives some protection. Revaccination of a previously immunized person is effective in preventing the disease if given within seven to eight days of exposure. That was of tremendous comfort to Sam. And Debbie's prognosis was good. Frank Gorzalka would need revaccinating. And where was the vaccine to come from if she couldn't use the *S* word?

In light of letting Jeffers know she was interested in Jess's plight and because Nguyen knew that Debbie was in the hospital, she would have to do something about Debbie's security.

"Am I going to get them?" Debbie asked. "The pimples."

Sam gave her a weak smile. "Let's not borrow trouble, as my mother used to say."

They had enough trouble; they didn't need to borrow any.

$\triangledown$

31

THE PLACARD, FRAMED in bricks and placed strategically on the lawn close to the busy street, read CELEBRATION OF DAVID CRIDER'S LIFE, 1 P.M. Sam circled the block, and then tried the second block before she found a place to park. A quarter to one and nary a seat in the house. She wanted to sit well in the back but found herself being ushered up the center aisle to a fourth-row pew.

She read the pamphlet, celebrating David's life, as she acclimated. She felt as uncomfortable in the church as most of the congregation would be in the hospital. The organist played soft music for the sad day.

Isaac Crider sat in a heavy dark wood chair on one side of the altar; a tall man bearing a family resemblance to Isaac sat in a matching chair on the other side. A lectern stood behind the altar, which was draped with a purple cloth. Twenty or so young people in choir robes sat in front of the baptistery that ran across the back wall, under the hanging cross. The mural behind the baptistery was of Jesus delivering the sermon on the mount. The scripture over the mural read: Hear, and understand. On the altar was an eight by ten photo of David. Flowers were all along the front.

Sam studied the picture, hoping to focus the fuzzy image by sheer willpower. The picture was no more clear than the image of him in her mind. It was such a strange feeling knowing she'd posted him, held every organ in her hands, and yet couldn't remember a blasted thing about him.

The mourners were younger than at most of the funerals she attended. David's friends sat in the row ahead of her, each with clean hair and collared shirts. The shirt directly in front of her was light blue denim, and the part of the tie peeking out under the collar was a yellow-and-orange plaid. Most of the boys looked ill at ease.

On the other side of the aisle, in the first row, sat a small woman dressed in white that set off her dark hair. Sam assumed her to be the boy's mother. Next to her sat a shriveled gray-haired woman, her arms wrapped around the mother. The third person in was a white-haired, sallow man on the small side. A woman resembling the woman Sam picked to be David's mother sat on the other side of the old man. David's supposed aunt was comforted by a balding blond man. A lone woman sat at the end. Sam took her to be Isaac's spouse.

Behind them were younger family members. Cousins of David. In the row opposite her were mourners like herself or like the protesters she had been seeing. If they realized who she was, they were keeping it to themselves out of respect for David's family or their place of worship. Either way, she was thankful.

More kids sat behind her. She knew because their whispers were reaching her ears.

"He won't. A thousand dollars says he'll never come home."

"Why would he leave before graduation?"

"Yeah, and why didn't he take his car?"

"How do you know he didn't?"

"I went out there after school last Thursday. His car was there. But he wasn't."

"Chimge poul filphith," the man beside her said.

"Beg your pardon?"

He stood, his eyes closed, and his head turned upward. "Dismorl sident hoe tornom. Juirman gus blurmer."

The kids in front of her turned around in surprise. Sam

whirled around as the woman on her other side stood and spoke in the same cadence. And then a dozen or so people in the congregation rose and joined in.

Pastor Crider walked to the podium and bellowed, "How is it then, brethren? when ye come together, every one of you hath a psalm, hath a doctrine, hath a tongue, hath a revelation, hath an interpretation. Let all things be done unto edifying."

Almost everyone in the sanctuary was on his feet. All speaking in tongues. The boys in front of and behind her were cackling in embarrassment.

David's mother stepped into the aisle and raised her arms above her head; others joined her in the aisle.

Sam wanted to leave but needed to stick around to speak with the boy's parents after the service. She also wanted to talk with the kids in the pew behind her. See if they were talking about Jess.

Then as the chatter died down the organ started playing "Rock of Ages." The choir stood and everyone joined in. So began the celebration of David's life.

Sam was home by three to wait for the delivery. The lumber was gone, but a cement mixer was taking up room in its stead. It had been there before when they poured the foundation; she didn't have a clue why it was back.

The contractor, or subcontractor, or whoever the hell he was, started toward her. He was about to be disappointed; she didn't have any answers. Sam met him at the edge of the red shale drive. The construction people had all but ruined the grass. She suspected Derek would have to reseed.

"Mrs. Turner," he said, tipping his John Deere cap.

"Good afternoon." She had no idea what his name was. Derek oversaw all that. "Warming up finally."

"Finally. Can I get you to move your outfit?" He pointed to the north side of the house, by the garage. "Need to turn the mixer around." He pointed to the truck with the huge mixer tumbling gray slush behind the cab.

"Certainly." A question for which she knew the answer. "What's the cement for? Thought you poured the foundation earlier."

"The hot tub." He nodded to a clearing, this side of the evergreens, next to the deer salt lick, marked off with stakes and twine.

So they were adding a hot tub. She'd enjoy relaxing in warm bubbling water with her husband after a hard day at work. Looking up at the stars, snow blinding her from November to April. Assuming her husband would be returned to her before the chlorine vapors killed the trees.

She got into the Jeep, backed it up, and turned it toward the garage. She pulled onto the asphalt in front of the garage. She'd put in a pad of asphalt after her first winter here to cut down on tracking mud into the garage and then on into the house. No sense raising the garage and parking inside; she had to go back into town once she was finished here. She owed it to the man to tell him before she told the rest.

Nicola, the blue corduroy straps of Woody's Snugli digging into her shoulders, planted a rubber boot on the lower plank of the corral, trying to coax the horses to come to her by waving a bunch of carrots. Roseola trotted over. Alanine, not wanting to miss out on anything, followed.

Sam sloshed across wet grass to join Nicola and the baby. She wanted to hold Woody but not enough to take the time to readjust the straps on the Snugli. "Hi," Sam said.

Nicola showed her gums and then jumped out of her skin, startling Woody, as Roseola picked that very moment to snatch the carrots. The horse blew a long string of mucus for a thank you. Alanine nudged her friend, but to no avail. Horses aren't into sharing.

Truth be told, horses aren't as smart as chickens. Chickens! She'd be raising them soon enough. The chick embryo chorioallantoic membrane culture was costly and time-consuming. Besides, it was unnecessary to see if virus-produced soluble hemagglutinin would grow on chick allantoic membrane now that she had a confirmation by way of a special visit from the family's deputy director of operations.

Nicola rapidly said something to her, and then rubbed the baby's back.

Sam pretended to understand. She held out her hand to Alanine, catching a bit of her mane. "She's a bad girl," Sam told the horse in a cadence fit for the baby as she patted its neck. "We'll see if there isn't a spare apple for you."

Roseola, through daintiness and impeccable manners, lost part of her prize. Alanine scooped it up out of the mud and chomped happily.

Nicola commented on the equitable solution, smiling and gesturing. Sam thought it was in English, but she spoke so excitedly that she wasn't certain. But it didn't matter; they'd shared the experience and communicated nicely.

Sam leaned over the fence and reveled in the beauty of the land. This made all the other shit worthwhile. The bison were two brown blobs on the horizon. One group grazed lazily on the flat, the other where the land sloped up the side of the mountain. They would stay in the foothills, well below the timberline; the thick pines left little on the ground to forage.

Above the timber, a patchwork of snow covered the ravines and shady areas of the north face of the Big Horns. Clouds were beginning to obscure the summit. Cloud Peak didn't get its name for nothing.

Without the banging and whirling and yelling from the construction folks, Woody's whimpering, and the horses' chomping and snorting, the place would have been as serene as a postcard from paradise.

"Pretty, isn't it?" Sam said to Nicola.

"Pretty, yes."

"Emil?"

Nicola gestured toward the bison and said a string of words, of which Sam was able to extract "Fido." It didn't surprise her that the dogs were with him, though they were too far off to see a lone man on horseback, let alone two hundred-pound, eighteen-month-old pups.

Sam should go into the house, take her medicine, and call Sharon while she waited. Perhaps she could learn more about Derek's plight. Was Derek in the "free hotel," as their guide Woods, for whom Woody was named, called the jail when they had toured the island? Was he at the clinic with her father? She would like to imagine he was being held hostage but with free rein of the island, which would mean he'd be with her father. Maybe if she called the clinic they'd let her speak with him. And maybe pigs were flying. She'd call Woods, but he was on the dark side of their family tree. And Derek's family seemed to change sides faster than politically correct terms. Or more accurately, change sides with political correctness.

She started toward the house, then she heard the truck. She went around front and waved it around by the garage.

"Where do you want it stacked?" Frank Gorzalka asked as he climbed out.

She motioned around the corner, the east side of the garage, where the green wood was ripening. "There's a wheelbarrow in the storage shed." She pointed toward the outbuilding between Jake's place and the barn. "Want me to get it for you?"

"I can get it," he said, apparently insulted that she would dare think of such a thing.

Sam caught his arm as he started off. "Mr. Gorzalka . . ." She lost her resolve. She would wait until he was finished stacking the wood. "It's to the right. Shouldn't be too hard to find."

He scratched his head as he went off in search of the wheelbarrow.

Sam went inside and used the kitchen phone to call her sister, keeping an eye on Frank Gorzalka. "Hi, it's just me," she said after the beep, "give me a call when you can." She stood at the counter and wrote out her list.

Ken
Eugene

Bob
Terry
hospital administrator
director of nursing
mortician
sheriff
chief of police
judge
mayor
county commissioner
fish & game
superintendent of schools
newspaper
president of college

Nicola came in. Sam took Woody out of the Snugli and hugged and kissed him and told him how much she loved him. His eyes tracked; he understood. The thudding against the wall assured Sam that they were getting their cord of wood. Woody and she stood at the French door and watched the pile grow.

When the wheelbarrow was on the way back to the shed, Sam put Woody in his swing, padded the blanket around him so he wouldn't fall to one side, cranked it up, and stepped outside.

"Come on into the library and I'll write you a check."

Gorzalka pointed to his muddy shoes. "I'll wait here."

"Don't be silly."

He followed her in, trailing mud from one end of the house to the other.

Sam pulled the library doors shut.

"Mr. Gorzalka, please sit down. I have something to discuss with you."

"About my son?"

She nodded.

He sat.

Sam sat on the other side of the couch. "Mr. Gorzalka, your son's girlfriend has smallpox that she caught from your son."

His eyes watered as she explained about the test tube in Washington.

"The reason I'm telling you all this is that I believe your son is dead."

Frank Gorzalka swallowed a lump in his throat. He was being too macho for his own good.

"You haven't heard from him, have you?"

He shook his head.

"He's never disappeared like this before, has he?"

He shook his head.

"Jess didn't accept any of the colleges he applied to. He missed the deadlines."

Frank stared at her.

"I believe, Mr. Gorzalka, that Jess went into the emergency room at the hospital Wednesday night, two weeks ago yesterday. I believe a doctor there did something with him. Kidnapped him, maybe, because Jess knew something."

Frank blinked back a tear but otherwise remained stoic.

"Mr. Gorzalka, I want to get even with these bastards, and I need your help."

32

Sam waited in the dark parking lot across from the county courthouse. When she saw the last person on her list go in, she got out of the Jeep and crossed the street.

She rode the elevator up. Ken was standing at the city council door, waiting to escort her in.

Hank was riding herd over the motley gathering, having arranged them along the long tables the city councilmen used on Tuesday nights. Ken patted her back as she headed for the chair that was set up for her, front and center. She felt as though she were about to be interrogated in the Spanish Inquisition. The chief of police pushed his chair back and started to rise, but Hank caught him and whispered in his ear. Funny, you'd think a bully of Bill's caliber would have made a perfect Spanish Inquisitor.

Sam stood behind the chair, leaning on it for moral rather than physical support. "Thank you all for coming. For those of you who don't know me—"

"The lucky bastard," Bill got in under his breath, but loud enough for everyone to hear.

The illustrious hospital administrator snickered. Thaddeus let a cackle get by his lips—how quickly potential lawsuit partners are forgotten. The judge looked on judiciously. Bob Wallace shot bill a disapproving look. Bless his heart. Terry and the director of nursing exchanged glances. Eugene looked on.

Pastor Crider bowed his head. The medium height, balking older man with black-rimmed glasses was either the superintendent of schools or the newspaper publisher. The middle-aged man with the silverish recruit haircut and a suit a shade darker and much thicker was the other. The distinguished-looking Mayor Sully and the rancher county commissioner she recognized from the flyers that were up all over town before last election. The Fish and Game Department warden wore a uniform. And the president of the college wore a name tag, for petesake.

"I'm Samantha Turner, coroner of Sheridan County. I've asked you here tonight because we have a big problem on our hands. Three of our teenagers have been stricken with a mysterious virus. On purpose."

"On purpose!" Larry scoffed. The others murmured.

"That's what the lady said," Ken shouted out from the door he was guarding. "Now be still and let her have her say."

"One of our children was exposed to a test tube of a virus on a school trip to Washington." She waited to see Crider's reaction: a bowed head. Neither Frank Gorzalka nor Pastor Crider was invited to this meeting, but Crider had insisted on coming.

"We have reason to suspect two doctors. As near as I can come, they—and we believe it is a conspiracy—came to Sheridan as ER doctors—"

"You mean Drs. Nguyen and Jeffers?" Larry asked. She didn't know if he meant it as an I-told-you-so, you're-the-one-who-wanted-ER-docs, or simply to clear up what she meant.

"Yes. But since we don't know who else may be involved we need to keep this under our hats."

"Outsiders, she means. Not locals," Hank explained.

"Anyway, they waited for the teenage boy to show symptoms of the virus. But due to his religious beliefs, he didn't present in the emergency room or at the doctor's offices. I was the first to see him, in my capacity as county medical examiner. After his death."

She glanced around at Ken to see how she was doing. He

didn't give her any help. "Apparently, we were getting too close to unraveling their scheme—"

"What was the scheme?" Bill asked.

"Could you hold the questions until I've finished?" Sam noticed Bill looked happy as punch to hold a thought. Probably wouldn't remember the question five minutes hence. "Anyway, everyone too close to the situation came down with another virus." Except for Eugene, who enjoyed a free trip to Switzerland. "Hantavirus. With which I believe these same people infected us, and then fortunately cured us when they had what they wanted from the first teenager."

"Is this the same virus?" the superintendent or publisher asked.

"Same virus infecting the teenagers, you mean?" Sam watched Bill shift arrogantly to let her know he didn't appreciate being told to hold his question and then having to listen to someone else's question being answered. She shook her head. "Hantavirus is an upper respiratory disease. Theirs was a highly contagious exanthematous infection."

"Exanthematous, meaning?" The middle-aged man with silverish close-clipped hair had to be the publisher. He asked questions like a reporter.

"Skin eruptions. Like chickenpox . . . only worse," Eugene answered, to let her know he'd figured out what was going on. Still pissed off that he went to Switzerland and she to the ICU, Sam hadn't told him what Ken and the sheriff and she were discussing behind closed doors. Just that he'd find out at the meeting.

"Something serious enough to kill the first teenager. His friend, who was exposed via the first, has disappeared, and in light of the evidence, is presumed dead. Now we have a third case, a close friend of the second teenager."

"What did they want from . . . the teenager?" Pastor Crider asked.

"The virus, Pastor Crider."

"But if they had the virus to give him the virus, why did

they want the virus from him?" the newspaperman asked, not surprisingly.

"It had to do with timing. They needed him to carry it unwittingly for them a couple of weeks, until they were ready to retrieve it."

Eugene looked as though he were about to say something. Fortunately, he thought better of it.

"This all sounds ridiculous," Bill offered.

"So why are you telling us instead of the CDC?" Larry asked.

"Because we don't have a body to prove our case. And Bob's patient is in the early stages of this. The CDC and the state health department aren't going to be impressed by speculation." They needed Jess's body, and she thought she knew a way of finding it.

"And we are?" Bill asked without the slightest compunction.

"Look," Sam said, collapsing in the chair, "I know several of you think of me as an outsider. Unlike many of you, I'm not a second- or third- or fourth-generation Sheridanite. But Sheridan is as much my home as it is yours. These people, whoever they are, chose us because we're isolated, and frankly, because they think we're country hicks."

She waited for the murmurs of indignation to die down.

"I don't know about you," she said, doing a pretty decent imitation of an evangelist, "but I don't appreciate that."

"Yeah, we should—" Thaddeus stopped short.

"String them up? Tar and feather them? How about"— Sam glanced at the mayor—"we run our own scam? It'll be our take on Ibsen's *An Enemy of the People*."

33

Friday, April 30

ONE OF THE protesters crashed a sign down on the hood of her Jeep and shouted, "Nebuchadnezzar, you burn in the fiery furnace."

Sam parked in the doctors-only parking, pushed through the protesters, and headed for the front door of the hospital. She turned on her light and started down the back hall to the pathology department.

"Dr. Turner," Larry called from his office.

Sam stopped and retraced her footsteps. "Wonder what he wants?" she asked Jean, Larry's secretary.

Jean shrugged.

"What do you want, Larry?" Sam called.

Larry rose from his desk and ventured out to Jean's. "Dr. Wallace wants me to call the CDC about a patient he has on the third floor."

"The girl in isolation?"

Larry nodded. "Have you had a chance to look at her lab work?"

"I haven't, but I'll ask Eugene. Think it's another case of hantavirus?"

He shrugged.

"Why bother the CDC? We know what it is. We can treat it without their help." Sam hurried on.

"Good morning, Kate," Sam said as she tossed her bag into her bottom drawer. "Going to be a pretty day."

"Hope the weather holds for the rodeo this weekend."

"Ah, yes, the college rodeo. Starts tomorrow?" she asked as she hooked her sweater to the coat tree and put on her lab coat.

"Opening ceremony eight A.M."

"Will hardly have time to melt the morning frost." Sam pointed to Eugene's office. "Is he in yet?"

"In the lab."

"Have to pass on a message from Larry. Nothing I like better than being Larry's messenger girl."

Sam found Eugene at the light microscope. "Early bird gets the microscope, I see."

"Hi, Sam. Working today?" he asked without looking up.

"Thought I would. Say, Larry wants to know if you've looked at Bob's patient's lab work. You know, the one in isolation. Bob wants to call in the CDC."

Eugene looked up. "Another hantavirus?" he asked, for everyone to hear.

"Sure hope not." Sam clutched her throat. "Still sore from that damned ventilator. Hate to see anyone else go through that."

"Hantavirus?" Terry asked as she lumbered over from her work station. "Does someone else have it?"

Sam shrugged. "Hope not."

Terry answered the phone on the wall, grabbed her equipment box, and headed out.

Eugene returned to his work.

"Terry forgot her . . . " Sam picked up a pair of disposable gloves and followed Terry to the ER.

Mayor Sully and his teenage daughter were there. The teenager was lying on the examining table, writhing in pain. Sam handed Terry the gloves as she caught Connie's eye. Connie was in on it. She and a select few nurses who would be responsible for these children on the floor had had a confidential briefing in the director of nursing's office. Connie gave her a beats-me shrug.

Dr. Nguyen was busy taking the girl's history.

Sam looked over his shoulder. He covered his work as if she were a schoolgirl trying to cheat off his paper.

The teenager's eyes widened to saucers as Terry prepared to draw blood. She apparently didn't appreciate this part of the deal.

"Dr. Wallace is our family doctor," the mayor told Nguyen. "We called him and he said he'd meet us here."

"What's wrong?" Sam asked.

The girl grabbed her forehead like a vise. "A headache. It's like . . . awful." She was never going to be the deputy director of operations with a performance like that.

"Backache and nausea," the mayor prompted.

"Backache and nausea," the girl repeated as she writhed some more.

"Backache and nausea. That's interesting." As an aside to Connie, Sam added, "Kind of like the one we had a couple days ago."

"Debbie Freeman? The one in isolation? No fever, though."

"Odd." Sam patted the girl's hand. "You'll be fine. I'm sure it's nothing," she said, giving everyone the benefit of her expertise.

She'd hardly gotten the words out when the bay doors opened and Leon Sayers, the newspaper publisher with the silver buzz cut, came in with a teenage boy, a nephew who happened to be a sophomore at Sheridan College.

"My, you're popular today. Guess I'd better get back to work," Sam told Dr. Nguyen and Connie as she stuck her hands into her lab coat pockets and sauntered to the door. She heard one of Terry's gloves snap off. "Busy day," Sam said aloud to no one in particular, no one at all. "Going to be a busy day."

Kate was cradling the phone when Sam walked into pathology after getting a cup of coffee out of the lab.

"Any messages?"

Kate tore one off the pad, added it to a stack, and handed them over. "They're at it again."

"Just hang up."

Kate picked up the ringing phone, all the time giving Sam the evil eye. "Pathology." Kate listened a second, and then put the phone on hold. "It's for you. ER. Dr. Wallace wants to consult with you."

"Tell them I'll be right there."

Sam pushed through the ER doors to find Bob comforting the mayor's daughter, who had a bad case of the chills now, as Connie took vitals on the newspaperman's nephew, who was doing a pretty decent imitation of the mayor's daughter's impression of a stomach ache. Nguyen was sitting at the nursing station, pretending not to be taking it all in. "What's up, Bob?"

"Doesn't this remind you of the Freeman girl?"

Sam shrugged. "No fever."

"The Freeman girl doesn't have a fever now, either."

"Have you discharged her?" Sam asked Bob.

"What kind of doctor would I be if I did that without knowing what's wrong with her?"

"Apparently whatever it was has corrected itself."

"Maybe, maybe not." He craned around to see Connie. "I think we'd better admit this one."

Sam walked over to the boy's examining table.

"Same thing," Connie told her.

"Fever?"

Connie shook her head.

"Who's the attending?"

Connie nodded to Bob.

"That's fortunate to catch him while he's here," Sam said sarcastically as she tapped Bob on the shoulder. "Here's another one for you."

Terry came through the hall doors with her equipment tray. That would go over in a big way with the boy.

"Looks like we're going to have a whole herd of zebras. What do you say, Connie?" Bob asked. "An epidemic?"

"An epidemic!" the mayor put in as Larry's wife brought in their oldest child, who was doubled over in pain. The mayor took Bob aside. "You have to keep this quiet until after the rodeo."

"Rodeo?" Bob asked too loudly.

"What rodeo?" Sam asked.

"The college rodeo," Terry explained as she put the rubber thong around the boy's forearm. "This weekend."

"How come I didn't hear about the rodeo?" Sam asked as she watched Connie talking to the new arrivals.

"Because you never read the newspaper."

"Read that excuse—" Sam stopped suddenly as she saw the newspaper man looking at her. "Connie, do you want me to call upstairs and have them bring a gurney for Miss Sully?"

"Tell them to send two," Bob told her.

Connie helped Larry's boy onto the last examining table. "Three, I think."

"Would someone please call my husband?" Larry's wife asked in near hysterics. She was in most of the community theater's plays, and no wonder.

"I'll call him," Sam said magnanimously as she joined Nguyen at the nursing station and paged Larry. "Why don't you have a look?" Sam whispered. "Bob's over the hill."

Nguyen pretended not to hear.

Larry rushed through the hall doors ahead of the first gurney. He looked around with thespian flair and ran to examining table number three and held his wife as they both stared down at their thrashing boy.

"I think he's going to die," the mother projected before she turned and sobbed into the folds of Larry's sport jacket.

Larry patted her back. "Of course he's not. We have the finest doctors in the whole country on our staff. We'll save him."

Sam shook her head.

"Larry, think we have a regular epidemic on our hands," Bob told him as he palpated the nephew's neck.

"We need to call the CDC in," Larry said.

Sam left the nursing station and headed for Larry. "And

look foolish? Really, Bob, these are not life-threatening complaints. Let's just wait and see."

"Life-threatening!" Mayor Sully looked at her in utter astonishment.

"Not! Not! Not life-threatening," Sam explained.

"Of course not, it's just . . . we need to know what this is," Larry said, all the time patting his wife's back as her sobbing ebbed and flowed. "We need to call the CDC in here."

"It seems to me," Sam said, her fists well established on the curve of her hips, "that we can wait twelve hours to see if this resolves itself. They'll think we're country hicks if we panic and call them back for nothing."

The president of the college caught the tail end of her speech as he brought in a couple of college kids he'd promised to dig up. She watched Larry counting heads, calculating what this little stunt was going to cost the hospital in lost income. Plenty. From the paper draping the examining tables and lab work to the nursing staff monitoring these patients. The crestfallen look on Larry's face was the one highlight of this whole dirty business. She would savor this moment forever. But now she had to hightail it so Bob and Larry could discuss the consequences of not calling the CDC. She would be interested to hear if Nguyen would put in his two cents worth.

34

Mrs. Freeman carried Debbie's personal belongings and the flowers Sam had had Daisy send. Sam carried a white plastic bag with PERSONAL BELONGINGS printed in blue letters, but instead of being filled with disposable hospital items like the pitcher and thermometer Debbie had used, it held a couple of gowns and masks and a box of disposable gloves. Debbie was in the wheelchair the private duty nurse was pushing. Debbie was burning up with fever, but that was beside the point. She was being discharged for her health.

"Excuse me, Mrs. Freeman," one of the three women behind the reception counter called as the wheelchair activated the automatic doors. Mother Freeman had already stopped by on her way up to get Debbie and signed the release papers.

The nurse pulled the wheelchair back when Mrs. Freeman waddled over to the counter. She didn't look nearly as wide in her basic black polyester pants as she had in orange. Maybe hospital gowns would become the fashion rage and she could wear the ones in the bag after the nurse had finished with them. They'd cover her dimpled thighs nicely.

"There's a fifty-cent charge for the phone that we can't bill the insurance company."

"Oh, let's see," Mother said, laying out Debbie's belongings and flowers on the counter. "Where's my purse?"

It was on her right arm, but Sam was more concerned

about getting Debbie into the car and out of here before anyone got close enough to the girl to notice her red rash. Tomorrow she'd have pustules, a milder case, thanks to the vaccination Jeffers had given her when she was in the emergency room with Jess. She prayed it would be a milder case.

Sam didn't do this on a regular basis and wished she'd choreographed it better. An escape car at the curb with flowers and personal belongings already in the trunk would have been superlative.

"I'm not sure I have . . . " Mrs. Freeman said, digging into her purse.

Sam joined her at the counter, juggling the personal-belongings bag as she poked her fingers into her Levi's. "I have it." She was certain she had some crumpled bills in her pocket. She couldn't remember spending them after the coffee machine rejected them.

"Fifty cents," the debt collector repeated.

"Right," Sam acknowledged, thrusting her hand farther into her right pocket.

"Here," Mother said, pulling a handful of change from the bottom of her purse, a twenty-nine cent red, yellow, and blue hyacinth stamp attached. The flowers had enough dirt on them to last forever, but the stamp was wilted around the edges.

Debbie groaned. Mother Freeman counted her pennies and nickels.

Not having full faith in the scant collection of change, Sam tried her hip pocket. What had she done with those crumpled bills? She didn't remember putting them back in her purse. Had she stuck them into her lab coat pocket? The lab coat that was currently hanging on the coat tree in her office?

"Twenty-three, twenty-four . . . "

Give her the stamp now and call it even.

"Mother!"

"Just a second," Mother said, "twenty-six—"

"Twenty-five," the worker corrected, struggling to keep annoyance out of her voice.

Sam's right hand crossed her body to get at the left pocket. There they were! She pulled a bill out between two fingers and threw it to the counter. "Here, take it out of this."

"I'll get your change," the clerk turned on her heels and headed to one of the desks under the windows that looked out over the field to the high school and the westerly Big Horn Mountains.

Sam threw her head toward the door. "Let's go."

"But your change?" Mrs. Freeman exclaimed.

"I'll get it when I come back in. Let's go," she said again. They were out the door with no further snarls.

"Why don't you drive the car around?" Sam suggested to Debbie's mother, relieving her of the water-sloshing flowers. "We'll wait at the curb."

Of course, Mrs. Freeman had parked at the far end of the parking lot. Sam was just thankful she'd parked in the front lot.

Sam squatted down beside the chair. "How you doing?"

"What are they doing?" Debbie asked about the protesters.

"They're David's people. David was cremated instead of buried. They blame me." Though now they were protesting at her request.

"But Daniel wasn't burnt in the fiery furnace. God spared him."

Sam patted her hand as she rose. The girl wasn't delirious, anyway.

The automatic doors opened and the clerk called out, "Dr. Turner, there's a phone call for you."

Bob was racing across the parking lot as a battered red Subaru with black exhaust was limping toward them.

"Transfer the call to pathology." Kate would take a message and add it to the pile.

Sam went around to the back of the Subaru and unburdened herself, anchoring the flowers in the flat spare tire so the water wouldn't spill out onto the gowns. The nurse helped Debbie into the passenger's seat, reminding her yet again that it was important for her to look well. That was why Debbie couldn't lie down in the backseat.

The nurse shut the door about the time Sam rounded the car. The Freemans drove off. The nurse took the wheelchair back inside, like any other time except that now, after returning the wheelchair, she would slip out the back and over to the Freemans' residence. Sam waited for Bob, who was frantically waving at her.

"What's up?" Sam asked Bob when he was beside her.

"Earl Jeffers called," he replied, a hand to his chest as if it helped him breathe. "He asked if I wanted a consult on the teenagers. Lee Nguyen must have called him."

Nguyen was the type of doctor who preferred diagnostic tools—lab results, X rays, monitoring results—to squandering his valuable time seeing patients. But Jeffers seemed to be a tactile doctor, touching, observing, and examining his patients, lingering to listen affectionately to their complaints. That was all well and good, but only Nguyen's method would serve Sam's purpose.

"What did you tell him?"

"I told him I had an emergency in my office and that I'd call him back as soon as I could."

"Quick thinking." She patted him on the back. "Okay. Call him back. Tell him you accept and ask him to meet you in the ER at four."

"You going to give the kids succinylcholine and hook them up to ventilators?"

"Heavens no! They're the monsters. We're not going to put the children in danger."

"Jeffers will know they're lollygaggers as soon as he lays eyes on them."

"Well, then we'll have to see that he doesn't."

"Then I'll tell him I don't need his help."

"No," Sam said, "his ER shift starts at five. Tell him to meet you at four. I'll come up with some sort of a diversion to make him miss your appointment."

"What kind of a diversion?"

"I haven't the foggiest idea, but surely I'll be able to cultivate a germ of an idea between now and then."

"That seems to be your specialty these days."

"Come on," Sam said, hooking his arm. "I'll give you a ride back to your office. I've got to go over to Debbie's house and reconnect her IV."

"ICU is crowded with healthy kids, and the one who needs to be there is on her way home."

"Maybe we'll get everything straightened out soon."

"In our next lives."

$\triangledown$

35

Sᴀᴍ ɢʀᴀʙʙᴇᴅ ʜᴇʀ lab coat.

"Derek called," Kate said.

"What? When?"

"Not long after you left."

"Where was he? Did he leave a number?"

"Said he'd try to catch you later."

"Anything else? What did he say, exactly?"

"Gee, Sam, don't get in a twit. He just wanted to chat. Said he'd call back later."

He might have said to Kate he just wanted to chat, but Sam bet *she* would have heard a different story. "But he didn't leave a number where I could reach him?"

"I asked, but he said he was out gadding about. Sounded far away." Kate answered the ringing phone. Sam held her breath, waiting to see if it were Derek calling back. It wasn't. Sam, remembering her purpose, went into the lab.

"Terry," Sam asked, interrupting the girl's work, "do you have the results for those kids?"

"Oh, yeah," she said, getting to her feet. "In the Out file." Sam followed her to the wire basket on the counter by the blood bank. Terry tore off the goldenrod copies on each of the reports and handed them to Sam.

Sam looked them over. "God! Did Eugene see these?"

"I don't think so; he's been over at the VA hospital most of the morning."

Sam marched into the ER and up to Nguyen, who was

reading the latest issue of the *New England Journal of Medicine*. Connie was nowhere to be seen.

"Dr. Nguyen, I need your help."

Nguyen looked at her over the top of the magazine. "Oh?"

She thrust out the tissue-thin goldenrod reports. "Look at the results from the lab tests of those kids who presented this morning."

He gave the first a perfunctory glance, skimmed the other four, and then read the first again. "These are the patients Dr. Wallace admitted?"

Sam nodded.

"Are you certain these are the correct numbers on the ESR and SGOT?" Erythrocyte—red corpuscle—sedimentation rate was less of a red herring than the serum glutamic oxaloacetic transaminase (SGOT) levels, which increased in myocardial infarction and in diseases involving destruction of liver cells. But they wanted Nguyen to be challenged, no run-of-the-mill diagnosis.

"Look at the leukocytosis if you think those are abnormal." A white blood cell count of 10,000 or more per cubic millimeter might be expected. These ranged from 60,000 to 100,000.

He leaned forward and supported his head with his hands. "They didn't have fevers."

"I wonder . . . " Sam picked up the phone and touched the zero. "ICU, please." She covered the receiver. "Let's see if that's changed." She turned her attention to the nurse on the other end of the line. "Yes, this is Dr. Turner in pathology. Could you look in the charts of . . . " She pulled the lab reports out from under the good doctor's arms and read the names.

Her beeper activated.

"Good, could you read me each of their temperatures and the times of the readings?" Sam pulled the beeper off her belt. The red phone number was Kate's. Was it Derek? "One hundred and four?" She nodded as she listened to the others and felt Nguyen's eyes burning through her. "Which one convulsed?" She nodded as the director of nursing's selectee chose one at random. "Not surprising, with *that* fever." Her beeper cycled again. "Thanks." She hung up and dialed Kate. "This is Sam."

"Sheriff's on the line."

The adrenaline, pumping madly because she thought it might have been Derek, diminished and left fatigue in its wake. "Have the operator transfer him to the ER." She hung up the phone and waited. "They have fevers. One zero three to one zero five."

He raised an eyebrow in disbelief.

"Two of them are on ventilators."

"And the others aren't?"

"Not yet."

She picked up the ringing phone. "Dr. Turner here."

"Hi, Sam, it's Hank. You called?"

"Another body?" She gave Nguyen a sorry-I'm-conducting-business-on-your-line shrug. Nguyen gave her an indifferent gaze.

"What? Are you talking to me, Sam?" Hank asked.

"Yes, Hank. A floater?" Sam watched Nguyen for signs of interest. He wasn't generous enough to show her any. "No. Sorry, don't know why I jumped to that conclusion. Guess because the last one was." She rolled her eyes for Nguyen's benefit.

"Sam, are you okay? You're not having one of those amnesia spells again, are you?"

"No, Hank, not at all. Blisters? What kind of blisters?"

"You talking to me, Sam? Oh, I get it. Someone's listening."

"Pus? All over his body?" Sam had Doctor Nguyen's full attention.

"Pus?" Hank repeated.

"How would I know! You're the one looking at the body." She was looking at the perp. All right, the *alleged* perpetrator.

"You want me to say anything, Sam?"

"Not necessarily. Why don't you transfer the corpse to the

mortuary. I'll have a look at it over there. If I can get through the protesters."

"Oh, yeah. Good thing about the protesters, huh, Sam? You want me to take a body over there for you?"

"Do you have one, Hank?"

"Well, no." The CIA wouldn't be recruiting him anytime soon. Just as well, he was always willing to listen to reason, something she couldn't say for the moronic chauvinist chief pig.

"Guess that takes care of that."

"Guess so." He paused a beat. "Do you want me to say anything else?"

"It's been unseasonably cold. That's the only reason I can come up with until I see the corpse."

"Everybody knows we go from winter to summer. Spring lasts about an hour in these here parts," Hank said, trying his best to keep up his side of the conversation.

"An hour's good. I'll see you then." Sam hung up. "God, I don't know why I ever ran for county coroner, a ten-thou-a-year job. Dealing with one country hick after another is not the most fulfilling life. He asked if I wanted to go to the crime site. Like I wanted to tramp around in this mud."

"Sheridan seems like such a quiet place."

"On the surface, anyway. I'm about to be sued because the undertaker's wife sent the wrong body to the Billings crematorium."

"Why would that have anything to do with you?" he asked, as if he didn't know exactly what it had to do with her.

"It was a coroner's case. I had it on hold. Last time I was named as corespondent in a malpractice case in which my only involvement was in signing a lab report, it cost my insurance company three thousand dollars to hire an attorney to petition to have my name removed from the list. And people wonder why their medical bills are so high."

"You have a murder?" he asked in an unsatisfactory segue.

"Looks like it." His face blanched a sallow yellow. Sam

sucked in her breath and got up. She was halfway out of the department before she returned and leaned on the counter across from him. "I almost forgot to ask you about those," she pointed to the lab reports. "Bob surely will need some help. Earl, I'm told, was my saving grace when I had hantavirus. . . . Wait a minute." She closed her eyes, mainly to keep a straight face after seeing the shock on his. "Hantavirus. What if . . . ? We need to call off the rodeo."

▽

36

Sam DUG IN her Levi's pocket to see if she had any change. A lousy penny would give her twelve minutes, and she had plenty in her desk drawer. She unlocked her Jeep and reached in for her purse. She hoped someone would come along to use the rest of her nickel's worth. She sure didn't plan to spend an hour in the mayor's office.

She pushed through the first set of doors, and then the second without waiting for the first to shut. It was a warm afternoon, no need to shut out the wind.

"May I help you?" The receptionist smiled. Sam would have preferred an old biddy snapping at her to the sweet older woman.

"I'm Dr. Turner. Here to see the mayor."

"Oh yes, he's expecting you." She pointed to the door marked MAYOR.

"Thank you." Sam knocked on the door as she entered.

Mayor Sully was behind his desk. Leon Sayers, the newspaper publisher, sat on the couch with the president of the college. The schools superintendent sat in a straight chair between the couch and desk. There was a chair for her on the other side of the couch.

"Gentlemen."

The four men rose, four greetings coming like a blast of shot. Sam went to the window and looked out. The trees were budding; she hoped it was a sign.

"Saw your boss when I was at the hospital visiting Veronica," Mayor Sully said, returning to his seat.

"I don't have a boss. To whom are you referring?"

"Larry's not your boss?"

"He runs the hospital, I have a contract with the hospital. That's a far cry from being my boss." She had a new appreciation for Derek's remark about politicians changing bedfellows when it became expedient.

"Anyway," the mayor continued, "he asked me to pass on the message that the CDC would be here on the evening plane."

"Thank you."

"Would you like to read the news release?" Sayers asked, holding out a piece of paper.

"Thank you," Sam said as she took it and then sat in the chair. She rummaged through her purse to find her glasses. It didn't matter what she was looking for, it was always at the bottom, a cosmic parallel to Murphy's law.

Situated with her glasses on, she read it over.

Mystery Illness Is Linked to Buffalo

The mystery illness that has stricken the Sheridan area may be caused by a virus carried by the herd of buffalo on the Turner Ranch.

Interviews with the six victims of the mystery disease, young and apparently healthy teenagers, revealed that each had come in contact with the animals during the previous seventy-two hours.

Primary findings by hospital personnel have not been confirmed, but a spokesperson for the Sheridan County Hospital told this reporter that the U.S. Centers for Disease Control and Prevention would be arriving shortly.

This will mark the second time this month that the U.S. Centers for Disease Control and Prevention has been summoned to Sheridan. The first time was for a breakout of hantavirus, a virus carried by rodents and transmitted in rodent droppings and urine. Hantavirus most recently was in the news when it swept through the Four Corners area of New Mexico and Arizona last year. Outbreaks of hantavirus can be traced back to the Korean War where it occurred among U.S. troops.

A spokesperson for the U.S. Fish and Game department confirmed the possibility that the buffalo might be carriers of a similar virus, if not hantavirus itself. They will test the buffalo and quarantine the herd until results are in.

Sheridan health authorities caution parents to watch their children for signs of fever, muscle aches, headache, nausea, reddening of the skin. As the disease progresses, fluids build up in the lungs, literally suffocating the patient.

This reminded her of how much she hated reading her name in the paper's police blotter every time she was issued a citation or her dogs were thrown in the pound. All that was before she stopped torturing herself and let her subscription expire. "Thank you," she said, handing it back. "We have to move up our timetable," she said to Dr. Jacobson, president of Sheridan College. "Four sharp at the hospital. In the emergency room."

"What about the CDC?" Larry asked.

Sam sighed. "Have to be a double feature. Once at the hospital, once at the airport." She pushed out of her chair. "I appreciate all of your help."

"It's our town, too," Mayor Sully said as he got up and leaned across the desk, his hand extended.

Sam smiled. It was more their town than it was hers, and it was sweet of him to turn it around. "You'll have my vote next election, Mayor Sully," she said, shaking his hand.

"You mean you didn't vote for me last time?"

Sam laughed, shook hands all around, and started out.

"Veronica will be home for dinner?" the mayor asked.

"After all the kids have done? No, we'll spring for dinner. Nothing like good ol' hospital food that sticks to your ribs. Oh, and have Bill post one of his men at the airport in case the CDC comes in on a chartered flight."

"Why would they do that?" the newspaperman asked.

Sam looked at him and wondered where the notion came from. She shrugged and opened the door and then turned back to the men. "You'll be sorry. I'm warning you, the rodeo needs to be closed down. We have an epidemic as it is. Whatever this is, it's affecting our children. Do we want it spread over the region like prairie fire?"

She slammed the door and stormed toward the outside door, then she retraced her footsteps and reopened the mayor's door. "I'm the county coroner. I have an unexplained death over at Thaddeus's, plus a teenage victim I can connect to the deceased, not to mention a missing boy I know came in contact with the first victim. That gives me the authority to close down the rodeo. And that's exactly what I'm going to do."

Sam slipped into the back of the courtroom. Her beeper activated before she barely had a chance to sit down on the cold bench. She pulled it from her belt and turned it down so she would not disturb the court when it cycled the second time. The number was Kate's. She couldn't ignore it. Kate might have news from Derek.

She got up and started out, but not before the beeper recycled at an all-time loud. Instead of turning it down, she must have turned it up. She fumbled with it as she pushed through the door.

"Dr. Turner," Judge Stanley Moots called, interrupting the lawyer.

Sam turned around, the door whooshing closed behind her. "Yes, Your Honor?"

"Have you interrupted these proceedings for any special reason?"

"No, Your Honor. I mean, yes, Your Honor. I need to speak with you at your earliest convenience."

"Would you care to elaborate for the court?"

Twelve jury members, two tables of lawyers and their respective clients, three dozen spectators—including Sherman, the shrimp from the newspaper—turned around and gave her their full attention. She hoped she could sound as convincing as Larry's wife.

"I need a court order to stop the college rodeo. We have a hantavirus epidemic in town."

The courtroom exploded in chaotic noise. She felt like she was back in David's church.

Judge Moots picked up his gavel and pounded. "Silence in the court." When the proper decorum had been reached, he straightened the collar of his black robe and gently picked up his gavel. "The court will take a ten-minute recess." He gave the wooden block one rap of the gavel.

"All rise," the court reporter ordered as the judge stepped down from the bar and headed for the side exit that would take him to his chambers. Sam went out the back and around the corner and followed him in. Sam waved at the bewildered-looking secretary. The judge held the door open, securing it after Sam was through.

"Have a seat," he said, pointing to a black leather wingback chair.

"I need to use the phone." She turned the phone around and dialed Kate's number.

Judge Moots sat behind his desk, opened his bottom drawer, and took out an ashtray with a gold lighter and a nasty-looking cigar in the middle. He put the ashtray on the desk and his feet on the open drawer.

"Kate, it's Sam. You beeped me?"

Sam watched Moots ignite the lighter on the third try.

"You said to beep if Derek called."

"Is he still on the line?"

"Of course not."

Sam sighed. "What did he say? Did he give you a number where I can reach him?"

The tip of Stanley's mangy half-chewed cigar turned a glorious red after ten puffs.

"No, he was at a pay phone. Said he would call later."

"Did he say anything else?"

"Well, yeah, he asked how I was doing. Stuff like that."

"*Exactly* what stuff?"

"Gee, I don't remember. How the weather was. How you were doing. Stuff like that."

"Did you ask him how he was doing?"

"He sounded fine. You going to be at a particular number for a while? If he calls back, I mean."

"No, I'm going to be tied up later." She rolled her eyes for Stanley's benefit. He chuckled for hers. They both knew she meant it literally. "But I'm on my way back. If he calls right back, keep him on the line. Or get a number."

"I'll try."

"Thanks, Kate. 'Bye." She hung up and turned the phone back so it faced the judge. She plopped down in the wingback chair.

He blew smoke high in the air, but it came down on her like curtains falling on the third act. "I feel like I'm playing hooky. Makes the cigar taste twice as nice."

Sam rested her elbow on the arm of the chair and held her hand under her nose. Some of the smoke still managed to get into her nostrils.

He puffed away half a centimeter while they waited. "Had some relatives in town last fall, wife's relatives, that is, from back east. Took them out to the Bradford Brinton Museum and then for a nice ride around the countryside. They were real impressed with your buffalo. Would have thought they'd never seen so much as a cow the way they carried on. How are your buffalo?" he asked as he rolled the cigar between his chubby fingers.

"Fine."

"Didn't you have a baby?"

"A boy. Woody."

"Woody? Is that a family name? Woodrow, maybe?"

"He was named after a friend who was there when he was born. Woods."

"Woods," he said as if searching his memory bank. "Woods."

"Woody was born on the island of St. Thomas in the Caribbean."

Stanley nodded as if she'd passed a test.

"He was premature. My husband and I were on a cruise."

"Met your husband once. At the doctor-lawyer Christmas party last year."

"Two years ago. We didn't attend the last one."

"Should have. It was nice. Real nice."

Sam smiled. "We'll be sure to attend the next one."

He tossed a manila envelope across the desk. She opened it to find the two documents. "Thank you."

"You sure about that second one?"

She shook her head. "It's the only thing that makes any sense."

"Doesn't make a lick of sense to me."

She nodded. "Amazing what people will do when they're not thinking straight. I liken it to a body in the bathtub. If it's dressed, it's most likely a suicide. If naked, either an accident or murder."

He puffed on his cigar as he let thought whirl. "How's that?"

"A suicide wouldn't want to be discovered naked."

He shook his head.

Sam rose and offered her hand. "Thank you, again."

"I just hope you're wrong."

"Doesn't make much difference, either way. Dead's dead."

37

"DID DEREK CALL?" Sam asked as she walked into pathology.

Kate shook her head. "Just these."

Sam took the messages and glanced at them. She pulled the one from Bob out of the pile and threw it away; she had stopped by his office to tell him the change of plans. She ran her hand over the message from Derek as if it would help tell her where he was, and if he were all right. It was the one from Thaddeus that she returned.

"This is Dr. Turner," Sam said into the phone after the twit who couldn't tell a seventeen-year-old from a seventy-year-old answered. "I'm returning Mr. Smith's call, Mrs. Smith."

"Just a sec."

It wasn't just a sec. Sam had enough time to scan the toxicology results from Tom Polvich's autopsy. Sam hadn't found a needle mark, but needles were so fine these days that she would have been surprised had she found one. Nor did the preliminary toxicology results show anything. Not surprising. Her gut instinct told her Polvich was injected with succinylcholine chloride—a man-made compound similar to the drug curare, of South American Indian poisonous dart fame—which is broken down rapidly into substances found naturally in the human body. Succinylcholine was an ideal murder weapon, and it was accessible. Bob, Terry, the Criders, Thaddeus, and she had all been paralyzed by it.

"Hello?"

"Thaddeus, it's Sam. You called?"

"Yeah, Dr. Jeffers showed up just like you thought he would." Didn't take long for Dr. Nguyen to share the news.

"And?"

"The protesters wouldn't let him through."

"That's it? He went away?"

"That's right."

Ken raced in, a stern look on his face. Barium on his right pant leg and shoe. An occupational hazard for radiologists. Not all patients can hold their barium long enough to get good barium enema films. And as Ken liked to complain, he was usually the one standing next to the table at the time.

"Thanks, Thaddeus." She hung up and gave Ken her full attention. "What's up, Doc?"

He took her arm and pulled her up and to the door. "Come on, I need to talk to you."

"What for?"

Ken pulled her across the hall, into the department's waiting room, through the hall of X-raying rooms, and into his office. He shut the door and stood in front of it. "I'm going in your place," he said, his arms stubbornly crossed.

"You will not!"

"Bob and I talked it over."

"He must have sprinted to the phone the second I left his office." Her hands flew to her hips. "And since when do you and Bob make decisions for me?"

"Since you're not thinking straight." He came toward her. "Look at me. A strapping man, able to defend myself. And frail you? I've never seen you in such bad shape."

"Gee, thanks." She skirted him. "Now, if you'll excuse me."

He grabbed her arm and swung her around. "No, you're not excused. You're not going. There is no reason why you have to be there."

"I can think of *one* reason. *I'm* the one who's closing down their rodeo. They'll be looking for *me*."

"Dr. Miller," said a voice coming out of the intercom on his desk, "there's a call for you on line two."

"Thank you, Joyce." He loosened his grip. Sam pulled away. "Sam—"

"Answer your call, Ken."

They stared each other down until Ken broke it to answer the call.

Sam slipped out of the room.

She raced back to pathology, put on her lab coat, took it off to don her cardigan sweater, then put the lab coat back on. Be cold after the sun was down, but to wear her jacket to the ER might tip someone off. It was early, a quarter to four, but once she was in the ER, Ken couldn't do a blasted thing about it. She pulled the headset of the transcription machine away from Kate's right ear. "Going over the ER for a minute. Transfer Derek's call." She snapped the earpiece back into position.

"Will do," Kate said without missing a beat.

She hurried to the ER, then composed herself before pushing through the bay doors. Gary was behind the nursing station. Dr. Nguyen was in a straight chair beside examining table two, reading a book. The examining tables on either side were dark.

She bet she'd hear about it from Larry once these two were gone. Dr. Nguyen seemed to have a lot of downtime. She'd never convince Larry to hire more ER doctors if the ledger showed red ink. She didn't suppose Larry would count the kids.

"Hi," she said, feeling as if she were sneaking up on Dr. Nguyen.

He gave her a weak smile and returned to his book.

"What are you reading?" she asked, leaning up against the examining table.

Dr. Nguyen looked up at her, and then back at the book. "*Fortran for Humans.*"

"I hate computers."

He smiled. Or smirked; on him it was hard to tell the

difference.

"What was the total count?"

Dr. Nguyen turned the flap of the jacket over the page to mark his place, and then closed the book. He laid it on his lap and gave her his full attention. "Five."

"No others came in?"

He stared into her eyes an uncomfortably long time. "No."

She smiled. "Good."

The bay doors opened. Sam turned away to see Ken. He didn't look all that happy to see her talking to Dr. Nguyen, but she knew he wouldn't cause a scene.

"Ah, Sam, here you are. They need you in pathology."

That was a dirty trick! The jerk had on his jacket. "Going home already, Ken?" She motioned to his jacket.

Ken caught her drift. She hoped he was the only one who picked up on it. "Oh, yes. Finished early. Thought I'd spend a little time with the kids."

"Well, guess I'd better see what they want." She touched Nguyen's arm. He recoiled noticeably. "Keep me posted." She glared at Ken as she left.

Sam sat at her desk watching Kate smoke the typewriter. She glanced at her watch. Five minutes. She picked up the phone and dialed the ER's extension. The nurse, Gary, answered.

"Yes, this is Sophie down in records. UPS dropped off a package for you. Can you come down and get it when you have a minute?"

"Sure. Be right down."

Sam hung up and picked up the manila envelope. She took the rodeo document out and stuck the envelope in her bottom drawer, locking it and her purse inside. She tossed the key to the back of her middle drawer and shut it.

She gripped the document in her hand and headed for the ER. It was still empty save for Ken and Nguyen. "You still here, Ken?"

He motioned to Nguyen. "We were discussing software. Time slipped away. What do you have there?"

"The court order to call off the rodeo tomorrow. Think it'll be necessary, Dr. Nguyen?" A truck pulled up in the ambulance dock. Young cowboys were jumping out of the bed. Where the hell was Jeffers? How was she going to tell the boys to wait with Nguyen standing here? "I've got to run." She touched Ken's sleeve. "See you later." She got to the hall before the four kidnappers, wearing team jackets, were through the outside door. She cracked the door enough to see.

"Where's this Dr. Turner who's trying to shut down our rodeo?" a lanky boy with bowlegs asked, as if he'd watched too many James Cagney movies.

"Why do you want to know?" Ken asked.

"You Dr. Turner?" an even scrawnier kid with sandy hair asked as he ambled over to Ken like John Wayne. He wasn't even close, but the six-shooter helped.

Two more slim fellows were back by the door, shotguns crossing their chests. James Cagney turned around to show off the back of his jacket. The design was straight off the Wyoming license plates, a cowboy on a bucking bronc.

"Yeah, I'm Dr. Turner," Ken lied. "Why?"

"Then you'll be going with us." The boy brandished the six-shooter toward the door. The other flipped a gunny sack over his head, and then over Nguyen's. The one grabbed Ken's arm roughly and led him to the door. The other followed with Nguyen.

Sam watched Ken and Nguyen stumble blindly to get into the bed of the truck. The two cowboys with shotguns rode on the ledge, Ken and Nguyen out of her sight line on the floor. The pickup pulled away, coughing black smoke.

This was turning out to be one hell of a disappointing day.

38

"YOU'RE CERTAIN ONE of them said 'hunting cabin'?" Earl Jeffers asked as he rode shotgun up red-grade. When it wasn't snow-packed or snow-slush, like now, the red-shale road leading into the Big Horns from the south could be seen from miles away, a red ribbon streaming up the side of the mountain.

"Hunting cabin." Be a good month before the road would be travelworthy, but Sam's Jeep was in four-wheel drive and they had a couple of hours to kill. Going up to Bob's hunting cabin seemed as good a place as any to kill them.

"Maybe we should turn back and call the sheriff. He could check it out."

"We're already halfway there. No sense turning back now. Don't worry, Gary will call Clarence if someone comes into the ER."

"That comforts me," he said sarcastically.

Sam smiled and glanced over at him before she turned back to the bumpy road ahead. She wished he weren't one of the conspirators, if not the murderer; he would have made a nice addition to the staff. Hadn't taken him long to form an opinion about Clarence.

"Would really like to take a look at Dr. Wallace's young patients. Find a regimen for their treatment. I don't believe your stay order for the rodeo was in time."

"Oh?"

"I was by the fairgrounds. From the looks of the trailers

and livestock and kids moving about, I'd say they're pretty well mixed together. We need to interview the victims, or at least their parents, get a list of associates, try to isolate and cut the chain of transmission."

He seemed so noble that Sam had to remind herself that she had been victimized by him and his fellow conspirators.

"Rule of thumb in these parts," Sam said as they came to a fork in the road and read the sign that showed two miles to the lake by Bob's cabin one way and eight miles the other, "is to take the longest route and save yourself a lot of time. Might be two miles, but you probably have to ford the same creek four times. They wouldn't have an alternative route otherwise."

Jeffers got out and looked at the two roads. He walked around to her side. She slid down the window. "Back around, up this one." He pointed to the shortcut.

"Why?"

"No one's come through here in quite some time." He nodded behind the Jeep. "Ours are the only tracks."

He had her there. She could do nothing but comply.

"Let's go back to town and call the authorities from the mortuary," he said after supervising the turnaround and getting back into the Jeep.

"Mortuary?"

"Let's have a look at the body the sheriff brought in."

"How did you know about that?"

"Dr. Wallace mentioned it when I spoke to him about his young patients."

Except Bob would have known better than to talk about it. Nor did Bob know when or how she was going to spring the body on Nguyen and Jeffers, because she didn't know until she did it. The only person who could have told him was Nguyen and, for some reason, Jeffers didn't want her to know that. "All right, I haven't had a chance to look at it. Really should; sounds like it might be foul play. Don't know why I ever wanted to be coroner. Medical examiner is bad enough. Most coroners in Wyoming are undertakers," she rattled on. "You can always count on a couple of hunting accidents and drownings, ranching-equipment accidents, the usual car accidents." She fiddled with her radio, getting static. "And the unusual ones."

"Unusual ones?" he asked as he took over the search for a radio station. It was a futile search for two reasons: the mountains blocked the radio waves, and her radio was on the fritz. But it gave him something to do.

"Horse, deer, antelope. A red fox caused one because the driver turned around to look at it and ran headon into an eighteen-wheeler. That's according to the driver of the eighteen-wheeler, of course."

They were out of the mountains, and he long ago had given up the search for outside entertainment. They had exhausted enlightening conversation when brilliance came to her, not to mention the turnoff. "Wait a minute! I know the hunting cabin they must have meant." Sam fishtailed as she pulled off the county blacktop onto the graveled road that led to the Bradford Brinton Museum. "The old trophy lodge by the creek on the Brinton place."

"Why don't we go back to town and tell the sheriff? You said the kidnappers had guns."

"They aren't killers." She didn't add, *Unlike you.* "They simply want the rodeo to go on. We'll drive by and see if we see their pickup."

He didn't voice an objection.

There was no pickup but tire marks and plenty of tracks covering the muddy ground down to the creek. Sam and Jeffers left the Jeep by the road, climbed the buck-and-rail fence, and followed the tracks to the foot bridge. Followed the mud to the porch. Sam's boots deposited their share along the way. Jeffers wore French Shriners, the city slicker.

Sam repressed a shudder as she opened the door and walked into the musty-smelling room. She was just as glad

Ken replaced her, since she was able to keep Jeffers occupied, to his obvious delight. She had no desire to spend time tied to a chair under the watchful glass eyes of the animals Bradford Brinton had bagged on African safaris.

Ken looked every bit the victim. The lasso circled the cowhide chair the entire distance of his trunk and ran between his legs and then wrapped around his ankles. His hands were tied loosely behind his back. She took the red bandanna out of his mouth first.

Jeffers saw to Nguyen.

"Sam!" Ken said after a gasping breath of musty air. "How in the world did you find us?"

"Wasn't easy. I ran into Earl in the parking lot as I was trying to get to my Jeep to follow the pickup, and he came with me. But the truck lost us."

"Tell me about it. I felt every bump in the road. Collided with the steel studs every jolt." He groaned as she struggled with the knot around his wrists.

Jeffers must have been a Boy Scout; he was unwrapping Nguyen a good deal faster than she was Ken. It occurred to her that the race between them might be of some consequence. Ken must have realized, too. He struggled to work his hands free. She left him to it and went around to untie his feet.

Nguyen was freed first, but only by a hair. Ken jumped to his feet, ready to pounce. But the tension passed.

"Let's get out of here," Sam suggested. "I've seen all the zebras I care to see."

Nguyen didn't seem the least bit amused, but Ken and Jeffers appreciated the pun. Ken made long strides to the door and held it open.

Jeffers put a hand to the small of Sam's back to let her out first. "As I used to tell my medical students," Jeffers said, "if you hear hoofbeats, think horses."

"You were at a teaching institution?" Sam asked.

"Do you see any of the hoodlums around?" Nguyen said.

"They're gone," Jeffers answered. He ignored her question in favor of giving her a hand off the porch.

She crossed the bridge first. The water was splashing over the sides, making the bridge slick. They were losing the sun fast. But she took her time; she had plans for these two, and timing was everything.

39

Sam closed the dogs up in the library and found the threesome in her kitchen with Nicola and the baby. Nguyen was sitting at the kitchen table sipping ice water and looking out the sliding glass doors into the darkness. Nicola and Jeffers were busy sweeping up a baby bottle Fido had knocked off the table with his wagging tail. Ken was swinging the baby, and generally being in the way. The cat was perched on top of the refrigerator, taking it all in. Sam had to keep her unwilling guests occupied for another twenty-five minutes.

"The sheriff said to sit tight, he'll be right out."

Jeffers nodded to the phone. "I should call the hospital and tell them where I am."

"Okay, and I'll see if I can rustle up some supper," Sam said, opening the refrigerator, "since some of us were tied up earlier."

Sam took the dust pan from Jeffers and replaced him as the chief bottle scraper-upper. "Use the phone in the library if you want a little privacy."

"Doesn't matter, this one's fine."

"Maybe you should call Mary after Earl's finished, Ken."

Ken nodded. "And to think I was going home early."

Jeffers was picking up the phone to dial when it rang. "Hello?" He held the phone out. "Samantha, it's for you."

Samantha. It was Derek! Her gut feeling said so. Practically everyone else called her Sam. She laid the dust pan, clanging glass shards, on the floor and rushed to the phone. Her soaring heart fell. Derek was going to kill her. "Hello."

"Who was that?"

She was at a distinct disadvantage with company present. "Earl Jeffers."

"Are you in trouble?"

"He was about to use the phone." She wanted to ask the questions. How he was. How her father was. She wanted to tell him about the visit from his boss, what they were doing, that she wanted him home. Her mind was a volcanic eruption of things she wanted to say, and at the same time she was paralyzed by fright. Afraid she'd slip off the razor's edge and say the wrong thing and blow the scam and never find out who killed Jess Gorzalka and Tom Polvich. "Where are you, Derek?"

"In Denver. Missed the plane." He was on his way home. Thank you, God. And thank you, God, for making him miss the plane. She had to wrap this up before he got home. He would ruin everything. "I'll arrive in Casper around ten-thirty. Emil's there, isn't he?" Translation: Is he at the bar? *I'll.* He was alone.

She looked from Ken to Nguyen, and then to the tile on the counter. To meet his plane Emil would have to leave at eight-thirty. She had plans for Emil that would make him late. What should she do? Tell him yes and leave him stranded at the Casper airport for an hour? Tell him to rent a car? "Sure. You won't recognize Woody. He's grown so much."

There was a long pause. "Are you in trouble?"

"No, Nicola's right here." Nicola stopped sweeping and looked up. "It's Derek," Sam said to her. Nicola smiled to the tops of her gums. "We're still having some trouble knocking down the language barrier, but we're surviving."

"Do you want me to call Hank?"

"Not at all. Listen, Earl needs to use the phone. And then Ken after him," she blundered on. "I'm glad you finished your article early, and I'll see you soon."

"What's going on, Samantha?" Derek was scowling, she knew he was.

She sighed and rolled her eyes for the guys. "It's a long story. Lee and Ken were hostages of some college boys who didn't want me to close down the rodeo. Everything's fine now, and Earl needs to call the hospital to let them know where he is. I love you. 'Bye." She hung up before he had a chance to ask anything else she couldn't answer.

"Wow, Sam, you probably scared the be'jesus out of him," Ken said, winding Woody's swing again. The tune and the clicking were getting on her nerves. Nguyen didn't look all that happy about it, either. Woody had a big grin for Ken. Or gas.

The wastebasket was next to the swing. Sam took it to Nicola to make certain Woody was not in danger of flying glass. Forget that she'd brought home two suspected murderers for him to meet. "Serves him right for leaving me here while he's off gallivanting around the globe being a foreign correspondent."

Jeffers picked up the phone.

Sam glanced at the clock on the wall as she heard a car engine. It wasn't eight yet. Were they early? "I hear a car. Must be Hank." Sam squeezed between Jeffers and Ken, into the family room, and around the corner into the hall. She looked out through the floor-to-ceiling plate glass window that provided passive solar heat during the winter day and froze them at night. She saw only her reflection. Ken was right, she looked awful. But that was the least of her worries. She opened the door and peered out. It was Larry with the other suspect. "Send in the Clowns" played in her head. "It's Larry," she yelled for everyone's benefit. She hurried to the car, her hands wrapped tightly around her against the chill.

"What in the world are you doing out here, Larry?" she asked as he opened the car door and stepped out. She didn't like the worried look on his face. He wasn't that good an actor. "What's wrong?"

Ken and Nguyen were coming down the walk.

A heavyset man, wearing a three-piece suit that put even Thaddeus to shame, paraded around the car. Getting out the back was a man in the medium height range, wearing an average suit and lacking the panache of the other stranger.

"Sam," Larry said in a shaky voice, "I don't believe you've met Dr. Charles Zimmerman."

"Dr. Turner." The man of panache extended his hand.

Sam shook his hand. "Dr. Zimmerman." She turned to the other one, who had to be Roger Ryder, the other conspirator she'd been waiting for. "Dr. Ryder, I believe we've already met." She offered her hand.

"No, Sam, this is Dr. Maximilian Ross, *director* of the U.S. Centers for Disease Control and Prevention."

"It's a pleasure to meet you, Dr. Ross."

"The pleasure is all mine."

"Dr. Ryder isn't with you?" Sam asked.

"No, Dr. Ryder resigned his post."

Sam didn't know what to make of that statement. Did they know about the faked report? Had Ryder taken a vial and fled the country?

"Dr. Zimmerman," Larry said, a strange smile glued to his face, "may I present Dr. Kenneth Miller and Dr. Lee Nguyen." He shook their hands one after another as Larry added, "Dr. Zimmerman is the deputy assistant secretary of the Department of Health and Human Services."

Oh, boy, were they in trouble.

Amenities out of the way, Sam asked: "Shall we go inside and get out of the cold?" And watch her dig out her medical license and kiss it good-bye.

Jeffers met them in the hall. Sam slipped away to use the phone. See if she could raise Hank on his radio and have him stop the main event. Nicola was on the phone, speaking Hungarian. Sam had a pretty good idea who had called back.

She was so happy she'd put the dogs in the library. She went into the family room and turned up the lights. The north windows always made the large room chilly. She ushered everyone in. "Have a seat. I'll get some wood for the fire."

"I'll help," Ken said as he raced behind her to the patio doors.

"Would anyone like coffee?" Sam heard Jeffers ask before Ken closed the sliding glass door.

"The director of the CDC and a bigwig from the Department of Health," Ken whispered.

"Hold out your arms." She started piling on the wood Frank Gorzalka had chopped.

"What are we going to do, Sam?" His voice was nearing panic. She knew the feeling.

"I don't know. Go to law school."

"How can you be so glib?"

"Would you rather I cry?"

He grunted as she rammed a log into his chest.

"I'll try to call Hank, see if he can stop them."

"No, the children, Sam. We don't have any sick kids to show these two. We'll have to make them look ill. Put them on ventilators."

"Definitely not! We can't do that to our kids."

"You'd rather the hospital lose its certificate of need? Not to mention our licenses."

"Yes, Ken, I would. What about our oath? What about the golden rule of medicine, 'First of all, do no harm?' "

He bowed his head, at a loss for words. "You have enough wood," he said humbly. "Malpractice attorneys. We'll be partners."

"Absolutely." She added one last log and smiled up at him. "But we won't defend Clarence."

$\triangledown$

40

Bᴇғᴏʀᴇ ᴛʜᴇ ғɪʀᴇ had a good start, the Fish and Game warden and a local vet, but not the one she used, were at the door. She invited them in, since she didn't have anything else to lose.

"We've had a report that your bison may be transmitting a virus. I'd like the doc to have a look."

Her heart wasn't in it now. Instead of protesting, she said: "By all means."

The two men looked at each other.

"Emil will take you out to them. You'll find him around back, next to the barn. Jake's Place is written over the door."

They stared, giving her one last chance to cause a scene.

"Is there anything else?"

"No, ma'am," the warden responded.

"Good night," she said as she closed the door and went in to face the music.

She sat down on the hearth. The doctors were in the middle of a conversation she couldn't grasp. Larry was nodding as if he were following their every word, though she suspected his train of thought was on the same track as hers—nervously waiting for the collision.

"Dr. Turner?"

She looked up to see who had spoken.

"May we speak to you alone for a moment?" Dr. Zimmerman asked.

Sam scanned the faces around her. If she took any solace

in her situation it was in hearing Nicola's faint foreign crooning. "Of course." She got to her feet.

Dr. Zimmerman and Dr. Ross made up the entire "we." They rose and followed her through the hall.

"Sorry the house is in shambles; we're doing some renovating."

"Don't apologize," Dr. Zimmerman said. "We renovated the kitchen last year. And I mean that literally. It took the *whole* year."

She smiled her thanks for the small kindness by the hangman.

The library's glass doors were streaked with nose prints where the dogs had tried to take in the evening's unusual activity. "Get back," Sam said as she opened the door and threw her leg out to block the dogs' escape. She grabbed The Little One's choke chain and gave it a tug, which always had an amazingly calming effect on the dog. The Little One stayed obediently to one side as she then chased Fido around the room. "I'll put them in the laundry room," she said after securing Fido's choke chain and his cooperation. They'd escape through the doggy door, but she no longer cared that they'd be running wild, bothering the vet and everyone else pretending interest in her buffalo.

The two doctors found seats on the couch, and Dr. Ross was brushing dog hair off the legs of his pants when she returned. She closed the doors, noting the sweeping pattern on the carpet. She made another mental note to say something to the carpenters. She sat in the rocker.

"Dr. Turner," Dr. Zimmerman said, "what's going on?"

"In what sense, sir?"

"Dr. Turner, we are trying to clear up—"

The phone rang. Someone else could get it. "Sorry. Go on, Dr. Ross."

"In a medical sense," Dr. Zimmerman said, cutting the red tape.

"I am not at liberty to say, sir."

"Patient confidentiality?"

"No. More on the lines of national security," Sam said, realizing she sounded like someone out of a B spy movie.

"If someone in the White House vouched for us, would you be up front with us?"

She'd rather enjoy a call from the president. He said "if" the way Derek did when he wanted to mislead someone. "Would someone from the White House vouch for you?"

"Yes," Dr. Zimmerman said, looking her straight in the eyes. He was telling the truth or was a sociopathic liar.

"The president?"

That took him back. He recovered with a smile. "I suppose we could arrange it." He glanced at his watch. "It's ten now . . . "

Eastern time. It was five to eight here, to be precise. She was satisfied. And unless the president called in the next four minutes, he'd have to find a Hungarian interpreter. "We have smallpox, Doctors." She could tell by their lack of surprise that it was exactly what they thought. "Three cases."

"*Three* cases? Not six?"

"Yes. Three. Currently, we have one. The other five you are alluding to are decoys." She studied them. "It is my belief that our one case would be placed in grave danger if her true ailment were made public."

"But the CDC was notified of six cases," Dr. Ross said. "How did you expect—"

"It was my feeble attempt to lure Dr. Ryder to town." She studied them. Ross's red-blotched neck made her suspect they knew about his part in the conspiracy. "His report was inaccurate. Tom Polvich, who is laid out in the mortuary, Ryder, and Nguyen and Jeffers"—she thumbed toward the door—"were part of a conspiracy. . . . But surely you know all that." It was more a question than a statement. They weren't committing. "We're hoping one of them, if not all three, will lead us to where he buried the body of the second smallpox victim, giving himself away as the murderer."

"And how—"

"What the devil is that?" Dr. Zimmerman asked, interrupting his colleague. The commotion outside brought all of them to their feet.

"Showtime, gentlemen. I trust you'll do nothing to impede."

"We'll be delighted to observe," Dr. Zimmerman told her as he started toward the door.

Yeah, be a real lark for someone with access to the White House to see how country hicks attempt to solve their problems. But, come to think of it, the White House didn't have all that much to brag about either. Sam stopped at the hall closet for her parka. "Be nippy out. Help yourselves." She left the doctors rummaging through the closet of coats.

Ken, Larry, and Jeffers were already outside. Nguyen was in the doorway. Sam shoved him out of her way, mumbling, "Excuse me."

"What's going on?" Ken asked, staring at the truck barreling toward them.

"The cowboys are back," Jeffers said, jumping to the wrong conclusion.

Sam strained to see by torchlight the hollering men leaning over the top of the cab and hanging over the sides of the pickup bed. Three in the cab, seven or so in the bed. "These aren't kids."

"Rednecks," Ken allowed.

The battered truck screeched to a halt in front of them.

Sam pushed through the doctors. "What do you men want?"

The driver got out of the cab and stood unsteadily on the running board. Even from this distance it was obvious that they'd fortified themselves at a bar before coming out. Frank Gorzalka held up the newspaper. "You read tonight's paper?"

"No, why?" Sam shouted back.

"Says here your buffalo are making kids sick."

Sam looked at the men around her, and then back to Frank. "That's impossible!"

"That's not what the paper says."

"You believe everything you read in the paper?"

"Come on, Frank," a sloppy drunkard yelled over the top of the cab. "Let's get it over with."

"What are you planning to do?" Sam asked, taking a couple of aggressive steps forward.

Frank reached into the cab and pulled a rifle off the rack covering the back window. He brandished it about. "Make sure no one else gets sick." He tossed the rifle to one of the men in back and got into the cab. He revved up the engine, and then pitched the pickup over the lawn.

"I'll get a shotgun," Sam said, racing back to the house.

"Where's the sheriff?" Nguyen asked as she raced by.

"Don't know. Call nine-one-one and tell them to let him know we've got more trouble and tell him to hurry," she called over her shoulder as she tore down the hall.

From the bedroom window on the south side of the house, Sam watched the truck lurch forward in the clearing between the evergreens and the new construction, bouncing over the concrete pad that might still be able to serve as the foundation for Derek's bubbling hot tub. She'd never hear the end of it otherwise. Hell, she would never hear the end of this anyway, if she knew her Derek.

Sam grabbed the shotgun and hurried down the steps. Bewildered, Nicola was at the bottom of the staircase, Woody in her arms. Sam put a hand to her back and led her into the nursery. "Stay here." Sam closed the door behind her. Sam went out through the laundry door to head the trucks off at the corral fence.

"Stay here" must loosely translate to "put the baby in the crib and follow me," if she could go by the thumping steps behind her.

Sam stepped into the headlights, cocked the shotgun, and took aim. Didn't take much courage to stand between a moving truck and a fence, knowing the truck would stop. Took a lot, though, when a person didn't. Nicola was standing beside her, ready to stop the speeding truck with her bare hands.

The truck slowed and then came to a stop ten feet in front of them.

"Just stay where you are, fellows." Sam motioned with the shotgun for the driver to get out. "You in back, throw the rifle over the side."

"Don't do it," a brave soul yelled out anonymously.

"The sheriff is on his way. Let's just settle down. Wait for him to get here."

The spectators on foot were gathered around. The pickup inched toward them.

"Don't do it!"

Ken opened the driver's door and pulled Frank out. "Didn't you hear the lady?"

"Maybe the lady didn't hear me," Frank responded, pushing away from Ken. "You called to say my son's dead and you won't even let me look at the body to make sure you're telling me the truth, and now the newspaper says he's dead on account of your buffalo."

"Frank? Frank Gorzalka? Is that you?"

Nicola giggled. "Gorzalka," she repeated, giggling again.

"The Fish and Game warden has a vet looking at the buffalo as we speak, Mr. Gorzalka." Sam heard Nicola giggle again. "I'm sorry about your son, Mr. Gorzalka, believe me when I say that."

"Gorzalka," Nicola whispered. Nicola wasn't in on any of this, and Sam for the life of her couldn't understand what she thought was so funny. She certainly hoped Jeffers and Nguyen didn't see the humor.

The middle man in the cab moved to the driver's seat and revved up the engine. Sam turned the shotgun up and pulled the trigger; the recoil sent her back toward the fence. Nicola, with quick reflexes, caught Sam and steadied her. The blast stopped the pickup. The men in the bed grumbled and waved torches.

Emil came barreling through the pasture in the old pickup, bouncing noticeably on shot springs. The dogs barked excitedly as they ran along beside it.

Sirens and red lights broadcast the sheriff's arrival. Two deputy cars followed in a parade of red lights. Frank jumped into the cab and backed up the pickup. It spun around, throwing a man out. His torch rolled across the ground, igniting something flammable around the construction site with an ear-shattering bang. The exploding debris shot up into the air like fireworks, sparks raining down. Rotten-egg sulfur fumes filled the air.

Flames raced up the sides of the naked wood frame.

Paralyzed, Sam watched the whirl of chaotic activity around her. Gorzalka's men swarmed over the sides of the truck, some running toward the orange blaze, others scattering to the four winds, searching for containers to start a fire line from the creek. Jeffers yelled something about getting the hose. The Washington doctors went with him. The local men knew better. Too early in the season to turn on the outside water.

The sheriff pulled to a stop, his spotlight bathing the construction site in white light. Emil's truck rammed through the corral fence. He was out and racing toward the fire before the truck had a chance to come to a full stop.

The buffalo stampeded heading off to the north.

"Baby!" Nicola said.

Sam and Nicola nearly collided as they raced to the house. Sam's heart was going faster than her legs. Her world was collapsing like a house of cards, but nothing mattered except her helpless baby. Her feet felt like they were stuck to glue, everything moving in slow motion, only her mind seemed to be racing in all directions at once. Every minute of the baby's life flashed through her mind. The house seemed a million miles away, the seconds an eternity. Yet she outdistanced Nicola by half.

She clawed at the door, and was through it before it opened completely, her hipbone smacking on the door's edge. The cat ran between her legs as it raced out. Smoke stung her eyes. She took a choking breath. She knew enough to crouch down, to get under the poisonous fumes, but she wasn't about to waste a second of her baby's precious time, his air.

A hundred desperate years passed as she felt hot metal on the doorknob and turned it. Woody was crying. Tears rolled over her cheeks. Her lungs burned from smoke fumes. Flames were dancing behind the crib, but on the outside of the window. The crib hit the wall as she bumped the side and leaned in, picking up the baby and pulling loose the crib blanket in one sweeping motion. He never felt so soft or wonderful. She raced out, wrapping Woody in the blanket as she went.

She had to take another breath before she could clear the smoke. She couldn't help it. She'd reached the breaking point and had to breathe. She dove to the floor, gasping for air. She scooted across the floor toward the laundry room on her elbows and knees, the baby squeezed tightly to her chest.

Nicola, coming toward her, took the baby and turned around to take him to safety. Sam scrambled to her feet and stumbled out of the house. She coughed, exchanging smoke for the sulfur air outdoors. Nicola gave her a hand and led her toward one of the deputy's patrol cars. The baby's healthy crying was music to her ears. As she recovered her senses, she breathed slower and deeper.

Sam had heard stories of amazing feats people performed when a loved one's life was in the balance, and now she knew what they meant. The body could do anything, given the right incentive. Sam sat in the passenger's seat, cuddling her child and watching the fire spread to the cedar shakes until it was one glorious conflagration.

She kissed Woody. "Boy, will your daddy ever be surprised."

SAM TURNED OFF the water to listen. She thought she heard the phone. No. She turned the faucet on and adjusted the temperature until it was perfect. She leaned back and delighted in the warm water.

It was after midnight, and they were finally squared away. Emil got off late, but he should have picked up Derek by now. The only call she was expecting was from Hank. His men were staking out the Gorzalka place, waiting for either Jeffers or Nguyen to venture out. The police were watching the mortuary to make certain no one broke in there.

She was filthy and exhausted and happy that no one was calling. Her heart wasn't in it now, and she suspected that from now on her life would be divided in two segments— before the fire and after the fire.

Even her teeth felt gritty. She'd have to call down to the desk and have them send up the forgotten-sundries kit the sign on the lavatory announced the Holiday Inn would be happy to provide. Ken's Visa card had bought out Buttrey's baby aisle and replaced her antibiotic prescription, but she hadn't done a red-hot job of remembering all the little things she used and took for granted everyday. Sunday, after the rodeo officials and participants' parents checked out, they would move to a suite, but until then, the adjoining double rooms were all they had.

Somehow she thought she'd rather room with Nicola tonight. Emil promised he wouldn't tell Derek about the fire until the last moment—she didn't want him to have too much time to dwell on it—but she'd have a lot of explaining to do.

The volunteer fire department had arrived in time to save the barn and outbuildings. Dr. Zimmerman and Dr. Jeffers had found the water valve around by the garage and turned on the sprinkling system, containing the fire to the immediate area around the house. That would be little consolation to Derek. She'd remind him that he never did like the house, calling it a big, dysfunctional barn. She'd also remind him that most of his belongings were still in storage in New York. She was the one who had watched a lifetime of memorabilia go up in flames. Sam wondered if Derek had any pictures of his father. Dr. Zimmerman had worn John's old blue parka he'd taken from the closet. She'd be sure to ask for it back. That, a diamond necklace, and her engagement ring in the bank's vault were all she had left of John, although she supposed she should count his son and grandson too.

Seeing Dr. Zimmerman was going to be a humiliating experience. He must have been mightily impressed by their bumpkin ways. She could imagine him telling about the fire at every Washington cocktail party from now to kingdom come. Men would guffaw so heartily the liquid would slosh over the sides of their martini glasses, and their women would titter politely as they offered up cocktail napkins. Be as funny as Nicola giggling at Mr. Gorzalka's name. Sam was certain Nicola didn't understand that Gorzalka was his name; she most likely thought Sam was insulting him by calling him a drunkard. Mr. Whiskey.

Sam shot out of the tub. Whiskey!

Sam screeched to a stop in a parking space outside the ER door. She got out of the Holiday Inn's courtesy van, which she had guaranteed to return by five, a good hour before they would need it to shuttle a pilot and crew to the airport. She had pleaded and begged and promised her firstborn to get the van. A call to 911 and a patch to the sleepy and gruff chief of police had secured the keys.

Like the front lot, the ER was deserted. Bertha was slumped forward at the nursing station, not surprisingly, her head buried in her crossed arms. Sam's wet hair was stiff as a board by the time Bertha responded to the doorbell and unlocked the door for her, all the time rubbing her tired eyes and appraising her. Injury or illness?

Ignorance.

"Thanks, Bertha. I'll only be a minute."

Sam's legs felt as if she'd run up a hundred flights of stairs as she hurried across the ER, pushed through the bay doors, and raced through the hall. Her legs felt as if she'd run up two hundred flights of stairs by the time she got back to the ER to call the boiler room to have maintenance unlock the pathology department. Before the fire, after the fire. She could see the beginning of a pattern.

"I'll lock up," she told Henry, the maintenance man, dangling the keys that she'd found way in the back of her middle desk drawer. Satisfied, Henry went back to whatever he usually did in the wee hours of the night alone in the basement boiler room.

Sam switched on the laboratory lights and made a beeline to the refrigerator. She opened the freezer section and scanned the specimens through the swirls of mist. She smiled. It was there. Plain as day. A vial of frozen smallpox labeled WHISKEY. And she pretty well knew who had put it there. Who better to know Gorzalka was Polish for whiskey than Polvich? Eugene had asked her about it, but that had been the end of it. They could have left it there for months, presuming someone in the department put it there for a reason.

She took out what she surmised was the motive for Tom Polvich's death. This frosty test tube held captive a disease that had changed the course of history time and time again. It was time to end this mass murderer's reign. And she would be its executioner.

"Dr. Turner, turn slowly around." The voice was calm and collected and Dr. Lee Nguyen's.

Sam hadn't heard anyone come in. She lifted her hand to return the vial to the freezer.

"No, Dr. Turner. I said turn around."

She complied. Nguyen stood in the doorway between the office and the lab, his right hand in his pocket.

"What do you have in your pocket?"

"Does it matter?"

"If it's a gun I'll be more inclined to stay than if it's your index finger."

He didn't seem amused, but he *did* bring out his hand. And a hypodermic needle. "Satisfied?"

"If it's filled with a vitamin B compound I'll be more inclined to stay than if it's filled with succinylcholine."

He looked at the hypo, and then gave a noncommittal shrug. He held out the other hand. "Bring me the vial."

"This test tube filled with whiskey?"

"It was important enough to bring you here in the middle of the night. Hence, it's the vial we've been looking for."

"I'm on my way up to ICU. I just stopped to make room in the freezer—"

"Don't insult my intelligence, Dr. Turner. Did you actually believe that I was fooled by this charade you and your friends have been playing?"

"What do you mean?"

"The sick teenagers, the rodeo boys who kidnapped me, the article in the paper about the buffalo, the two men posing as officials from the CDC and the Department of Health. You went to a great deal of trouble to keep us from discovering the vial the double-crosser Tom Polvich hid from us."

It crossed her mind to tell him the officials were the genuine article, but she decided to keep it to herself. As she would Debbie, who was cultivating more of what was in the vial. "The police are following you; you won't get away with it."

"No one followed me." True, the deputies were staking out Gorzalka's place, waiting for Nguyen or his friend Jeffers to show up there. They were working under the criminal-justice-textbook supposition that the perpetrator would return to the scene of the crime, make certain Jess Gorzalka was still buried. That was the whole purpose of the visit from Frank and his friends, to make sure the suspects understood that she had Jess's body. Since it cost her the house, she would have appreciated Nguyen's cooperation.

"What happened to Jess Gorzalka?"

"Tom killed him."

"Dr. Jeffers saw Jess in the ER Wednesday night. The CDC didn't show up until Thursday. How do you explain that?"

"After Earl turned over the ER to the night nurse that Wednesday, we paid the boy a house call," Nguyen explained. "He was concerned about the boy being alone so he convinced him to come to our apartment where we could keep an eye on him until his father came home."

"Well? You were going to let him live? How were you going to explain the scars?"

"He had an extremely involved case of acne vulgaris. That along with claiming chicken pox." Nguyen shrugged.

"In that case, why did Dr. Polvich kill him?"

"The boy wanted to go to the police, tell them about how David became ill."

"The perfume researcher in Washington, you mean?" He looked surprised that she knew that. She wished she'd kept her big mouth shut. "Why would Dr. Polvich care about such a wild accusation? It's all over town. David told it to everyone in school." She tried to sound nonchalant to protect her source.

"Because Dr. Polvich was that person," Nguyen explained.

A good prosecutor might have been able to make something stick to the slimy Dr. Polvich, but it would not have been first-degree murder. Yet he committed a first-degree murder to cover it. "What happened to Jess's body?"

"We didn't know what to think when we discovered the boy had died," Nguyen said. "We took the body back out to his trailer."

"And buried him."

"No, we put him in his bed. We assumed, at first, that the federal authorities had disposed of his body in the same manner they had the first boy."

"At first?"

"Until your phone call from the sheriff yesterday. The body with the yellow pustules."

"Right," she lied for the sake of argument. She was almost positive Nguyen was wrong about the authorities disposing of Jess's body. She looked beyond Nguyen to her desk. The manila envelope Judge Moots gave her was locked in the bottom drawer. But that made a great deal more sense now that she realized Jess hadn't been buried by these two. Her purse was in the drawer, also. It hadn't burned in the fire. She had credit cards. And she wouldn't have to replace her driver's license. Thank you, God, for the little things. And the heavy thing—Derek's 9mm Ruger. "Explain about Tom Polvich's death."

"I confronted Tom with my suspicion that he'd murdered the boy and told him to go to the authorities or we would. We struggled . . . " He left the rest unsaid in favor of motioning to the needle.

Since she had lost her house to the cause, she would have preferred hearing that Polvich was going to sell the virus to an unnamed rebel group that planned to start an epidemic in the opposing military force, or who wanted to wipe out a village over zealous religious differences. "On what did you base your suspicion?"

"The empty vial we found under the boy's bed."

"A vial of?" Sam asked.

"Lidocaine."

Lidocaine was a drug used to stabilize heart rhythms. She would have found it in tissue samples. But then, she never saw the body. "How did that tie in Polvich?" Sam asked.

"Your name was on the vial."

"My name?"

"We deduced from the black bag Tom stole."

She did have Lidocaine in her bag, and had ever since John's cardiac arrest. So that's what happened to her black bag. "Why did Tom steal my black bag?"

"For the smallpox grids."

"Grids?"

"You'd called the CDC after using an electron microscope."

"We don't have an electron microscope."

"In Billings."

She'd driven to Billings to use theirs? She'd called Billings looking for Jess. Why hadn't she thought to ask the pathology department if they'd seen her? Why hadn't Derek known? More than likely he had. She would forgive him if he walked in the door this very minute and rescued her.

"Whose idea was it to give me succinylcholine and stick me on a ventilator?"

"The CDC. Roger Ryder and Tom Polvich."

That would have been the thing to give Jess. They must have been buying it in gallon buckets.

"Dr. Turner." Nguyen held out his hand.

She looked at the test tube. The frost had evaporated. "I don't suppose you'd be willing to push whatever you have in the hypo into your arm to win my allegiance?"

Nguyen shook his head. "It's scopolamine, to produce retroactive amnesia. I'd hate to forget my purpose."

Apparently, he wouldn't mind if she forgot hers.

"Dr. Turner," Nguyen said again, his fingers beckoning for her to bring him the vial.

Sam glanced to the blood bank door as she heard the lock click. The door opened and Jeffers walked in. She would have preferred the cavalry. She turned back to Nguyen; she needed to get to her desk and the Ruger. She took the liberty of closing the freezer door. She was standing in a draft.

"Is that it?" Jeffers asked, motioning to the vial in Sam's hand.

Nguyen nodded. "Get it from her."

Sam felt hollow as she gave up the vial, making an easy

echo for Harrison's words about hoping they could keep *their* vial in a safer place. She watched Jeffers and Nguyen exchange vial for syringe. Watched, too, as Jeffers uncapped the needle. She prayed that it *was* filled with scopolamine. Nothing had prepared her for what she next witnessed. Jeffers jabbed the needle into Nguyen's forearm and pushed the plunger. Nguyen struggled awkwardly, trying to hold on to the vial.

"Get the vial, Sam," Jeffers commanded.

Sam sped toward the falling vial, diving and sliding into the shattering glass. Nguyen crumbled to the floor, trapping her. She heard choking sounds and felt cutting pain as a sliver of glass embedded deep into the palm of her right hand as Jeffers rolled Nguyen off her.

Jeffers was on the phone, calling Bertha in the ER to bring a crash cart. Sam looked from the melting icicle of smallpox to Jeffers, to her desk where she could retrieve the Ruger, to Nguyen's blue face. He had lied to her. The only thing *his* "scopolamine" was making him forget was how to breathe. She pulled the glass from her hand, blood filling the wound, and then tilted Nguyen's head back. She cleared the airway passage with her left hand and cupped her mouth over his. Somehow she knew that if he had succeeded in sticking her with the syringe, he wouldn't have been as kind. Sam had been breathing for Nguyen a good minute or more before she felt Jeffers edge her out of the way.

"Cardiac arrest?" Bertha asked as she assisted Jeffers.

"No, he overdosed on a muscle relaxant. Let's intubate him," Jeffers told Bertha as he placed an S airway tube down Nguyen's throat. He bagged Nguyen until Bertha had turned on the oxygen, sending 100 percent oxygen down Nguyen's maw.

"Who are you?" Sam asked as she searched the crash cart drawers for antiseptic to clean the wound and a gauze pad. She was thankful the virus was frozen.

Jeffers looked at Bertha. "We'll bring you the car when we're finished."

She looked questioningly at him.

"We can manage him alone now," Jeffers insisted.

Bertha turned to Sam.

"It's all right."

Bertha gave the cart a fleeting glance as she left. The nurse was understandably concerned; she would be held accountable for any drugs that disappeared from the cart.

Sam went to her desk and unlocked the bottom drawer. She readied the Ruger just in case her faith in Jeffers had been misplaced. "Will you answer my question now, please?"

"I'm an employee of the World Health Organization," Jeffers said. "I infiltrated Lee's group after a virologist came forward with the allegation that he had been approached by a small group of virologists and microbiologists dedicated to the preservation of microorganisms to remove a vial of the smallpox virus from the government laboratory where he is employed."

At the CDC in Atlanta, of course. "Is it all right if I destroy it?" she motioned to the puddle on the floor by Nguyen's feet.

"Please!"

She headed for the nearest Bunsen burner, but ended up in the storage room. She was having a bad fire day and figured the hospital would burn down if she so much as lit a match. She poured bleach over the virus and then in a widening circle around the spill. Execution by bleach. A fitting end for a slayer of millions, dating back to ancient Egypt.

"I take it you won't be staying on in Sheridan as our ER doc?"

Jeffers smiled.

Nguyen's color was returning. He was coming out from under the succinylcholine. He struggled to raise a hand to fight the tube, but he couldn't manage the task. He tried again in a jerky, determined maneuver.

"What are you going to do with him?" Sam asked.

Jeffers shrugged. "Nothing for me to do." He nodded to the bleach and broken vial. "You finished my job."

Sam went to the phone and called the sheriff. Though she didn't know why she bothered. Something told her that the federal government would insist on a plea-bargaining arrangement. They would never allow his case to go to trial where the smallpox issue could come out.

"WE'RE GOING TO be late," Derek warned from the doorway to Nicola and Woody's bedroom.

"Okay, okay," Sam replied, struggling to get the bootie on Woody's kicking foot. He was putting on weight nicely now, despite the crowded and chaotic conditions in their three-bedroom apartment. It would be the end of summer before they could move into the new house.

Nicola finished stuffing the diaper bag and shoved the box of newborn Pampers under her bed. They no longer needed to cut the diapers in half.

Derek brushed his lips across Sam's temple as she and the baby came out, a step ahead of Nicola.

Her father held the apartment door open for her and whistled his approval of the new black sheath Derek had picked out. "You should wear all of your clothes that short, Sharon."

"Samantha," she corrected. Her father was still a little confused, but the precursor graft had given him a whole new lease on life. Then he whistled at Nicola. Derek had brought him home a week ago and had taken him back to the nursing home for a lack of anywhere else to stay. But he lasted only two days before the administrator called her at the hospital and told her to come get him. He was flirting with all the ladies, and apparently two, or three, of his admirers tangled in a wig-pulling argument. Sam blamed herself; she should have expected her father to take after his roguish son-in-law after filling his head with Derek's genetic makeup.

"*Koszonom szepen*." Nicola tweaked his black suit sleeve and gave him her full-gum smile. Her face had cleared up nicely now that she was on a regimen of Accutane.

"*Szia*," Sam's father replied.

"*Szlvesen*," Sam corrected. "She said thank you very much and you said hello, not you're welcome."

"*Szlvesen*," her father said as he caught up with Nicola in the hall. His arm went around her waist. His hand wandered down her backside, but Nicola brought her hand around and moved his back up.

"He's met his match in Attila," Derek said as he closed the door, and tried it to make certain it was locked. As if they had anything to steal. The Ruger, she supposed.

Derek hadn't been detained at the airport, as Sharon told her. It was a little matter of explaining away two stamps arriving into the country less than a week apart, and no stamp out. He had left by military transport instead of through normal channels. Someone from the embassy vouched for him, and then he flew off to the WHO head-quarters in Geneva to check out Nguyen and Jeffers.

Derek's excuse for being unnerved the night he left Sheridan was that he thought she'd kill him if she found out he had involved her family. There was probably a little more to it than that, but whatever the cloak-and-dagger shenanigans were had been resolved to *his* "family's" satis-faction. And it served to cancel out her fear that he would kill her over burning down the house.

She felt Derek's hand cup her buttock as they followed Nicola and Sam's dad. "You want something to hold?" She handed him the baby.

Thaddeus held open the door of the black limo for them. Sam slid in first and sat beside Frank Gorzalka. Debbie sat facing them. Sam reached over and blended a blob of pancake makeup that concealed one of Debbie's few scabs. Luckily, Debbie had had a mild case.

They picked up the hearse, and a long line of cars, in front of the mortuary. No-chin Skip rode one of the two motorcycles at the lead.

Wasn't hard to find the plot in the cemetery; family members and Jess's schoolfriends sat in the chairs that had been set out on three sides of the grave, and more stood four deep in a horseshoe configuration behind the chairs. The mourners in the procession filled in wherever they were able.

The mortician led the way to the six seats saved in the front row. The six empty seats to the right were for the pallbearers. Pastor Rider was standing over the open grave, his Bible in both hands. The double grave marker the city council allocated, or appropriated, had replaced Mrs. Gorzalka's smaller one.

Thaddeus had done a nice job cleaning the seven-thousand-dollar casket, Sam noticed as the pallbearers—Judge Moots, Mayor Sully, Dr. Jacobson the college president, the police chief, Leon Sayers from the newspaper, and good ol' Larry—carried it up the green slope from the hearse. Jess's casket had been quite muddy after the sheriff and his men exhumed it. Frank had dug the hole too close to the creek bed, and water had crept in around the casket he'd taken from Thaddeus's showroom.

"Thank you," Frank whispered to Sam as he wiped away a single tear.

"They'll be together now," Sam whispered back.